# Autumn in Yalta

*Library of Modern Jewish Literature*

*Other titles in the Library of Modern Jewish Literature*

# Autumn in Yalta

## A NOVEL AND THREE STORIES

· · · · ·

David Shrayer-Petrov

Edited and with an Afterword by Maxim D. Shrayer

 *Syracuse University Press*

Syracuse University Press, Syracuse, New York 13244–5160

Copyright © 2006 by David Shrayer-Petrov and Maxim D. Shrayer

Original works copyright © 1992, 1996, 1999, 2004 by David Shrayer-Petrov

Notes copyright © 2006 by Maxim D. Shrayer

Afterword copyright © 2004, 2006 by Maxim D. Shrayer

*All Rights Reserved*

First Edition 2006

06   07   08   09   10   11        6   5   4   3   2   1

Publication history of each work is described in the work's first note found in the Notes
to the Text section. Permission to reprint these works, the notes, and the afterword is
gratefully acknowledged.

The paper used in this publication meets the minimum requirements of American National
Standard for Information Science—Permanence of Paper for Printed Library Materials,
ANSI Z39.48–1984.

**Library of Congress Cataloging-in-Publication Data**

Shraer-Petrov, David.

[Selections. English. 2006]

Autumn in Yalta : a novel and three stories / David Shrayer-Petrov ; edited and with an
afterword by Maxim D. Shrayer.— 1st ed.

p. cm.—(Library of modern Jewish literature)

ISBN 0–8156–0820–9 (hardcover : alk. paper)

1. Shraer-Petrov, David—Translations into English. I. Title. II. Series.

PG3549.S537A2    2006

891.73'5—dc22        2005035104

*Manufactured in the United States of America*

# Contents

◆  ◆  ◆  ◆  ◆

David Shrayer-Petrov was born in 1936 in Leningrad (St. Petersburg) and debuted as a poet in the 1950s. After studying medicine, Shrayer-Petrov served as a military physician in Belarus before returning to Leningrad to pursue both literature and medicine. He moved to Moscow in 1964. Although Shrayer-Petrov managed to publish a collection of poetry and two books of essays in the 1960s and 1970s, literary exploration of Jewish themes put him in conflict with the Soviet authorities, limiting publication of his work and prompting him to emigrate. A Jewish refusenik and a dissident from 1979 to 1987, Shrayer-Petrov lived as an outcast in his native country but continued to write despite expulsion from the Soviet Writer's Union and persecution by the KGB. He was finally allowed to leave in 1987, settling in Providence, Rhode Island, where he lives with his wife, the translator Emilia Shrayer. Shrayer-Petrov's arrival in the West brought forth a flow of publications, including six collections of poetry, six novels, two volumes of memoirs, and numerous contributions to literary magazines in Europe and North America. In 1992 Shrayer-Petrov's novel *Herbert and Nelly* was long-listed for the Russian Booker Prize, and in 2004 his novel *Savely Ronkin* was long-listed for the Booker-Open Russia Prize. His works have been translated into a number of European languages. Dr. Shrayer-Petrov divides his time between writing and doing cancer research at Brown University, where he is on the faculty of the Medical School. The latest among his nineteen Russian books are *Form of Love* (2003), a poetry collection; *These Strange Russian Jews* (2004), two novels in one volume long-listed for the 2005 Bunin Prize; *Carp for the Gefilte Fish* (2005), a collection of stories; *Judin's Redemption* (2005), a novel; and a revised edition of *Herbert and Nelly* (2006).

* * * * *

Maxim D. Shrayer, professor of Russian and English at Boston College, where he codirects the Jewish Studies Program, is a specialist in Jewish-Russian literature and a prolific literary translator. He is a recipient of fellowships from the National Endowment for the Humanities, the Rockefeller Foundation, and the Bogliasco Foundation. Among Shrayer's books are *The World of Nabokov's Stories* and *Russian Poet/Soviet Jew*. Editor of the definitive two-volume *Anthology of Jewish-Russian Literature* (2006), Shrayer has edited and co-translated a number of his father's works, notably the collection *Jonah and Sarah* (2003), also published by Syracuse University Press.

# Acknowledgments

The author would like to thank Raduga Publishers (Moscow) and the Russian-language periodicals where these works appeared in the original.

The author and the editor would like to thank all the contributing translators: Arna B. Bronstein, Aleksandra I. Fleszar, Emilia Shrayer, and Margarit Tadevosyan, for creating faithful and elegant English versions of the Russian originals. We admire their love of letters and commitment to the cause of giving literary works a new life in translation.

Stephen Vedder and Michael S. Swanson of Boston College's Media Technology Services have done a splendid job with the cover photos. Ellen S. Goodman of Syracuse University Press has been an enthusiastic supporter of this project. We wish to thank her and the entire staff of the press for their dedication and professionalism. We also thank Jeffrey H. Lockridge for his editorial work on the manuscript.

The editor thanks the Boston College Graduate School of Arts and Sciences for a grant that has supported the translation of part of this book. A Boston College Faculty Fellowship has given the editor of this book a respite from teaching, and he is most grateful for it. A Fellowship from the Bogliasco Foundation and the staff of the Centro Studi Ligure per le arti e le lettere (Bogliasco, Italy) have provided the editor with the peace and comfort that he needed to complete a large portion of his work in October–November 2004. *Mille grazie!*

Emilia Shrayer and Karen E. Lasser read the manuscript and

offered invaluable comments. They inspire and sustain us each day of our lives. Without them, many of these pages would have remained blank—in Russian or in English. No words can express our love for them and our gratitude for their devotion.

D.S.-P. and M.D.S.

Autumn in Yalta

# Strange Danya Rayev

A NOVEL

I was born in Lesnoye on the Vyborg Side of Leningrad in January 1936.* My father Pavel Borisovich (Fayvl Borukhovich) Rayev was an automobile engineer. My mother, Stella Vladimirovna (Shayna Wolfovna) Kogan, a chemical lab technician. Father came from a hardy family, where Jewish cultural and religious traditions were observed. Mother came from an ultraorthodox family. My grandfather on my mother's side was a rabbi until the October Revolution. Mother's maternal ancestors were also rabbis. Mother broke with all of that, leaving home early to make her own way in the world.

My name is Daniil. At home they call me Danya or Danik.

My first memories are filled with sunlight. Or fringed with sunlight. I remember my father and mother's voices. "Pavel!" mother calls. "Stellochka!" father answers her. Again layers of sunlight. I remember myself at the age of three or so. It's summertime. We have two rooms. One—a big corner room filled to the brim with sunlight. Huge windows look out onto the park of the Forestry Technology Academy. Birch and birdcherry branches are pushing their way into the windows. There was always summer and joy. Father and I are going out early to buy grapes for mama. The grapes look like longish little lanterns. Yellow green. The grapes have not been washed. They are covered with germs. We are not allowed to eat the grapes until we get home. The grapes are called ladyfingers.

*Editor's notes on cultural, historical, and geographical allusions in the text can be found in the back of this volume.

1

Nanny's name is Nyura. She feeds me and takes me for walks in the park. My mother works at the Forestry Technology Academy. Nanny Nyura came from a village. That's all I remember about her. But it was from Nyura that I first heard the word "village." It seems that I heard a few other village words from her: cow, *izba* (a peasant log house), mushrooms.

Although, I might have heard these words used at the dacha, where they took me and my cousins, Mika and Malvina, to get us out of the city. I don't remember anything about the dacha.

My mother is pretty. And here is my first winter memory. Mother is pretty. She is wearing a floor-length green winter coat. The coat has a collar made of short black fur. Her hat and muff are made of the same fur. The muff keeps mother's hands warm. They call the seal fur kitty. The name is just as wondrous as ladyfingers. It stays with you for life. It's winter. Mother and I are in the park. I'm wearing a fur coat and a hat with earflaps that tie with straps. I'm hot. Mother pulls me on a sled along the park alleys. Together we sit down on the sled and slide down the hill. Mother hits her knee on a birch tree. The birch trunk is striped like a zebra.

My parents took me to the zoo. There were zebras and tigers and elephants there. And polar bears. And walruses. And ice cream.

Again it's winter. I'm at home. The windows are covered in icy patterns. Mama and nanny are also home. It's an early winter afternoon. Mama's face is tear-stained. I hear a loud whirring on the other side of the window. A gigantic dragonfly in the winter? Papa is wearing a short, white, belted sheepskin coat. I know these words: map case and holster. The map case holds maps. The holster holds a pistol. Papa's not taking off his coat. Downstairs a tankette waits for him. He is a commander. He's going off to the Finnish War. Papa kisses mama and me. "I'll return by spring!" We go out into the courtyard after him. A green tankette stands in the snow-covered courtyard. It looks like a little tank. Like a motorcycle covered in armor. Papa opens the door of the tankette. Mama does not let go of him and cries. Papa kisses mama. The tankette is chugging, clattering, and rattling. Then it goes out of the courtyard and onto the street. And now it disappears around the corner.

Papa returned from the Finish War. He was wounded slightly in his left arm. His arm is in a sling. Papa is happy to be back. We have a gramophone. Finnish records keep spinning on it. New words: foxtrot, tango, boston. I like all the records, even though I don't understand the words. But one record is special. Among the unintelligible songs (papa says they are in Finnish), there is one that I understand. I remember the words:

Come buy the pretzel rolls, hot tasty pretzel rolls,
Send me those ruble notes, send them my way.
And on this rainy night, pity your seller's plight,
Pity this trader's sight and quickly pay.

Some fifty years later, I will hear this song in New York.

Autumn. Autumnal park. Mother and I are going to visit Professor Vladimir Nikolaevich Krestinsky. He is dying. He has cancer. I'm taking him an orange. Yellow leaves float on the pond. The wind chases them along the water, and the rain blocks them, fastening them to the shore with its nails. The professor's house is in the middle of the park, right next to the academy. I put the orange on the side table next to the couch where Vladimir Nikolaevich is lying. Mother is telling him all about what's been happening in their department. She's smiling. Mother is so pretty when she smiles. Vladimir Nikolaevich also smiles and asks me what I saw on the way over. I tell him all about the wind, the water, the leaves, and the rain. We visit Professor Krestinsky every Sunday. He plays paper dolls with me. They slide along the table when you blow on them.

One day mother says, "Danik, today we won't be going to see Vladimir Nikolaevich. We won't go next Sunday either."

"Why not?" I ask.

"He died. You know, Danik, he had cancer."

Yes, I know. I can even imagine how this big, red, cancerous crawfish drags Vladimir Nikolaevich into a horrible black cave. I have seen red crawfish on a sign at a beer stand, when Nanny Nyura and I went to Svetlanovsky Market for wild strawberries. Nanny told me that crawfish are bad. They live in the river in caves, and they steal children who don't listen.

Why did they take Professor Krestinsky? . . .

Again sun. A sunny morning. I wake up because mama and papa are kissing me. They have just come home. Just off the train. They sped through the night on the "Red Arrow." I know that Indians shoot arrows. The leader of the redskins. "Red Arrow"—that's an express train on which mama and papa flew from Moscow to Leningrad. They went to an Agricultural Expo. Papa is tall and kind. He lifts me up all the way to the ceiling. Mama is holding a bike. A real two-wheeler. A child's glistening two-wheel bike. Papa puts me down right onto the seat.

Papa and I take the bike into the courtyard. Summer. Morning. Sunday. The courtyard is empty. Only Mishka Shushpanov, the local hoodlum, sits on the stoop of the laundry, making a slingshot. Mishka is sparrow hunting. Once, I heard him chant, "Kill the kikes, save Russia!" as he was shooting the sparrows with his slingshot.

Papa is teaching me to ride. I'm getting the hang of it. I make circles around the courtyard. The windows swing open. Those are the neighbors. We live in a two-story house made of stone. The inhabitants stick their heads out and say to papa, "Good morning to you, Pavel Borisovich! What a present you brought your son from Moscow!" Some of the neighbors come out into the courtyard and shake papa's hand. Papa smiles in return. He asks, "How's your health?" Papa is tall and kind. Papa was a Red Army commander during the war with Finland. Papa is a chief engineer. Everyone likes and respects him. Everyone enjoys shaking his hand.

Mama and papa are at work. Nanny Nyura and I are in the courtyard. We have just returned from the park, where I rode my bicycle. Nanny hurries me home. I have to eat and take a nap. I'm still of preschool age. I have to take a nap during the day. I plead with nanny to let me ride a little more in the courtyard. She leaves. I ride in circles. A rock hits the back wheel. I brake, jump off the bike, look around. That's Mishka Shushpanov. He aims at me from the balcony. He's scoping me out with his slingshot and shouting, "Kike the Jew was selling worms, carried them on a plate, asked a kopek for the bait! . . ." He's picking on me and shooting rocks at me with his slingshot. A faint memory of conversation overheard at home and at my grandparents' tells me that "Kike the Jew" is something insulting, and this something insulting refers to me. I get back on the bike, and just to spite Mishka Shushpanov, I circle the courtyard. Rocks hit the spokes, the wheel, and the seat. I feel I've been hit on my head and fall down. It hurts. I am bleeding. They take me to the hospital, bandage my head, and give me a shot. In the evening, papa says, "Danik, now you're also a fighter!"

Mama and papa—that's my whole life. In the morning, I'm already thinking about how they'll return from work and play with me. With papa I play more, and with mama I read. Until I was four, mama would read to me, and we would memorize poems and fairy tales. Many poems. And particularly Pushkin's fairy tales. And of course the entire collection of those wonderful books: *The Hunchback Pony, Mr. Scruba-Dub-Dub, The Mail, Uncle Styopa, The Three Little Pigs, The Jungle Book,* and many, many others. When I was about four, I started to read by myself. I read endlessly. I used to read a lot especially when I was sick. There were a few times when I was really sick.

Papa and mama. Mama and papa. It even seemed to me that they existed together not just because I always saw them together, or because they were always together. But they are actually one complete unit: mama–papa—papa–mama. I don't remember them fighting. I don't remember any such thing. It probably took place without me. Or I loved them so much and I so believed in their kindness, that I could not imagine any discord between them.

Only later, much later, did I find out that mama was hot-tempered, quick to take offense, and easily hurt. I found out that while she loved papa madly, she caused him a lot of grief, was jealous without reason, suspicious without reason, torturing herself and papa for nothing. And the cause of all this was my difficult birth. I was a large baby. The midwife was inexperienced. Postpartum sepsis set in. There were no antibiotics then. Mama was unconscious for more than a week and hung between life and death. She did not breast-feed me. I was breast-fed by Auntie Musya, the wife of mama's brother Mitya (Meyer) Kogan. She, herself, had a year-old boy, Borya. Auntie Musya came from a Russian Orthodox family. There was a rumor that she had secretly christened her son in church. Borya called his mother's friend Anya "Godmother." And I copied him. When mama started to get better, papa's parents insisted that I be circumcised. Mama felt sorry for me; I was more than a month old. On top of that, she'd been a member of the Komsomol and participated in the proletarian "Blueshirts" movement. When she was in a good mood, she would hum the song of her youth, "We are the Blueshirts, the union is our home . . ." But they convinced her, cajoled her, talked her into it. They named me Daniil in honor of my grandmother's brother who had died young.

Probably because of the difficult birth, because of mama's illness, I wasn't a terribly strong child. Family history tells that when I was two and a half, I got really sick with pneumonia. Lobar pneumonia. Sulfa drugs had only just come out. One of them, streptocide, was imported from abroad. You could only get it at the druggist with a special prescription, which was issued only by the city's leading pediatricians on special letterhead. I was dying. Father's older brother, Uncle Yanya, went at night to see the famous Professor Tur and brought him back to our house. They cured me. My pneumonia was so bad that it resulted in complications to the muscles in my eyes, leaving me cross-eyed.

This grave event of my early childhood did not stay in my memory. I found out about it much later. In any case, I can't exclude the possibility that subconsciously, or rather, without my being conscious of them, thoughts about illnesses, dying, and recovery, about these processes which resemble the changing seasons, began to occupy my imagination. The illness and the death of Professor Vladimir Nikolaevich Krestnitsky. Papa's stories about the war with Finland—how he was wounded, how he himself shot and killed the enemy. Conversations about sick people and about illnesses, which were conducted in our house not in layman's terms, but professionally (one of my aunts and one of my uncles were doctors), all of that imbedded itself in my memory, sparking an interest in observing nature. And later, an interest in curing people as elements of nature.

Mama knew a lot about trees. Of course that was a part of her profession. She was a senior lab technician in the Department of Organic Chemistry at the Forestry Technology Academy. For mama, chemistry was not an abstract science but a reality. It was about that magical, as well as natural, life of plants that mama would teach me when I was a young boy. We're in the park. A summer evening. Mama points to a very tall tree. The tree has yellowish-red layered bark. Little grooves between islets of bark. Thick sap oozes from inside. It hardens on the bark scales. The branches of this thick long-needle conifer start somewhere in the sky.

"This is a pine, Danik. A Siberian pine tree. Remember when Uncle Kolya gave you pine nuts?"

Of course I remember pine nuts!

"And do you remember when our neighbor Ekaterina Nikolaevna got sick, and they gave her a shot?"

I don't really remember the shot. Then mama breaks off a condensed drop of the sap, rubs it between her fingers, and lets me smell it. Yes, yes. Now I remember: that was the smell in Ekaterina Nikolaevna's room after the shot. I also remember another wondrous word: camphor.

"That was the smell of camphor, mama!"

"That's right, Danik! Camphor is made from the pine sap. These aromatic substances are called terpens. Got it?"

I repeat, "Terpens."

In the spring, the ponds of the Forestry Technology Academy begin to swarm with life. You only have to watch very carefully. Jelly-like clumps of frogs' eggs bob in the silty water. In a week or two the eggs disappear. Water plants are swarming with little, black, large-headed creatures. You dip your net in, and these half-fish, half-froglets are swimming in a glass jar, which you brought from home. "How can that be—from these little eggs? And what's going to happen to these tadpoles after this?" Another week or two, and there are no tadpoles in the ponds. The wet grass is swarming with little frogs. And the grown-up frogs croak in the pond. The bottom of the pond is inhabited by newts that look like crocodiles. "How's that? And how did I get here? All at once? Or did I start from an egg and then turn into a tadpole?"

I'm already five years old. I observe, I read, I ask questions. I know that they brought children to the USSR from distant Spain, that they are Spanish Young Pioneers. Rescued from the fascist dictator Franco. Parents of these Spanish children perished fighting for freedom. Who Pioneers are, I know. A girl named Liza lives in our house. She goes to school with a red Pioneer scarf around her neck. She loves her red scarf so much that she even plays stickball in it, although her mother, Aunt Katya, does not let her. "It's a silk scarf, it's expensive. You'll rip it, Liza, and I won't buy you another one!"

Our courtyard is big. The most interesting things happen in our courtyard in the spring and summer. In the winter, everything dies down. It's dark. Rain. Frost. Snowdrifts. Paths heading from the house to Novoseltsevskaya Street and to Engels Prospekt. A path leads through the courtyard to the laundry. There are narrow paths from the house to the sheds. Each family has their own shed in the yard. We burn wood in our stove every day from October to May. Nanny Nyura brings in the wood and stokes the stove. I help her.

Our courtyard is big. On the sides there are two houses. Our building—a two-story brick house covered in yellow stucco. And a cottage of the same color, but one story. The laundry takes up half of this building. The other half is occupied by the Iodkos. They are Polish. Iodko himself is the director of security for the Forestry Technology Academy. He's bald and important. He wears a blue cap and a belted blue field shirt. He has shiny boots with his breeches tucked into them. The breeches are rounded, as if Iodko rides on a wheel. Everybody is afraid of Iodko. Except for my papa. Iodko has an orchard behind the wrought-iron fence. The other Iodkos take up half of the first story in our two-story house. They also have an orchard, an apple orchard. And they have a strawberry patch. On the first floor there are two more apartments. One long one. There are all sorts of Uncle Vasyas living there with their wives and children. And a Circassian family. The drunkard Uncle Fedya with his wife, Lyusya, live in the other small apartment, under our staircase.

There are two apartments on the second floor. In one there are people we know and some we don't know. Of them I know Mishka Shushpanov, who had once shot at me with his slingshot. And the yardkeepers live there. Yardkeeper Uncle Vasya is also a horrible drunkard. Every day he pounds on his wife. They have two children: the deaf and dumb Valka and the inveterate crook Vanka. Vanka the Steward. When Vanka the Steward is not in prison, he stands in the yard, blows smoke from his *papirosa,* and talks with Alka the Circassian. Alka sticks her face out the window, giggles, and twists her head. Friends of Vanka the Steward come to our courtyard: Sashok, Mishanya, and Maksyuta. That is, if they're not behind bars.

Mama, papa, nanny, and I live in the other apartment on the second floor. We have two rooms. Four families live in our communal apartment: the Dralinskys, another Dralinsky family, the Krylovs, and us. Each family, except ours, has one room. The elderly, the adults, and the children together. For everyone who lives in our apartment there is one kitchen, one stove, one sink, and one bathroom. It's scary to go to the bathroom at night. And it's cold. A white earthenware potty with a green glazed cover stands under my bed. Later, when we're evacuated, mama will take this potty with us. I'll describe the evacuation later.

In the middle of our courtyard, a bit closer to the laundry, the top of a manhole sticks out. Yes, it sticks out like a well. Its cast-iron cover is not on the ground or on the asphalt, like for all the other manholes. It rests on a concrete base. In the middle of the cover is a cast-iron ring, which you pull to get into the manhole. The Big Bad Wolf and the witch Baba Yaga live in this manhole. We children are strictly forbidden to open the cover. We're not even allowed to sit on the edge of it. Sometimes I do sit on the edge, when Nanny is busy with her chores. But I never touch the ring, and I never stand on the cover. But Slavik from the apartment where the yardkeepers live got up onto the manhole cover and started to jump. He was jumping on the cover and singing about the "The Three Little Pigs":

Who's afraid of the Big Bad Wolf,
The Big Bad Wolf, the Big Bad Wolf . . .

Slavik kept jumping and singing until the cover moved over. The cover moved over, and Slavik fell into the manhole. It's a good thing that Uncle Vasya, who was just coming out to sweep the yard, saw everything and saved Slavik. I remembered this event the entire three years we spent in evacuation in the Urals. For some reason, I really wanted to see Slavik when I got back. I wanted to see him and to tell him about the real wolves that had come up to our *izba* in the winter. But when we returned to Leningrad, Slavik was not in the yard. He had died during the siege.

They would often take me to the theater. Frightful scenes of those early days of my childhood have been engraved in my memory. From *The Nutcracker*—when huge gray rats with bloody eyes appeared in the purple rays of the spotlight. From *The Bluebird*—when Sugar was so generously feeding his frail, sweet fingers to the children. From *Eugene Onegin*—during the scene of the duel between Onegin and Lensky. Papa would later describe how, during each of the frightening scenes, I would ask to be taken out of the theater.

The circus—now that's entirely a different matter. There is a little man in the arena, and he's made up to look like Charlie Chaplin: a round black hat, a thin, brush-like mustache, a baggy and ill-fitting jacket and pants, huge boots, which make the clown trip over the carpets in the arena, every so often falling into the sawdust. That's the clown Caran D'Ache, or simply Pencil. He always performs with a black and white dog. Her name is Manyunya. The circus is filled with people from floor to ceiling. Everyone is laughing.

January 1941. Mama is taking me to a New Year's party at the Palace of Young Pioneers. That's on Nevsky Prospekt. From our neighborhood of Lesnoye we ride for a long time on streetcar number 20. It's freezing. I blow on the window to make a little peephole in the frozen glass. We're crossing the Liteiny Bridge. The Neva River is covered with ice, on top of which are snowdrifts. Here and there you can see black figures of fishermen. They're ice fishing. We get off the streetcar near the circus. Again my favorite circus! Mama takes me by the hand. We walk along the Fontanka toward Nevsky Prospekt. We are by the bridge, which crosses the Fontanka on Nevsky. "This is Anichkov Bridge," mama says. Huge bronze horses stand on each of the four corners of the bridge. Muscular bronze men can barely restrain them.

"How strong they are!" I cry with delight.

"You will be just like them—Danik!" Mama tells me. And then she adds, "They were done by the sculptor Klodt."

We cross Nevsky. We're at the Palace of Young Pioneers.

Besides mama and papa, I also have Grandma Freyda, Grandpa Borukh, Uncle Yanya, Uncle Abrasha, Aunt Berta, Aunt Tsilya, Aunt Enya, Uncle Moysha, Aunt Tanya, Uncle Israel, Aunt Dora, Aunt Difa, Aunt Mirochka, Uncle Miron, Cousin Malvina, Cousin Mika, second cousins Tedik, Alik, and Yadik. There are other relatives. This is all on papa's side—our *meshpucha*. "Our *meshpucha*," says grandma with pride. Our *meshpucha* lives in different areas of Leningrad. For example, grandma and grandpa with Aunt Berta, Uncle Yanya, Aunt Tsilya, and Malvina all live together on the Petrograd Side. Once a week on Sundays we go to the Petrograd Side. Sometimes we go to visit other relatives for a birthday party. We call it going to Zhukovskaya or to Kolokolnaya or to Lermontovsky. Or to the Mokhovaya to see Aunt Musya Rekhter. Her husband was papa's cousin. No one knows anything about him.

Sometimes during our Sunday excursions to the Petrograd Side grandma or grandpa digs out a mysterious letter from somewhere and talks quietly with my mama and papa. They take pictures out of an envelope. They speak in Yiddish. They utter names: Munya, Rusha, Remik, Danik, Palestine. Little by little, I start to understand: my papa's older brother, Uncle Munya, lives in Palestine with his family. They are from our *meshpucha*. His youngest son is also called Danik. He's going to become a famous Israeli painter.

Uncle Mitya Kogan's wife, Auntie Musya Trushina, breast-fed me when mama was very sick. Their son, Borya, is my favorite cousin. They live on the opposite side of town, beyond Nevskaya Zastava. An old outpost on the bank of the Neva. Aunt Musya has a brother, Uncle Kolya. He lives in the same building, but in a different apartment. He lives with a friend, Uncle Yura. They're bachelors.

My other grandfather's name is Wolf. He is mama's father. Grandpa Wolf lives in Belarus in a town called Polotsk. Once, before the war, mama took me to Polotsk. I was about four. I don't remember the trip. What I mean is, how we got on the train, who saw us off, who met us. I do remember Grandpa Wolf. He's old. He has a white beard. For some reason he's wearing a long sheepskin jacket. Does that mean it was winter? Yes, winter. He's sitting by the kitchen window. You can see the street through the window. Snowdrifts. The roofs of the wooden houses are covered in snow. Smoke billows out of sooty-brown, brick chimneys. I'm sitting on Grandpa Wolf's lap. He's feeding me a sweet roll and milk from a mug. "This is Polotsk, son," says Grandpa Wolf. "But there was a time when we lived in golden Lithuania, in Shavel." From what mama told me, I know that Grandpa Wolf, Grandma Eva, mama's sisters, Rivochka and Manya, brother Mitya, and my mother ran away from Lithuania fleeing the White Poles. The Poles killed Rivochka. Grandma Eva died from sorrow and typhus. Grandpa settled in Polotsk with the rest of the children. He used to be a rabbi. He became a teacher in a Jewish school. At that time there were still Jewish schools in Belarus. Then he married an orphan Grandma Eva had, at one time, taken in. Mama's stepsisters, Pesya and Fanya, were born. They grew up and finished school. Pesya is now studying at the Pedagogical Institute. She's going to be a math teacher. Fanya is at a junior teachers college. She's going to be an elementary school teacher. Pesya and Fanya look like my mother. They have blue eyes, and they are a lot of fun. They play with me when Grandpa Wolf gets tired or is praying.

Mama's older sister, Manechka, and her husband, Monus, and their two children, Osya and Bella, live in Minsk. Osya is big. He's not a good student, and soon they'll send him to Leningrad to a trade school. My papa is going to keep an eye on him. It's been decided that once Osya finishes this trade school, my papa will get him a job at his factory.

My mother's oldest brother, Uncle Eyno, still lives in Lithuania, in Panevežis. He is a bank president. Mama says that he is "noble like a magnate." I know what a magnet is. It attracts iron. What does a magnate do? Attract people? Uncle Eyno lives with his wife and two sons. We have pictures of them in our album.

Osya came to Leningrad. He's studying at the trade school. He's going to be a lathe operator. He has a black coat with silver buttons with hammers embossed on them, a wide leather belt with a buckle and a uniform cap. "You, Osya, look just like a Gymnasium student," papa jokes. All the local riff-raff are afraid of Osya.

Mama recalls how I was the first to notice that the war had started. Although it was Sunday, I woke up very early. I left my room and went into my parents'. I started to wake them up so that they could turn on the radio. Mama was upset with me, but papa got up and turned on the radio. Molotov was speaking. The war with Germany had begun.

To this day, I can't understand why they sent our kindergarten to the summer place in Akulovka even though the war had started. Akulovka was in the Novgorod Region. It was there that the Germans were heading. The kindergarten where Auntie Musya Trushina worked as an accountant. Her son, Borya, and I went with Auntie Musya.

Our bedroom in Akulovka was on the second floor. My bed was next to Borya's. A few other boys also slept in this room. I remember that night clearly, when I first saw the war. Borya woke me up gently, so as not to scare me. So as not to scare me and the other children. Borya was a bit older than we were. I got up and went to the window. Lightning crisscrossed the sky and there was rattling thunder. But it wasn't lightning and thunder. It was searchlights, cannons, and bombs. In the beam of a searchlight, I saw a plane flying over our house. There were crosses on its black wings. "That's a Junker. A fascist fighter-bomber," said Borya, who knew everything in the world.

It was a miracle that they were able to get the kindergarten back home from Akulovka.

There's a new word they keep repeating in our house—evacuation. It's the middle of August 1941. Nanny Nyura went back to her village in the Ryazan Region. Papa is serving in a tank battalion outside Leningrad, near Pulkovo. Again he's the commander. From time to time, he tears himself away to see us. Mama does not want to be evacuated. Papa tries to convince her to leave "for Danik's sake." I also don't want to go to that incomprehensible, distant evacuation. The Germans are encircling Leningrad. Finally mama agrees to go. The trade school, where Osya is studying, is still in Leningrad. Osya comes to say good-bye. Mama pleads with Osya to come with us. I remember how she tells Osya, "Manya would never forgive me, Osya, if something were to happen to you!"

We set off for the evacuation. Besides mama and me, there are other relatives in our train car: Aunt Tsilya (the wife of Uncle Yanya, who is in the hospital) with my cousin Malvina, Madame Bekman with Uncle Buzya (Malvina's grandparents), Aunt Enya, Grandpa Boruch's older sister and Moysha's mother (he is in the army), with Aunt Tanya (Moysha's wife) and a distant relative Maria Osipovna. She's traveling with her typewriter. Maria Osipovna is a typist. "I will survive anywhere with my armored car!" says Maria Osipovna and shows me her little black suitcase bound with a belt. That's the case for her typewriter. Maria Osipovna is afraid that they'll steal her typewriter, and so she seldom leaves her compartment.

Everyone says that our train is the last. After that the Germans will totally encircle Leningrad, and the siege will begin. After the night air raid by German Junkers over Akulovka, I understand what war is. We are going eastward. Our train speeds toward the Urals. In Leningrad I have a big children's book called *A Tale about the Great Plan*. From this book I remember that there's a lot of iron in the Urals. They make steel from the iron ore in metal factories. From this steel they made the rails on which our train is riding, and the tanks in which my papa is fighting the Germans. We're being evacuated to the Urals.

Madame Bekman looks into our compartment and says, "We are so lucky. We're riding in a train car with compartments, just as if we were on vacation." Mama nods her head out of politeness. But I see tears in mama's eyes. She keeps thinking, What's going to happen to our papa? What's going to happen to Osya?

Beyond the train windows are potato fields, a village here and there, forests and swamps. Sharing our compartment is Aunt Tsilya with Malvina, who is three and a half years older than I. Malvina and I play children's dominos. The domino game is called "The Orchard and the Garden." You have to add the same type of vegetable, fruit, or berry to each other. For example, a carrot with a carrot. Or an apple with an apple. Or a strawberry with a strawberry. Malvina thinks for a long time before each move. Sometimes she makes a mistake and puts an apple next to a pear. Or a blackberry with a raspberry.

Suddenly, our entire orchard-garden flies off the table. The train screeches and grinds to a halt. The engine's whistle toots. The buffers clank. Our train car stops in the middle of a forest. The conductor runs along the car and yells for "everybody to leave the train immediately." Mama grabs me by the hand. Aunt Tsilya shoves Malvina out of the compartment. The corridor is crowded. Everybody is yelling, shoving, and hurrying each other. Mama jumps off the iron train car steps. I jump into her arms. The conductor yells, "Get down! Get down!" I hear the noise of the planes. I hear the shooting and the cannonade. "Lie down! Lie down!" the conductors are shouting. Mama pins me to the ground; she covers me with her body. Somewhere next to us I can hear an explosion. And a long and horrible howl. I lift my head up. A huge black plane with white crosses on the wings, smoking and howling, falls from the sky directly onto our train. I push my face to the ground and wait to see what's going to happen next. Somewhere farther away from us, on the other side of the train, we can hear a crash. Everything becomes still. "Into the forest! Into the forest!" orders the conductor. We run into the forest.

The passengers are all crowded in a clearing. Among them are our people: Aunt Tsilya with Malvina, Madame Bekman with Uncle Buzya, Aunt Enya with Aunt Tanya and our distant relative Maria Osipovna with her "armored car." The conductor comes. The German Junkers had shot up the train. The engine is damaged. They'll exchange the engine by evening, and then we'll keep going toward the Urals. "But our ack-ack guns shot down the fascist. He fell down right there." The conductor points to somewhere into the forest on the other side of the train. "The vile thing burned up! Nothing but smoke is left!" I see the black smoke rising over the forest.

We've been riding for a very long time. The train wheels clickity-clack like drums. Between the clacks I put words with a beat: papa, tank, mama, field, forest, rain, meadow, bridge. We stop at various train stations. Mama, Aunt Tsilya, and Aunt Tanya run to get hot water for tea and bread for our whole *meshpucha*. They're the youngest. That's what Madame Bekman says. She never leaves the train car. Even when the train is there for two or three hours. Even when they let us get a breath of fresh air. Sometimes mama is lucky. She's able to exchange something for milk, brought to the train by peasant women dressed in quilted jackets and thick scarves.

Uncle Buzya Bekman exchanges tobacco for milk. He brought a stash of it from Leningrad.

The train stops at a town called Vereshchagino in the Molotov Region. We have arrived at the Urals. We drag our packages and suitcases off the train. Finally we are here. As it turns out, we have arrived, but it's not our journey's end. It turns out that we still have to travel forty versts to our final destination. To a big village called Siva. That's what we were told by the "local authorities."

"As long as they aren't the local secret agencies," Madame Bekman says to my mama and my aunt Tsilya.

Elderly Aunt Enya hears everything and just in case shushes her, "Sh-h-h, Madame Bekman! Haven't you had enough trouble by them?"

Uncle Buzya Bekman puffs on his pipe and makes arrangements with the elderly peasants from the collective farm to get us to Siva. He makes arrangements and treats them to *makhorka*. That's a strong homegrown tobacco. The smoke is so pungent that it's impossible to stand near him. Malvina says, "Phew!" and runs away from him.

We make our way from Vereshchagino to Siva in two wagons. A horse pulls each wagon. The first wagon is filled with our packages and suitcases. Malvina, Aunt Enya, and I sit on top of them. Aunt Enya is very old and frail. Madame Bekman and Maria Osipovna with her "armored car" sit in the other wagon on top of all the stuff. Mama and all the others traipse behind the wagons. The peasants stroll, holding the reins in their hands. The horses obey the reins.

"All this mud. The Egyptian plagues," says Aunt Enya. She's all hunched over from old age. It's even hard for her simply to sit in the wagon. But I'm interested in everything. From time to time, the horse lifts its tail and dumps a green bomb right under the wagon. A black forest surrounds us.

Finally, toward evening, when the red sun is setting behind the black forest, we come out onto a wide road. I have never seen such roads. In Leningrad we had asphalt roadways. Sometimes cobblestones. Here the road was paved with round pieces of wood. After the mud and deep puddles on the forest road, the horse pulled the wagon load easily along the wooden roadway. "The Ural Postroad!" said the peasant driving our horse. Then he added, "And here's our native Siva!"

We drive onto a bridge, which spans a wide river, also called Siva. Over the bridge from the very banks of the river and on, and on, almost to the mountains overgrown with trees, you can see *izba*s. "We're here, at our place of evacuation, Danik. That's the village Siva," says mama.

Evening. They put us up in the schoolhouse. It's the end of August, dark outside. We set ourselves up on the floor and fall asleep. I dream of horses. They look like the ones mama and I saw on the Fontanka Embankment. Papa, tall and strong, is driving the wagon. We're rushing into battle.

I wake up late. Malvina has already washed and combed her hair and is playing ball in the corner of the classroom. Mama, Aunt Tsilya, and Uncle Buzya have gone to rent us a place to live. The local authorities assigned a place right near the school for elderly Aunt Enya and for Tanya, who has a heart condition. Maria Osipovna went directly to the Village Council. Madame Bekman, who is feeding Malvina and me, tells us all about this. "A typist! Who's going to argue—it's a golden profession! They'll grab her right up! And they'll give her a worker's ration card at that!" says Madame Bekman about Maria Osipovna. I don't know what a worker's ration card is. I can't figure out if Madame Bekman is happy for Maria Osipovna or not.

Toward evening, mama and the others come back. They're dead-tired. Their galoshes and boots are covered in sticky brownish clay. They really lucked out. Almost at the end, without any real hope left, they decided to knock at the door of a large, handsome *izba* at the edge of the village, not far from the river. Mama rented a room for us in the Teryokhins' *izba*. And Aunt Tsilya and her father, Uncle Buzya, next door. That *izba* belonged to the Teryokhins' son who was off fighting the Germans.

A dull autumn rain is lashing at the windows of the school. I look out the window: when will the carts come to get our things and us? Finally I see a horse and wagon. A man all wrapped up in an oilskin coat sits at the reins. He ties the horse up to the post at the bottom of the school steps. He shakes off his coat and scrapes the clay off his boots with a wooden scraper. He walks into the school.

That's the owner of the *izba,* where we will spend the evacuation. His name is Andrey Mikheich. He has thinning gray hair and sad gray eyes. He's well shaven. Under his oilskin coat—a worn-out jacket. Under the jacket—a gray canvas shirt with a high collar, like a field shirt. On his feet—boots. We load up our things and set off for our room in the Teryokhins' *izba.*

The horse whose name, Starlet, Andrey Mikheich from time to time calls out, goes through the wide, tall double gates and stops in the middle of the yard. On the left of the wagon I see an *izba,* built from large, golden-brown logs. The chinks between the logs are filled with moss. There are tall sheds with thatched roofs on the right. Later I find out that that's the horse barn, the cattle shed, and other outbuildings, one with a hayloft. A horse, a cow, sheep, chickens, geese, and a pig live there. In the back of the yard, I see the brown wasteland of the vegetable garden. A small cubicle sticks out between the garden and the outbuildings. That's the outhouse. In the left corner of the vegetable garden, under the mountain ash blazing with red-orange berries, there is a small hut. That's the bathhouse.

Andrey Mikheich helps Aunt Tsilya, Malvina, Uncle Buzya, and Madame Bekman carry their suitcases and packages into the *izba* next door. The Teryokhins' daughter-in-law, Olga, lives there with her son, Mitya. Mitya's father, the Red Army soldier Nikolay Teryokhin, is fighting the fascists, just like my papa.

A teenager runs out onto the steps. He's wearing a belted canvas shirt and pants all decorated with patches. On his feet he wears longish baskets trimmed with cloth. These baskets stay on his feet with the help of strings. Later, I find out they are called *lapti*—bast shoes. They are woven from bast, which is stripped from the inside of tree bark. There are lined winter *lapti* and light summer ones. I will spend three years wearing bast shoes. Mama will, too.

"My name is Pashka," says the teenager. "And what's yours?"

"And my name is Danik," I answer. "And this is my mother, Stella Vladimirovna."

"That's a hard one!" Pashka says in amazement. "So, who would you be?"

"We're from Leningrad!" I say with pride and even with some boasting.

"And they say you're the vacated ones!"

I don't immediately get it that "vacated" is a distortion of the word "evacuated."

Pashka is to become my older friend and teacher of village life.

In the meantime, mama begins to bring our things inside the *izba*. An older woman, Elena Matveevna, helps her. Elena Matveevna tells me to call her Baba (Grandma) Lena." She's the owner of the *izba*. Andrey Mikheich is her husband. I will call him Ded (Grandpa) Andrey. Pashka is their son. In time these hosts start to refer to mama as Vladimirovna and she calls them Matveevna and Mikheich—by patronymic, after the village fashion.

Baba Lena has a kind, round face and brown eyes all framed by wrinkles. She looks like my Grandma Freyda. Baba Lena is plump around the middle. She wears a long black skirt, bast shoes, and a dark headscarf.

I miss my Grandma Freyda and my Grandpa Borukh. They were evacuated to Sverdlovsk together with Uncle Abrasha and his family. Uncle Abrasha is a talented designer. He's needed behind the front lines. He works in a military factory.

Pashka takes me inside the *izba*. We go up the stairs onto a high landing. The wood railing of the landing is decorated with wooden carvings. A heavy door opens wide into the entryway. It's cold there. A dull light coming through the window barely illuminates up the entryway. We go into the kitchen. A huge white stove looks like a fortress inside the *izba*. The stove is made of bricks. It stands sideways to the door. From the side, almost all the way to the top, you can see grooves. As if a few bricks were taken out from top to bottom. These are steps. They use them to get up onto the stove. It's warm there. You can sleep there. You can also sleep on the *polati*. That's a platform of planks between the stove and the kitchen wall on the entryway side.

"Come on into the main room, Danik," Baba Lena invites me into the next room. A picture in a gold frame hangs in the left corner of the main room. It's a picture of an old man. He has an elongated dark face and a long beard. He is wearing a robe made of a gilded cloth. The old man holds a stick in his left hand. His right hand is turned to me. The fingers on this hand are folded into a pinch. An little lamp with a wobbling wick hangs on a chain under the picture. I saw those in mama's laboratory. Maybe not exactly like that. Baba Lena walks up to the picture and quickly touches her forehead, her stomach, her right shoulder, her left shoulder, all with the fingers of her right hand, also folded into a pinch. She's touching with her pinched fingers and bowing at the same time. I stare at her in amazement. "That's an icon of Nicholas the Wonder Worker," Baba Lena points to the picture. "And that's an icon lamp." She points to what I thought was a laboratory spirit lamp.

The icon lamp in front of the image of Nicholas the Wonder Worker is always burning. Baba Lena keeps pouring oil into it. Actually, Nicholas the Wonder Worker is like a live person in the *izba*. Later I will often see Baba Lena talking to the icon. Andrey Mikheich never crosses himself. He says that he doesn't believe in God. He's an atheist. He's manager of the local Zagotzerno, grain production office.

A long bench stands in the main room along the wall with two windows. A table stands next to it. And another bench. On the other side of the table. The windows open out onto the street. We get a small back room. The main room has a curtain, with a wide bed behind it. There are bronze cones on the headboard of the bed.

Floral-print pillows rise in a pyramid up to the ceiling. That's Baba Lena and Ded Andrey's bed.

How difficult it is to separate those sixty-year-old impressions from my present memories of those impressions!

The first autumn and the first winter of our evacuation were particularly difficult. We had no bread, no potatoes, no meat. Mama had no job. We had no ration cards either. We did have some clothes, which mama traded with the neighboring peasants for necessities. Or, on Sundays, mama and I would make our way to the market square. You could sometimes exchange or buy some food products (using papa's military pay, which was transferred to us each month from his unit) at an unbelievably high price. But you couldn't get to the market square until the end of October, when the slimy clay, which sucked in your boots, would harden with the frost. Our hosts also helped us some. They gave us food now and again. More often to me. Mama was too proud to accept any.

Yes, it seems that all the adversities had passed my mother by. She lived for papa's letters and postcards, from her brother Mitya, from her sisters, Manya, Pesya, and Fanya. The war had scattered them all. Finally the first news arrived. Her older sister, Manya, ended up in Chelyabinsk with her little daughter, Bella. They came there "barefoot and naked" in the full meaning of that expression. Miraculously, they made it out of Lithuania, where they had gone a day before the start of the war to visit their older brother, Eyno, and his family. Mama sent Manya and Bella some of our winter things. The fate of Manya's son, Osya, remained unknown. The Germans had encircled Leningrad. Papa wrote from the Leningrad front that Osya's trade school was evacuated along the "ice road" over the frozen Lake Ladoga. Papa and Uncle Mitya were fighting in the tank units. Pesya and Fanya were serving in the signal corps.

At the end of October, the snow fell. The northern winter had set in. The snow would be so high that sometimes we couldn't go out through the door. And Baba Lena had to milk the cow and feed the farm animals early in the morning. She would wake Pashka up. Usually he slept on the stove or on the *polati*. Pashka would get up on the roof through the chimney, jump into the snowdrift, and dig out the door.

All winter Pashka skied to school. That was a pleasure in comparison to the trips along the streets filled with clayish autumn-spring mud.

Soon I learned to sleep on the *polati*. Onions were spread along the length and width of the wooden plank. The yellow-brown bulbs were warm and springy. Sheepskins were thrown on top of them. And we were on top of that: Pashka, the cat called Vaska, and I. And when it was so drafty in the *izba* at night that we got cold on the *polati,* we would move to the stove. The smooth stones, polished by many years, retained the heat. The stove and the *polati* were our club, our auditorium. Pashka and I talked about everything in the world. With his stories he was getting me ready for summer life in the village. I would try and tell him as much as I could remember about my Leningrad, about papa, about our courtyard.

The *polati* were in semidarkness. The onions rustled under the sheepskins. Their rustling mixed with the rustling of the cockroaches that occupied the *polati* in countless hordes. Dark brown and nosey, they came out of everywhere and stared at me, twitching their long whiskers. Soon I got used to them and didn't pay any attention. All you had to do in the morning was to go out into the entryway and shake the cockroaches off your clothes.

The cat Vaska was a huge, black and white lazybones, who spent a large portion of the winter on the stove. In March he started to disappear at night, and in the morning, all covered in soot, he would get back inside through the chimney, sometimes with a scratched face or a ripped ear. But the Teryokhins valued Vaska for his indomitable bravery. He would catch wild hamsters and rats in the horse barn or in the cattle shed and bring them to the stoop to show his masters.

We're lazing around on the *polati*. Pashka, the cat Vaska, and I. Pashka and I are playing cards. Vaska is snoozing. Below, at the kitchen table, are mama, Baba Lena, and Ded Andrey. A kerosene lamp on the table is giving some light. The wick is twisted, so it barely lights up their faces. It's evening. The latest news is coming over the radio from the district center. Then you can hear a song. Baba Lena cries when they play songs on the radio. Baba Lena and Ded Andrey have three sons at the front: Nikolay, Aleksandr, and Ivan. The eldest son, Nikolay, is Mitya's father and Olga's husband, from the *izba* where live Uncle Buzya, Madame Bekman, and Aunt Tsilya with Malvina. Their hostess, Olga, is from a Permyak village. The Permyaks live not far from our village Siva.

Often there's no kerosene for the lamp. Then they set up a tripod, called a *svetets,* and in the center they stick a long, dry sliver of pine. It burns and crackles. Burning coals, hissing their farewells, fall into a bowl filled with water.

Sometimes mama tells fortunes with cards.

Sometimes she sings. Mama has a good voice. She remembers many songs. When mama sings, Baba Lena doesn't cry, like she cries at the radio. If there is no wash to be done, no dinner to be made, and no cleaning to be done, mama reads. Mama likes Pushkin and Esenin best of all.

Mama writes poetry. She sends her poems to papa at the front. In papa's last letter there was a newspaper clipping of a Simonov poem. "Wait for me, and I'll return . . ." Mama often reads this poem out loud. I like it. But I don't understand what "wait for me" means.

Mitya, who lives in the *izba* next door, is a hunter. He is Baba Lena and Ded Andrey's grandson. He's sixteen years old, in the ninth grade. Next year he will finish secondary school and go to flight school. He wanders off into the forest for a long time on his skis with a double-barrel shotgun and with his dog. Yes, I forgot about the dogs. A red, fluffy dog, Polkan, lives in our yard on a chain. Mitya, the hunter, has a black and fluffy one, Zhuchka. The dogs have doghouses with a semicircular opening. Inside they have hay for warmth. On particularly cold nights Baba Lena lets Polkan inside the *izba*. And Mitya lets Zhuchka in. Mitya is a successful and generous hunter. Often he gets hares. Sometimes forest pigeons. Mitya brings a part of his loot to Baba Lena. She treats mama and me.

In the spring, Mitya picked up a little white hare in the forest. He lived in the *izba* until the summer. He hopped, chewed on cabbage, left puddles, and spread dark little nuts all around.

Mama tells fortunes with cards. Her fortune-telling is called "playing solitaire." Sometimes mama ponders the cards. Sometimes she quickly moves them from one spot to another. Baba Lena asks to have her fortune told. Mama foretells a letter from the front. And a letter comes. Little by little, in the nearby *izba*s they find out about mama's fortune-telling powers. Then in the faraway *izba*s. The peasants come by. "Be so kind and tell our fortune, Vladimirovna dear. Don't refuse us, dear one." Mama spreads the cards out and sees: if the cow will successfully give birth to a calf, if it's dangerous to chop wood in the forest for fear of wolves, will the back pain let up or should they go to the hospital to see a doctor, will the awaited news from the front come. The peasant women go home satisfied with the knowledge of the truths opened to them. And when Baba Lena closes the doors for the night, she brings in gifts left by them for mama in the entryway.

There is only one thing that mama will not foretell—will a soldier come home alive or will they send a burial notice? It happened after mama started to tell the fortune of Antipovna's husband. Her *izba* was across the road from ours. Mama took a look at the cards, cried out, mixed up the cards, and locked herself in our room. And the next day the postwoman brought a burial notice to Antipovna.

Our first winter in the village has ended. It may have ended according to the calendar, but not according to the frost. True, the days are getting longer, and occasionally the sun is starting to make its way through the snow clouds. Pashka got a pair of unpainted, birch skis from somewhere and brought them for me. I started to ski on the snow-covered fields, to the nearest underbrush and back. It was fun to slide along the sloping meadow surface, clad in a snow crust that melted by day and froze by night. Down to the banks of the Siva and down, down, down onto the ice, enshrouded in the deep snow.

Pashka promised, "Daily fishing will start when the river opens up, when the ice breaks!"

One night, spring came to our *izba*. I woke up from the mad dashing around and the doors slamming. Pashka was not on the *polati*. I put on my felt boots and went down. Pashka had just run into the *izba*.

"What's happening?" I asked him.

"Manka is having her calf!" Pashka shouted and again ran out with a pail of hot water.

I grabbed my hat and ran out onto the stoop. A light beamed from the cowshed. I ran across the yard and peeked inside. Manka the cow was lying on the straw and moaning long, drawn-out moos. Baba Lena was petting her and saying, "Be patient, Manka, be patient, our provider, not much longer, my sweet!" Manka's tail was raised. Suddenly a small brown head of a baby calf started to appear from under her tail. Ded Andrey was right there. And now the entire calf was in his hands. Baba Lena cut off something with a kitchen knife, and tied it up with a brown thread. I saw blood, jumped, and ran back to the stoop. The gates of the cowshed swung open, and Ded Andrey brought the calf out into the yard and was coming toward the stoop. I opened the door into the *izba*. Ded Andrey gingerly put the calf down onto the kitchen floor. And the little brown creature dug its tiny hoofs into the floor and got up on its

skinny legs, which bent like twigs. Soon Baba Lena and Pashka
came. Baba Lena kept on running between the calf in the kitchen
and the icon of Nicholas the Wonder Worker in the main room.
She kept on crossing herself and repeating, "Glory to You, O Lord,
Jesus Christ! Our dearest Manka has given us such a wonderful little
bull calf! Oh, what happiness!" They laid down straw in the kitchen.
The calf lived in the *izba* for a week or two, until he got stronger,
and the frost let up.

Shrovetide was coming. Ded Andrey, with Mitya and Pashka, set
up swings in the yard. Because I was so young, I didn't notice all the
changes in our lives. That's how a child accepts every new day in his
life. For the first time, I saw the railroad and the train, a plane in the
sky, an elephant at the circus, colorful birdcherry trees. Just as naturally I accepted life's rhythms in the Teryokhins' *izba*. For instance,
there was always a bowl of boiled beets in the kitchen. A wooden
spoon was in it. Actually, they ate with wooden spoons. There were
neither forks nor table knives. There were a few kitchen knives.
When I got hungry, I would take a piece of the juicy reddish brown
beet. I'd eat it and follow with a sip of the red beet broth. In the
same way, when necessary, I would clean an onion and bite it with
passion and tears, chew it, and swallow the juicy and bitter delight.

Onions served many purposes, besides food. A couple of times
each winter, we would all get seriously poisoned by fumes. In an effort to keep in the heat, our hostess would sometimes close the
dampers early. Fumes from the stove would come right into the
*izba*. In the morning, we had trouble getting up. Headaches. Nau-
sea. Baba Lena would cook onions. We would put pieces of cooked
onions in our ears. In an hour or two, the stupor would go away.

Another picture that stays with me. I walk into the main room.
There are two women from neighboring *izba*s there. Prokhorovna
and Nikiforovna. I knew them both. They would often stop by to
see Baba Lena. And I would sometimes end up in their *izba*s as well.

Pashka would take me along to play with the neighbors' kids. Or Baba Lena would take me there, why I don't remember. I walk into the main room and see Baba Lena sitting on a bench by the window, spinning wool. Baba Lena has a distaff for that. Something like a long back of a chair on a post with a footboard. A big tuft of wool was tied to the distaff. Baba Lena was holding the distaff with her leg, pressing it against the floor. With her left hand, she was spinning wool, turning it into thread, and with her right hand, she was spinning the spindle (which looked like a top) and winding the yarn around it. She was singing all the while. Prokhorovna also sang. A third neighbor, Nikiforovna, with no scarf on her head, was sitting on a bench by the other window, her head on the lap of Prokhorovna, who was picking through her hair with her left hand. In her right hand, she held a kitchen knife. From time to time, with a click of the knife, she would crush something that had been sitting in Nikiforovna's hair. I was disgusted and horrified. I ran to our room, to mama. Mama had been writing a letter to Aunt Musya in Nizhnye Mully near Molotov, which is what Perm was called at the time. Uncle Mitya's wife and my cousin Borya had been evacuated there from Leningrad.

"Mama, what is that horrible thing that Prokhorovna is doing there? She has a knife in her hand!"

"Sweetheart, she's looking for lice."

"What are these vile things called lice, and why do you have to look for them?"

"Lice are a real misfortune. They attack people and bite them. It's not pleasant. They don't let you sleep. They don't leave you in peace. But the worst thing is that they carry diseases from which people die. Your grandmother Eva, my mother, died from typhus, which is carried by lice."

"So what is it, mama? Can you kill lice only with a knife?"

"Oh no, Danik. Of course it can be done otherwise. With

chemicals. With kerosene, for example. But kerosene kills only the lice themselves. Their nits need to be destroyed by hand. And then you can wash them off with soap and hot water."

That was on a Thursday before Shrovetide. On Thursdays the Teryokhins fired up the bath. First to wash were Baba Lena and Ded Andrey. Then Olga. Then Pashka and Mitya. Then mama washed me, and Aunt Tsilya washed Malvina. Then they dressed us, and we waited for our mothers in the entryway of the bathhouse. Madame Bekman and Uncle Buzya would come at the end, when the heat subsided. Madame Bekman always came with her besom and Uncle Buzya with a wooden jar of kvass, which he made from fermented bread crust, according to his own recipe.

Times were hard. Each evening our host and mama would sit by the radio listening to the latest news. The news on the radio was not happy. Even though the Germans were stopped near Moscow, they reached the Volga River, made it to Stalingrad. They conquered half of Russia, Belarus, Ukraine, Crimea, and a part of the Caucasus. We got a letter from papa, who was in the hospital. He had been wounded in the shoulder by a fragment of an antitank mine. News from Teryokhins' sons seldom came.

But still, everybody in our *izba* celebrated Shrovetide. Baba Lena baked a lot of blinis. She invited mama and me to the table. I never ate such tasty and beautiful blinis. Maybe they seemed so special because we never had enough bread. In the main room, in the middle of the table, in full splendor stood a large plate with a mountain of huge, golden-white blinis. Baba Lena was in the kitchen baking the last blinis, artfully greasing the frying pan with a hare's foot soaked in melted butter. Then we took our places at the table. You would take one from the pile of blinis, pour honey and butter on it, fold it in quarters, and bite off a piece. With the blinis we drank milk with dried raspberries. Just before Shrovetide, Manka the cow began to give milk again.

Now, when over half a century has passed since the evacuation,

I think about the striking changes that had taken place in my mother's life during the war years. Not to mention in my life. I drank in this new life the way a newborn sucks in milk. An infant will take milk from any mother and will grow on any milk. But mama—what about her? She was numb from constant fear for papa, for her father (she had no news of Grandpa Wolf until the end of the war), for her brothers, for her sisters, and for her nephews and nieces. All the external events, not connected to her primary pain and brooding, passed her by. Her world of happiness was destroyed by the war. As evacuees, we found ourselves in a new world of daily life. Mother accepted this new world with resignation and detachment. This is the only explanation I can find for her indifference to my childish active participation in the village Russian Orthodox holidays. If I had received something in the way of a Jewish upbringing from Grandma Freyda, Grandpa Borukh, and briefly, but vividly from Grandpa-Rabbi Wolf, it all blew away in the Ural blizzards, all dissipated in a stream of new words, objects, and customs.

Paskha, the Russian Orthodox Easter, was already approaching. Not the Jewish Passover, with matzo, with tales of escape from Egyptian slavery and the forty-year wandering over the sands in search of our old native land—Canaan. No, not that Passover. We did not celebrate this Passover. No one spoke to me about it. Probably mama and our relatives decided not to disturb my young imagination by reminding me about our Jewishness. Most likely, I forgot about being Jewish. It's true, I did forget. So the delicious Easter cake *kulich,* the Easter eggs, which were dyed with paint made from onionskins, and which had to be rolled down a little hill made of wood, as well as the other culinary delights tempting an eternally insatiable boy, all impressed me as a real holiday. Mother decided not to deprive me of such a celebration. It is true that Elena Matveevna Teryokhina was the only one in the *izba* who was a believer. She was the only one in the family who prayed and crossed herself in front of the icons. So Shrovetide, Easter, and then Trinity

Sunday, Nicholas's Day, and Christmas in our *izba* were less religious than folk holidays.

Yes, I totally forgot who I was by birth. And this is what happened to me about a year after we came to Siva. By that time I felt myself totally at home with the children of the Urals, blue-eyed with high cheekbones from a mixture of Permyak and Russian blood, pugnacious from the severity of the climate and from a hunters' fervor that lived in every Ural *izba*. Even today I burn with shame at my treachery. A family of evacuees had come to our village. They didn't come at the beginning with everybody else, but much later. I considered myself to be totally local, a Sivan. Actually, I didn't consider anything, I just didn't think about who I was. My Leningrad prewar life seemed like a colorful dream, a July morning, grapes called ladyfingers, something fantastic and gratuitous. There was a boy in this newly arrived Jewish family. Dark-haired, swarthy, Mediterranean-looking. I confronted this boy after class, behind the school. We were surrounded by local boys and by evacuated boys. But these evacuated boys had bonded with the Urals and made friends with the locals, having spent a year among the fields and vegetable gardens, fishing and running in the forests with them.

"Hey, you, vacated kid." The new boy stood there silently, staring at me with astonishment, unable to comprehend what it was that I wanted with him.

"Hey, you, vacated kid, let's fight." There was no stopping me. Flabbergasted by the boy's indifference to my pestering him, I continued, "What you staring at with your slimy eyes?"

Suddenly the boy answered me quietly. "Look at yourself. You're just the same!"

I looked at him and for the first time, as if in a mirror, I saw myself through the eyes of the boys around me, both the locals and the evacuees.

The birdcherry trees bloomed in the middle of May. White petals covered the front garden. The ice broke up. There was a thunder coming from the river. It got cooler. "Time to put up some ice," Ded Andrey decided. They hitched up Starlet to a cart. Ded Andrey, Pashka and Mitya went off to the river. They brought a cart full of ice from the river. They put the ice in the cellar. Covered it with straw. An icehouse was ready for the summer. There they kept milk, sour cream, cottage cheese, butter, eggs. They used this icehouse until October, when it got so cold in the entryway that milk froze in pots and meat dumplings froze in bags where they were stored. And by that time the ice was almost gone.

One day in June the Teryokhins set off for the cemetery, taking with them food and drink. Baba Lena, as usual, brought me along. It was Trinity Sunday. The inhabitants of Siva (women, old men, and children) were going to the cemetery to remember the deceased. Dark, hollow-crusted snow was still lying between the graves. Baba Lena spread a piece of canvas cloth on her mother's grave, in the shadow of an Orthodox wooden cross with two cross-pieces. One was horizontal, and the other attached at an angle. That's the kind of cross you could see everywhere. From a woven basket they took out the memorial spread: hard-boiled eggs, bread, salted mushrooms, salt pork, potatoes, *kutya*. The main course was the *kutya*: wheat grain cooked with honey. In the middle of this strange table, a birch-bast container of home brew stood high. The sun was hot. We were all thirsty. One by one, we took mouthfuls of the home brew, generously flavored with dried raspberries, which, in these parts, just like honey, were often used in the place of sugar. In August, raspberries were harvested by the pailful and on hot days set out to dry on the roof and on rainy days on baking sheets inside the Russian stove. We all ate and threw crumbled hard-boiled eggs and *kutya* around the grave for the birds. Baba Lena and Ded Andrey reminisced about various events in the lives of their parents, or of their brothers, or sisters, who had, by then, passed away. It was on this Trinity Sunday that I first heard about angels. Angels, like birds, had wings. Angels flew around the graves unseen, carrying our conversations to the ears of those we were remembering. Birds were akin to angels. I also sipped the home brew with the meal. No one stopped me until I became very tipsy. Mama got really distressed over this incident and, maybe for the first time since she had bid farewell to papa, she came out of her deep melancholy.

High hills rose on the south side of our village. A thick, wild forest started behind the hills. The hillsides were overgrown with raspberry thickets. There was a valley down below, between the village and the forest. The snow had come down from the high hills. Then the valley turned green with all different kinds of grasses. Compassionate locals had taught us that certain wild plants called *pestiki* grew at the foot of the hills and in the valley. Peasants collect and eat them. *Pestiki* appear only in early June, and soon they overripen and become inedible. The four of us, mama and I, Aunt Tsilya and Malvina, walk through the entire village. The clay has dried up some. The sun is hot. It's easy, light, and fun to walk in summer bast shoes. Mama and Aunt Tsilya carry wicker baskets. Malvina and I have bast baskets. We run around chasing each other, happy in the morning and the sun. Aunt Tsilya and Malvina are particularly lively. Yesterday they got a letter from the hospital from Uncle Yanya—papa's older brother. He is being honorably discharged from military service because of a kidney ailment. Soon he'll join us in Siva. We pass by the *izba*s on the edge of the village. Very tall pines stand up ahead on the hills. We walk along the green valley toward the hills. Patches of worn-out and porous snow hide in the hollows. Where are these magical *pestiki*? I read in some book that in distant southern lands there are breadfruit trees. But right here, on the edge of our village? What if they were just teasing us? Or maybe we won't recognize these unusual plants in the grasses. Mama sees distrust in my face. "Danik, sweetie, people never lie for nothing. And what would be the reason to lie in this instance?" And just as if to confirm mama's words, Aunt Tsilya yells to us, "Here they are—the *pestiki*! Come quickly!" We run to Aunt Tsilya. All around her, like pewter toy soldiers in hats with long feathers, stands an entire army of green stalks with elongated bluish tops. Many years later in America, when I saw asparagus, I remembered the *pestiki* from my Ural childhood. We fill our wicker and bast baskets with *pestiki*. I seem to recall you can even eat them raw.

In the first year of our evacuation, the most important thing was the vegetable garden. Mama realized that we could not possibly last another winter without our own potatoes and other vegetables. And our elderly hosts also knew that for mama with her independent character, it was easier to grow her own garden than to be indebted to someone else. Ded Andrey gave us almost a third of his own plot, which started right at the rear of the *izba*. He even plowed our garden together with his. He plowed it with Starlet harnessed to a plow. Ded Andrey walked behind the plow and the horse. Layers of earth rose and twisted from under the plow blade— the plowshare. Pashka and I ran behind the plow along the furrow and picked the supple, reddish-purple worms for fishing. After plowing the garden, Ded Andrey broke up the earth with a harrow, which had a multitude of teeth that crumbled the large earth clumps. Baba Lena gave us the already sprouting tubers of potatoes, and mama cut them up into as many pieces as there were sprouts. This was much more economical than planting an entire tuber. Mama and I also planted cabbage and tomatoes from our hosts' seedlings. Cucumbers, beets, carrots, dill, turnips, and rutabagas were planted from seeds, which were kept in a wet rag on a plate for a day or two.

Now it's impossible to imagine that my mother, the daughter of a pious Jew, had to take another unthinkable action in order to survive our second hard Ural winter. Without the slightest doubt, and of course with absolutely no knowledge of the religious roots of their renter guests, our kind hosts persistently advised my mother to get a piglet. Thank goodness they had, at least until August or September, an abundance of small potatoes that had begun to sprout and were unfit for cooking. "Don't be afraid, Stella Vladimirovna, start living the village life. And then everything will fall into place. Just you see, you can make it through the winter with the meat and the bacon."

And here we have our very own piglet, Fifer, snorting in the shed, and smacking with impatience, devouring potatoes boiled and mashed with nettle and goosefoot. And also we have two geese, waddling and walking back and forth between the meadow and the river, under my unremitting care. Mama and I have a large dominion: a garden, a piglet, geese. We are real villagers.

But, for me, fishing turned out to be the greatest joy of village life. When Ded Andrey plowed the garden, we put our worms into a small pail with soil. Pashka had the gear ready: the rod, the hooks, the fishing line, the floats. I had to make a fishing rod from scratch. Pashka said, "Danka, you'll have to cut a proper fishing rod in the forest." It was only a short distance to the forest. Our *izba* was on the edge of the village. Over the meadow we went down to the river. A path wound its way down the banks. It led into the forest. Several times Pashka stopped next to young birches. He measured them against my height. He just couldn't decide which one would suit me just right. Finally he chose one. Cut it down. Cleaned the bark off. The fishing rod turned out to be long, light, and bendable.

"Now our main task is a fishing line for your rod," said Pashka.

"Where can I get a line, Pashka?" I asked my older friend and teacher of village life.

"Go ahead and guess! You must have read dozens of books. So think about it and tell me who are we going to ask for a line?"

"Ded Andrey?"

"No!"

"Mitya?"

"No!"

"We'll buy it at the village store?"

"No way!"

"Then Pashka, I don't know, God knows, I don't know! Tell me, where, Pashka? Tell me! I'm asking you nicely," I started to whine.

"Oh, you. You'd never guess."

"Never, Pashka." I agreed.

"From Starlet!" triumphed Pashka.

"How?" I was perplexed. Starlet is the horse that Ded Andrey rides when he goes on grain production business. She's tied to the post on the stoop. She's buried her muzzle into the bag, which hangs around her neck. There's hay in the bag. Starlet chews the hay and, satisfied, swishes her tail that looks like a huge brush for a giant artist. The tail is made of hundreds of bluish hairs. Pashka pulls Starlet's tail.

"Here's your fishing line. All you have to do is to ask Starlet politely. Danka, you stand on the stoop. Stand and learn, while you still can!"

My older friend jokes and orders me around. He strokes the horse's neck. He whispers tender words to her. Starlet nods her head, as if giving permission. Pashka goes up to her side.

"Can't do it from the back!" Pashka explains. "She'll end up hurting you."

Carefully, one by one, from the horse's tail, he pulls out hair, strong like a wire. We sit on the stoop and twist a fishing line from the resilient horsehairs. Three strands for one thread. By evening my fishing rod is ready. We go down to the river with our fishing rods, worms, pails for the catch, and two chunks of bread. Pasha is lucky. A small pike, a little perch, a fat gudgeon—one by one, they strike at his hook. Pashka takes the gudgeon off the hook, cuts its fat back in half down the spine, and salts it with salt we had brought from home.

"Take a bite!" Pashka offers.

I take a bite from the salty fish back. "Yummy, Pashka!"

Finally I also have some luck. I catch a moment when the float jumps up a bit and dives. I pull out a little perch.

"Good job! Danka! You've become a real Uralian!" Pashka praises me.

That was child's play. But, one day at the end of summer, I saw real fishing. On that day, Ded Andrey had been checking the drag-nets since morning. A dragnet is a long net with a pole tied to each end. It looks like lengths of hammock with a bag sewn into the middle of them. Mitya came in late afternoon. Ded Andrey and Mitya dragged the nets to the river. Pashka and I tagged along. On the shore they unwound the dragnet. Mitka took his shirt and pants off, grabbed a pole with one end of the dragnet, and swam to the other shore. He stopped where it was not so deep, and you could stand on the bottom. From that moment, both of the fishermen, Ded Andrey and Mitya, began to make their way knee-deep in water, each along his own side. They stopped, having gone about a hundred meters, and Mitya swam back, dragging his end of the net. They pulled the net out onto the shore. The bag was filled with fish and crawfish. Crawfish were not red at all, as I had thought before, but dark gray. Many of the crawfish got stuck in the mesh of the net. They dropped the crawfish into a pail, and at home they cooked them in salted water. And that's when they turned red. I saw drag-net fishing several more times. Once something big hit the net very hard. It was a huge pike, about a meter and a half long. Dark, with steely colored spots. It got tangled in the net, but its sharp teeth were dangerous. Ded Andrey broke this tangled-up pike over his knee like a stick. Then it quieted down. Baba Lena baked the pike whole inside a pie. The pie was the length of the entire table.

The garden demanded daily attention: watering from a can, pulling weeds, hoeing around the potato plants—and, once or twice each summer, feeding the tomatoes and cucumbers. The watering can was heavy. On hot days, mama had to use a yoke and carry two pails at once from the well to the garden. And getting the water from the well was not an easy job, even for the village women. Mama never complained. When I hugged her and felt sorry for her, she would kiss and reassure me.

"It's not all that hard, Danik. You just have to get used to it. I'm almost used to it. Soon it will get easier. But, look, we have our own fine potatoes and cabbage!"

I picked up on this idea. "Our juicy tomatoes! Our tasty cucumbers! Our sweet carrots! Our rutabagas!"

And we both burst out laughing. It wasn't hard to feed the tomatoes, cucumbers, and cabbage. It was just strange, and even nasty. But it had to be done! Nothing besides potatoes, carrots, and beets grew in this clayish Ural soil without manure or some such form of fertilizer. It's a good thing that the garden was fertilized only once or twice a summer. Before the cucumbers and tomatoes blossomed. It was fertilized with the stuff that accumulated for a year in a dugout hole in the yard, under the outhouse. Our hosts would put peat into this hole. Ded Andrey lifted out this smelly muck with a pail attached to a long pole. Baba Lena, Pashka, mama, and I would carry this fertilizer in our pails (I had a small one) to the garden. In the evening, they fired up the bathhouse with aromatic fresh birch branches. A lot of water was used to wash our clothes, and ourselves, and even so the stinky smell didn't leave our bodies and our clothes.

Uncle Buzya Bekman grew tobacco. It turned out to be profitable. He would sell or barter the tobacco right in his *izba*. And sometimes he would even trade at the market.

A mischief maker, Pashka had a foul mouth. A mischief maker, he taught me how to crawl over the fence into Uncle Buzya's garden and swipe tobacco leaves. I gave the leaves to Pashka. He dried them secretly on the roof of the bathhouse and smoked the rolled leaves of the *makhorka*. I didn't smoke. I just coughed. Paska taught me many fun things. For example, how to ride on the back of our pig, Fifer, when he got bigger. Pashka was the only son of Baba Lena's who was not sent to the front—because he was still too young. She forgave him a lot. Ded Andrey wouldn't have, but he didn't know much, always being on the road working around the district. Pashka could, for example, run into the *izba,* grab a pickle out of a bowl, and, shaking it, come out with the following: " 'Son of a bee hive!' said the Merry Queen when she first saw the Persian Prince's dick." If mama was there, she pretended not to notice. Baba Lena would shout with delight, "Oh, you foul-mouthed boy!" And I stood there with my eyes bugging out, struck not so much by the content of what had been said (and from which a romantic connection between a certain Merry Queen and the terrible Persian Prince had developed), as by its energetic rhythm and clear sound, and I pondered the mysterious words "son of a bee hive" and "dick." Soon after that, Pashka explained to me the meaning of what had been said, without any storks or cabbage patches.

"They take you and Malvina to the bathhouse together, right?"

"Yes, they do, Pashka," I answered reluctantly, ashamed of my obedience in the matter of being washed together with my girl cousin. And also doubly ashamed to be having this conversation with my teacher of village life.

"Did you see she has a crack cut through the place where we have our wiener?"

"Yes, I saw. So what about it, Pashka?!"

"Oh, nothing. And here we have the grand Persian Prince showing the Queen his dick—that's just another word for wiener— and the Queen shouted with delight: Son of a bee hive!"

I didn't understand much of that, but Pashka stubbornly kept teaching me life's basics, those basics which were perfectly natural for village kids. For example, when a rooster would jump onto a desperately squawking hen, Pashka would say, "The rooster's humping the hen, and she's screaming for joy!" Or he'd show me the live, thick stick with a glossy knob growing out from beneath a stallion's belly. In August, he got me to follow the cowherd, early in the morning, when he was taking the cows out to graze. He lured me over and showed me how a bull straddled our cow, Manka. "The bull jabs the cow. The cow will bring us a calf in the spring," Pashka explained. One of the last stages of my natural education was connected with the visit of Teryokhins' daughter, Rayka. It took place in the fall or in the winter. Rayka worked in a factory in the city of Molotov. She was a redhead, a blabbermouth, and loose. Having partied all over the village, she would climb onto the stove to catch a nap. This was the moment that Pashka was waiting for. He called me over and told me to look up at her from the bottom.

"Do you see?" He questioned me.

"Uh-huh."

Aunt Tsilya decided not to grow a garden. She was waiting for Uncle Yanya to get out of the hospital. Which he did at the beginning of the summer of '42. We were all ecstatic about his arrival. If it was possible for one of our people, then the others would also return from the war. He brought presents for everyone. Probably, for the first time since our arrival in Siva, our entire *meshpucha* got together. Uncle Yanya kept on kissing Malvina. He kissed me, too, and pinched my cheeks saying, "Danchik, what a *groys menshele* you've become!" I loved Uncle Yanya a lot. It was he, as the family legend goes, who found Professor Tur, the one who cured me of the deadly pneumonia. Soon Uncle Yanya got himself a job as an accountant in some office on the other side of Siva. It was hard for Uncle Yanya to walk from one end of the village to the other. Aunt Tsilya, Uncle Yanya, and Malvina found a different place to rent. A valley surrounded by hills of forests was right next to their *izba*. Mama would take me there to play with Malvina. She was three years older than I, but we were friends. Together, we would read *Russian Folk Tales,* collected by Karnaukhova, although, to tell the truth, I had read this book long before. But I loved Malvina and, with her, I patiently reread the tales of Emelya, of the Princess Frog, or of Sister Alyonushka and Brother Ivanushka.

As chance would have it, we had ended up like Sister Alyonushka and Brother Ivanushka in the fairy tale. One early summer morning mama brought me to play with Malvina. Mama went for the whole day to the collective farm to weed the peas. Aunt Tsilya and Uncle Yanya went to work. I was sitting in the kitchen, reading Kipling's *The Jungle Book*. It was one of my favorites. Finally, Malvina came out into the kitchen. Her eyes were red from crying, swollen from tears. One could see by her face that she had been hurt.

"Why were you crying your eyes out, Malvina?" I asked, pulling myself away from a page where Mowgli, brought up by the wolves, sees his real mother for the first time. Instead of answering, Malvina cried even harder. She was hysterical. I'd never seen anyone cry like that. Except for nursing infants. To cry like that, and not from pain but from God knows what! Malvina was sobbing, and I tried to console her. But how could I comfort her, how could I console her?

Through tears and bursting sobs, she asked me, "Danik, my dearest cousin. Swear that you'll not share my secret with anyone!"

"Swear to God, I won't!"

"Promise to do what I tell you!"

"I promise!"

"I've decided to run away from home! Will you come with me?"

"How? Why? And what about my mother? And Aunt Tsilya and Uncle Yanya? Are we taking them with us?"

"No! There's no way! The thing is that I'm running away from them! From my mother and father! I hate them! They no longer love me! They don't need me at all! They only love each other! Will you come with me, Danichek? You promised!"

"I'm not saying no, Malvina, but what about my mother? She still loves me. Maybe we'll take her with us?"

"No, Danik, we can't. I'd take Aunt Stellochka. I love her a lot. She always sings my favorite songs with me. But Aunt Stellochka is a grown-up. All grown-ups are alike. She'll squeal on me and we won't be able to run away."

And that really was true. All the adults did stick together. There's a reason they were made differently. Pashka told me about this more than once. And, nevertheless, I wanted to know why Malvina had come to hate Aunt Tsilya and Uncle Yanya so much. Well, Aunt Tsilya yells a lot, although she's a kind person. And how about Uncle Yanya? He spoke quietly, stepped gently, never argued with anyone. They say such people would never hurt a fly.

"Malvina, I promised you. I'll run away to the forest with you. Yes, to the forest! But tell me, Malvina, what happened?"

"Danichek, I'll tell you on the way."

She took a little basket, put a chunk of bread in it and a pitcher of water, closed the door, and we set off on the road toward the forest and the hills. And, along the way, Malvina started to tell her story. Occasionally she'd get so upset by what had happened the night before she would start to cry bitterly all over again. Here's what she told me.

"I woke up at night because my mother was moaning and groaning. As if someone were choking her. I got scared, Danik. I'd never heard mama groan or moan or yell in her sleep like that. Sometimes she did have nightmares, when papa was in the hospital. She'd yell out, but then she'd wake up right away. Now she was moaning, and yelling, and crying, and papa, for some reason, was not comforting her. I ran to their bed, Danik, and I saw a horrible picture. Papa slammed mama onto her back, and he was choking her. He was choking her and jumping up and down and crushing her, and she was moaning and sobbing and wasn't even trying to get out from under papa. She was even kissing him. I stood right next to them, and they didn't even notice me. I thought they had gone crazy. I was standing right next to them. Papa was jumping on mama, choking her, muttering something, and she was moaning, sobbing, and asking papa not to stop. They continued this horrendous game. Finally, mama saw me. But, even then, she didn't stop all this. Angrily, she told me to go back to bed. Then, later, they both calmed down and came in to me, together and separately. But I didn't want to see them any more. I was disgusted. I understood,

Danichek, that they no longer needed me. That they don't love me at all, that they only love to play this crazy game. That they'd just plain forgotten about me. You know, maybe I wasn't born because they loved me and wanted me to be with them. Maybe, Danichek, they just loved to play this crazy game, and I was born by accident. I don't want to be an accident. That's why I've decided to leave them forever. Only it's lonely and scary by myself."

Much of Malvina's tale was, of course, incomprehensible to me. But, for some strange reason, Pashka's lessons, my observations of animal life in the village (the rooster jumping onto the hen and her desperately happy squawking, dogs' weddings, the bull jabbing the cow and the cow's beckoning moo), and my cousin's tale about Aunt Tsilya's and Uncle Yanya's nighttime games, it all came together in one picture, complete, forbidding—and impossible to explain. Malvina and I were walking and talking openly. Only now do I understand how naïve and how insightful she was in her resentment.

The hills where in early spring we had picked the *pestiki* were now red with wild strawberries. We ate these large, sweet, and delicious-smelling berries. We ate and could not get enough. The sun began to set over the forest. The water from the pitcher was gone, and the chunk of bread eaten. I imagined what mama was doing. How she would come to get me, and Malvina and I would be gone. And Aunt Tsilya and Uncle Yanya wouldn't be happy either.

As if reading my mind, Malvina asked, "What do you think, Danik, are they worried? My mother and my father?"

"Certainly!"

"So it means that they love me, at least a little bit?"

"Sure!"

"Then let's run back!" Malvina shouted, and we ran as fast as our legs could carry us to the country road that led back to the village.

There were times when, from early morning all through the day, there was no one in our *izba*. Everybody went to work on the collective farm. Baba Lena, Pashka, mama. I don't know why they just didn't leave me next door with the Bekmans. I just don't know. To this day, I just don't understand it. So, mama went to the collective farm for the summer. She had to earn at least some grain for the winter. Grain was scarce and was given out according to days worked in the field. Sometimes mama would take me along. I remember the field of flax. Flax has blue, blue flowers, like mama's eyes. Mama is pulling out the crabgrass. I help her. Together we earn *workdays*. And here's a second field. It's rye. A field of ripened rye in August. Mama is cutting the rye with a sickle. She grabs as many stems as she can, stems with rocking, dark yellow spikes with long bristles. Mama holds the stems tightly in her right hand. In her left hand, she holds the sickle—a sharp half-moon knife with a wooden handle. Like on the flag. Mama is partly a lefty. She writes with her right hand, but does heavy work with her left hand. Mama cuts the stems and puts them together until she has collected a whole sheaf. When she gets a whole sheaf, she ties it together using the rye stems, like twine, and stands them one next to the other. This is called tying up the sheaves. They'll stand there for a while and dry. Then they'll be taken away to be threshed.

The yard by the granary is swept clean and lit up by a lantern. All around is darkness. A cool breeze is wafting in from the river. A late August evening. Threshing. Why did they have to thresh at night? Sheaves of rye lie on the clean swept part of the yard, and it even seems there's a tarpaulin spread on the ground. Among them are a few of the sheaves mama and I earned for workdays. Ded Andrey is threshing the rye. He threshes the rye with a flail. A flail is a heavy, short, cast-iron chain, nailed to a thick handle. Like a whip. Instead of a strap—a short chain. Ded Andrey is threshing, constantly hitting the ears, making the grains fall out. From time to time, he stops. Baba Lena and mama take turns bending down and picking up handfuls of grain still mixed with the ears and throwing them up in the air. They're winnowing the grain. Separating it from the ears and from the sharp, prickly beards of the chaff. They are cleaning the grain from the chaff.

We got a letter from papa. In a letter there was a picture of papa. Papa was wearing a navy uniform in the picture. Lieutenant-commander's bars on a dark navy jacket. And the hat was also a navy hat with a crab-shaped cockade. In the letter, papa wrote that he had been transferred to the Baltic Fleet. He is now commanding a unit of torpedo boats. Mama shows papa's picture to everybody. Mama and I are very proud of our dear papa.

And around that time, on a day when summer was nearing its end, a burial note came for Teryokhin's son Aleksandr. A burial note is a letter that comes from the military unit headquarters that says that such and such soldier or officer had been killed in action. Baba Lena spent whole days sitting in her black scarf and crying under the icon of Nicholas the Wonder Worker. Everything in our *izba* turned quiet and dark. Even Pashka stopped his mischief. When Ded Andrey came home, he sat on the stoop and smoked into the night. Uncle Buzya brought him tobacco. Uncle Buzya had a son, Samuil, at the front.

"How's our papa doing at sea?" I would ask mama. But, inside, I kept on thinking about that horrible burial note.

"Sweetheart, our papa is the bravest, the strongest, the luckiest! He made it through the Finnish War! He'll make it through this one. You should see how the Germans are afraid of him."

"How? Tell me, mama!"

"All the fascist subs scurried back to their Germany when papa's boats appeared on the horizon. Listen to what they say in the paper."

"Go on, mama, hurry up and read!"

Mama reads from the newspaper: "The heroic Baltic Fleet torpedo boats sank an enemy submarine that was on course from Königsberg to Kronstadt."

"Maybe those were papa's boats?"

"I'm sure they were!" mama smiles, lifts me up, and kisses me. I woke up because I heard mama crying.

"Mama, what's wrong with you? Mamochka, why are you crying?"

"No, it's nothing, Danik. I'm just . . . I'm stopping now." I sleep on a wide bench covered with a mattress stuffed with straw. I'm trying to fall asleep. I'm imagining how tomorrow I will go fishing with Pashka. And again I hear that mama is not sleeping; she's crying. I climb onto mama's bed. I hug her. I calm her down, and I kiss my mama. We fall asleep.

We have important news. A messenger, the watchwoman Klimovna, came from the principal of the elementary school to summon mama. In confidence she tells mama that the principal, Zoya Vasilievna, wants to hire mama as a teacher of German and singing in the school. Mama puts on a fancy dress. The same one she always wore to department meetings at the Forestry Technology Academy. Before the war. I'm told to wait at home. I whine. I want to go through the village with mama when she's so dressed up. And she's going to the school principal herself! Finally, we come to an agreement that I will walk with mama almost to the school, and I will wait for her at Aunt Enya's.

Aunt Enya and Tanya live not far from the school. Tanya is the wife of Uncle Moysha Grinberg. Moysha is Aunt Enya's son. He's fighting on the Leningrad Front. Aunt Enya likes it when I visit her and Tanya. Aunt Enya is very, very old, but very smart. She has a "brilliant memory," as they say in our *meshpucha*. Maybe it has something to do with a story she once told me. I don't remember when she told me about it—was it during the evacuation, or after we returned to Leningrad? Aunt Enya was the eldest daughter in the Rayev family. When she was marrying Khaim Grinberg, Moysha's father, her parents gave her a gold ring as a part of her dowry, and gold earrings, a gold necklace, and a gold bracelet. These gold ornaments were sprinkled with diamonds. The Rayevs were rich millers. The family owned twenty flour mills. During the Revolution all the Rayevs, including my Grandpa Borukh and Aunt Enya, were arrested by the officers of the Cheka and tortured. Everybody, including Grandpa Borukh, quickly told where they'd hidden things. Everyone, except Aunt Enya. They even made her drink her own urine. She stubbornly kept on saying that she didn't have, and hadn't had, any diamonds. Then came the Ukrainian Petlyurites, then the Whites, the Black-Reds and Yellow-Blues, the White Poles, and the Reds again. They forgot all about Aunt Enya. "So, where are the diamonds now, Aunt Enya?" I asked during the evacuation, or later in Leningrad. Aunt Enya looked at me slyly, and wiping her hands on her apron, she put a small plate with a small piece of bread on it in front of me. The bread was spread with a paper thin layer of butter, and on top of that just as thin a layer of honey. She cut the bread into centimeter squares and fed me square by square, with her long, aristocratic fingers. Starting in the fall, I spent a lot of time at Aunt Enya's and Tanya's. Sometimes mama would take me with her to school to her German lessons or to her singing lessons. But mostly she took me to Aunt Enya's and picked me up after her lessons. I loved to listen to Aunt Enya's stories of the Rayev family, of the mills, of the horses, of the Polish magnate Count Wisniewiecki, from whom my great-grandfather and later my grandfather, leased land along the river with dams where the mills stood. And also stories about the German colonists, who had leased the open expanses of the steppes from the same, His Excellency Wisniewiecki. The colonists grew wheat. And the Rayevs milled the grain. "You know, Danik, at that time we all spoke Yiddish. That's a Jewish language. The colonists understood Yiddish very well. And Yiddish and German are very similar! In the old days, all Jews knew Yiddish and understood German. When, during the First World War, the Austrian army entered our city of Kamenets-Podolsk, there were Jews among the officers. Oh, these were people of high culture! And look what's happening now: Germans are destroying the Jews as if they were their worst enemies." I didn't understand everything about Aunt Enya's stories, or her reasoning. But for some reason I was ashamed of the fact that the Jewish language was so similar to the language of those with whom my papa was fighting. It was a disgraceful shame, but it was true. Aunt Enya always had a present tucked away for me. For example, in the middle of a deep and impassable fall or a winter buried in snow, she would pick a red ball out of her felt boot, a tomato that had ripened in its darkness and warmth. Tanya, Aunt Enya's daughter-in-law, was always sick. She had a heart condition. Tanya and Moysha didn't have any children. I was Aunt Enya's favorite grandnephew. But when in Siva or after the war in Leningrad, I would remind her: "So, then what ever happened to the diamonds?" Aunt Enya would just smile mysteriously, wipe her thin fingers on her blue apron, and go get a present for me from a secret chest. Radiant with her high bun of gray hair, hunched over, and mysterious.

Mama had a wonderful ear for music. And she had a remarkable memory. She knew many poems. Songs with words and melodies rang out in mama's soul like the voices of birds. Besides Russian, mama knew words in many other languages: German, Lithuanian, Belarusian. Yiddish and Russian were mama's main languages. I remember mama lamenting that there were no German textbooks in the school, no dictionaries. She would make up German phrases and give them out to the students on handouts. She would put together a little German-Russian dictionary for each lesson. There was no piano in the school. Mama would teach the children songs a cappella. My cousin Malvina had a good ear for music, and she would help mama with the singing lessons. I was supposed to start school the following year.

It appears that the most important things in village life happened during our first year. Of course that wasn't so. It was just that everything settled into the sieve of our first year, and later it was difficult to separate all the events of our evacuation. For example, when did

I first start to ride a horse? At six or at seven? How did I manage to climb onto Starlet's back? There was no saddle. Boys rode around without saddles—on a canvas sack thrown over the horse's back. Or my first observation of surgery? Usually they herded the cows back from pasture around six in the evening. The cows walked and mooed loudly asking to be milked quickly. Our cow, Manka, also mooed loudly, particularly when she was approaching the gates of our *izba*. Here Baba Lena would spin like a top. Quickly she would bring Manka to the cowshed, wash her pink teats, which were sticking out from the swollen and heavy udder, set up the milking pail under Manka's stomach, and would start to milk her. A stream of milk would hit the pail. It was a sweet sound. And the sweet steam would waft up from the milking pail. I was ready with my mug. Baba Lena would cover my mug with gauze and pour in the steaming milk, which I would drink on the spot. Mama considered this to be very good for my lungs. Once, before Baba Lena could finish her milking and give me my medicinal milk, we heard a frantic clucking in the burdocks that grew along the fence around the yard. Baba Lena flew up like a frightened bird. We ran to the fence. Baba Lena's favorite egg-laying hen was clucking desperately, stretching her neck and rolling her eyes back. Baba Lena grabbed the hen, put her under her arm, and ran for the house. I ran after her, full of compassion and curiosity. In the kitchen, Baba Lena found the scissors, threaded a big needle with a brown thread, and told me to hold the hen's head tight. I held it, being conscious of the importance of my mission. Baba Lena cut open the top part of the hen's chest, opened up her windpipe, which jutted out like a sword, and pulled out a potato peel that was stuck sideways. Next, Baba Lena sewed up the windpipe with the coarse thread, and then the skin, and the hen immediately quieted down. Baba Lena took her favorite egg-laying hen back out into the yard.

"God be with you! It should hold!"

The hen ran off to her friends to drink water from the wooden trough.

"Baba Lena, who taught you that?" I asked, admiring her surgical art.

"Village life will teach you everything, Danichek. You'll grow up and you'll remember me, maybe you'll become a surgeon yourself. Vladimirovna mentioned that there are surgeons in your family."

Mama did tell me that our Uncle Israel is the chief surgeon in one of the armies that was fighting at Stalingrad. And Aunt Berta is a surgeon in a mobile hospital unit at the Northern Front.

It was almost time to dig up the potatoes and to pick the other vegetables. The tomatoes were filled with green juice. We picked the tomatoes and put them in dark places, such as felt boots, so they could ripen. Cucumbers also did well. We picked them all summer, and now we could salt them for the winter. It wasn't yet time for the cabbages. They would be picked on the eve of the first frost. But before the potatoes and other garden chores, we still had to harvest the raspberries. And in between digging up the potatoes and cutting down the cabbage heads, the mushrooms had to be picked and salted for the winter. All these chores were repeated every year of our stay in the Ural village. Mama immediately grasped how important these tasks were for our survival, and she religiously followed Baba Lena's advice. Mama really respected her. It seems that the Teryokhins also respected and admired my mother for her open disposition, her honesty, and for the interest she took in all the events of our hosts' lives.

Mama would go raspberry picking with a whole group of village women. She even looked like a local in her long, black, gathered cotton print skirt, her faded kerchief pulled all the way down to her eyebrows, her summer bast shoes trimmed with cloth, her yoke with pails hooked onto it, masterfully thrown half over her shoulder. Time and again, mama would go for the whole day, leaving before dawn in the company of women from neighboring *izba*s and returning in the evening, her pails filled with dark red, almost purple, juicy, aromatic berries. We dried them for the winter, to sweeten our tea and to use as a cold remedy. But once, mama returned all scared, without her pails and yoke. She had been picking raspberries from a bush that was so thick with berries there seemed to be no end to them. Suddenly, she heard the crunch of branches breaking and a growling coming from the other side of the bush. The branches parted and the huge, brown head of a bear appeared before mama's face. She dropped her pails and her yoke and took off running, her legs carrying her all the way to the village.

Fall had come. Heavy and persistent rains began. Mama would conquer the impassable mud and go to school to teach the children German and singing. Usually I would stay in the *izba* with Baba Lena. She would bake bread, and I would wait impatiently for the appearance of those hot, golden-brown rye loaves as they came out of the crucible of the Russian stove. She would cook cabbage soup in a cast-iron pot, and in another cast-iron pot, a huge one, she'd boil small potatoes for the pigs. Or she would spin. Or she would weave cloth. And always she talked to me. She'd tell me about her sons, in particular about Aleksandr, the one who was killed. But she also talked of the other ones, including Pashka, the son Baba Lena had when she was over fifty. "I went to milk Daisy—the cow we had before Manka. I came, set up the milking pail, washed the teats, and got set up to milk, when suddenly I got all twisted up, everything moved, I barely managed to grab my baby boy, Pashka. The whole house is sleeping. It's early, early morning. So, little by little, I did everything myself. I cut the cord with a knife and tied it up with a coarse thread . . ." I listened to all of this and tried to envision what Baba Lena told me, using my own imagination. After all, I did manage to visualize pictures out of Jules Verne's book *A Fifteen-Year-Old Captain*. A ship. A broken compass. The African jungle. The young captain Dick Sand. So the union of the spoken and the written word became for me a major source of knowledge, imagination, and pleasure.

In the forest not far from our *izba* grew an infinite number of large, orange mushrooms called saffron milk caps. The four of us would go to the forest: Baba Lena, Pashka, mama, and I. They would also give me a woven basket and a little knife. The milk caps stood like little people in round orange hats adorned with barely visible pale designs. And they died like soldiers. You cut the stem and an orange-colored liquid, which looks like blood, drips from the wound. We would eat salted milk caps all winter.

Potatoes were, of course, our main task. We earthed up our potato plants in the summer. And closer to the beginning of August, we would dig them under, when they had already blossomed and were flaunting their green berries, which looked like tiny tomatoes. Mama explained to me that tomatoes, potatoes, and even tobacco, which Uncle Buzya grew to sell, belong to the nightshade family. We eat tomatoes. But the berries on the potato plants are poisonous.

"By the way," mama added, "the same with the tobacco leaves. They contain a strong poison—nicotine."

I was very surprised, imagining Uncle Buzya in the role of a secret, evil poisoner.

I didn't get a chance to ask, so Uncle Buzya supplies poison? when mama, seeing doubt and question in my wide open eyes, said, "My darling, people are used to doing all sorts of strange, unusual, dangerous and even horrible things. For example, killing each other in war. Or fighting, stealing, lying, in a word, doing all sorts of base things. So that their conscience or fear doesn't torture them, they take small doses of poison. For example, they drink home brew or wine (remember how you got home-brew poisoning?), or they smoke tobacco. In the home brew and in wine there is a poison called alcohol. In the tobacco smoke, which they inhale when they smoke the tobacco, there is a poison called nicotine."

"But, mamochka, Baba Lena and Ded Andrey also drank the home brew."

"People drink wine or smoke tobacco to quiet their conscience or their anguish. Or as a stupid habit. Or just by chance, like you, silly."

When their leafy tops had dried up and turned brown, the potatoes had to be dug up. We went to the garden armed with pitchforks and sacks. Mama poked the pitchfork under the potato plants and pulled them out by their tops. The potatoes were attached to the plant roots and were half-covered with clay soil. I pulled the white tubers away from the weak roots, shook the soil off of them, and put them in a sack. Many just fell off the roots even before that. You had to look for them in the ground. We dug up several sacks and decided to go back and check to make sure that some of the potatoes hadn't remained in the ground. And then mama, probably because she was so tired or because I had stuck my hand in without warning her, ran her pitchfork clear through the index finger of my left hand. Blood spurted out. Mama bound my finger. They took me to the rural hospital. I got a tetanus shot. A nurse cleaned my wound, applied Rivanol, and bandaged it up. It took a long time for the finger to heal. The wound festered. Mama was afraid of blood poisoning but, this time, it turned out all right.

When mama was cleaning the cabbage heads of their green top leaves, which were not usable for sauerkraut, she would show me the green, fat, slow-moving caterpillars she found. They would swarm among all the leaves in the scrap pail, continuing to crawl and chew, even though they didn't have much longer to live.

In a single night, fall had turned to winter. We woke up to see the yard, the vegetable garden, and the road covered in snow. Immediately, it became more fun, but also more formidable. For the November holidays, Ded Andrey and Mitya had slaughtered our piglet, which had turned into a hog. For the winter, we had potatoes, sauerkraut, pickles, and salted mushrooms, meat, and a little bit of flour. We kept getting letters and postcards from papa. Once, we got a letter from mama's sister, Fanya. Inside the envelope was an article and a picture of Fanya from the army newspaper. In the picture was our Fanya in an army field shirt with the Order of the Fighting Red Banner pinned to her chest. In the article they said that a sergeant of the signalers, Fanya Kogan, had performed an act of heroism. For several hours, with her bare hands, she connected wires that had been torn apart by enemy shells. When her hands became numb from the cold, Fanya kept the wire ends tightly together with her teeth, until other signalers found and rescued her. All this took place at Stalingrad. Baba Lena cried and prayed to Nicholas the Wonder Worker.

In the middle of January, we got a package from papa. It was a bit late for New Year's, but it came just in time for my birthday. I was turning seven. In the package there was a blue silk scarf for mama. At that time, the radio kept on playing a song called "A Blue Scarf." For mama—the scarf, and for me—a black naval greatcoat, made just my size, and a black winter hat with earflaps and a real gold crab-shaped cockade. And a black regulation belt with a brass buckle decorated with an anchor. I put on all these gorgeous things and didn't want to take them off until night. Neighbors stopped by to see me, to see this real little sailor who had appeared in the Teryokhins' *izba*. Mitya Teryokhin had a camera with an "accordion." He took my picture, developed it, and we sent it to papa in the Baltic Sea. A picture was taken of mama in the blue scarf and me in my coat, cinched with the regulation belt and in my black hat with earflaps and a golden "crab." To tell the truth, the blue scarf came out black in the picture.

The year 1943 had begun. The streets, covered with snow and leveled by sleighs and stomped down by horses' hooves, seemed wider. The frost-covered window casings of the *izba* looked like the silver settings of icons. I strolled with mama in the village, which had come a bit more to life on Sundays, when sleighs filled with produce from the local farms would make their way to the market square. They carried sauerkraut, potatoes, salted mushrooms, honey, frozen milk. Once we went to visit Maria Osipovna. She worked as a typist at the Village Council and lived near the market square. On the way, we bumped into a strange man called either Babukh or Babuk (I don't recall). The flaps of his winter hat were tied down with straps. The collar of his sheepskin coat was turned up. He had a big hooked nose and black eyes, half-covered with heavy eyelids. Mama greeted him, and we continued on our way.

"Who was that, mama?" I asked guardedly. With the hooked nose he looked so different from everybody I knew and had met so far.

"He's a Karaite, Danik. The Karaites lived in Crimea and in Lithuania. The Germans killed almost all the Crimean Karaites. Miraculously, Babukh survived."

"There's a war there? The Karaites fought the Germans?"

"Like everybody else. The men are at the front. And the old men, woman, and children fell under German occupation. And perished."

At this point, we met up with the local policeman, Dodonov. He was just about the only policeman in the village. Everyone knew Dodonov and felt sorry for him. He was wounded in the head right at the beginning of the war and was discharged from the army. The women (and in each *izba* there were only women, old men, and children left) were always happy to see the policeman and to treat Dodonov to some homemade salty snacks to go with the home brew. He'd stop by our *izba* as well. So mama knew him. Dodonov saw us, greeted mama.

"Good health to you, Vladimirovna!" He stretched himself amusingly before me, saluted me and loudly presented a report.

"Comrade Naval Cadet, Police Sergeant Dodonov reports as ordered!"

I stopped, staring at Dodonov in bewilderment and didn't know how to answer. After all, I hadn't ordered Dodonov to do anything. Mama smiled politely at the policeman's joke and started to pull me by the hand, taking me away from trouble. Unfortunately, the Karaite Babukh, who was circling around the market looking at and choosing affordable produce, decided to butt into our conversation. He simply bumped into us like ships bump into each other in a fog. Horses and people were wrapped in clouds of steam, so that at a distance of two meters all one could see was a silhouette. It was so cold that, with each breath exhaled or with each word spoken, a thick cloud of steam would escape.

Babukh materialized out of the fog and said, "If one were to subscribe to the conventions of the masquerade, then one would have to address the boy as a naval officer. The crab-shaped cockade appears only on officers' hats and caps."

Dodonov was silent for a couple of minutes. He was taken aback, first of all, by Babukh's impudence, and second, because he had not understood half of what had been said. For example, the word "masquerade." Although his peasant sense told him that this hooked nose type was trying to make fun of him, the police sergeant Dodonov. This impudence had to be cut short.

And so Dodonov yelled at the Karaite Babukh, "And what gives you, Citizen Evacuee, the right to interrupt the conversation of a representative of the authorities with the populace. All of you with hooked noses, you can't even roll your r's properly, and now you've descended on us and try to install your way of life. I spilled my peasant-worker's blood for the Motherland, while you, creeping reptiles, were lounging around behind the lines. What do you think, I, a severely wounded frontline soldier can't tell an officer from a cadet? I'll show you, you rotten hooknose, such a masquerade your own mother won't recognize you."

Babukh was stunned and, without a word, vanished in the frosted fog. Dodonov kept on shaking his fists in the Karaite's direction. I understood that something horrible was happening when mama grabbed me by the shoulders. Pressing me to herself, she looked at the policeman with hatred and despair, as he continued to shake his fists and spill out threats at the now departed Babukh. Finally, Dodonov woke up.

"See, Vladimirovna, what scum we defend from the Germans? We spill our blood for the hooked noses and for the ones who can't roll a Russian r. Maybe we should have just killed them all ourselves, then there wouldn't be a war. Am I right, Vladimirovna, eh?"

"Are you right, Dodonov? Are you right?" mama repeated the policeman's words. She repeated them slowly and without emotion, as if in a dream, when she was tortured by nightmares, and I would wake her up and comfort her. "If you're right, Dodonov, then shoot my boy, and me, and shoot my husband, who is spilling his blood at the front. Because I, Dodonov, and my son, and my husband, and my sisters, we all are hook-nosed and misroll our r's. Why don't you start here, Dodonov, and take out your gun and shoot me and my boy because we are hook-nosed and can't roll Russian r's properly. Because we are Jews, Dodonov!" Mama was shouting and crying and couldn't stop. I tried to lead her away from Dodonov, but it was useless.

People gathered all around us. The policeman Dodonov was making excuses.

"Just look at yourself and your little guy, Vladimirovna. What kind of Jews are you? You're Russian judging by your appearance and by your speech. I wasn't talking about you."

Mama couldn't be stopped. Out of her coat pocket she took her passport, which, ever since we were evacuated from Leningrad, she always carried together with my birth certificate. Mama opened up her passport and read, enunciating clearly, "Shayna Vulfovna Kogan. Nationality—Jew." Dodonov was silent. Mama unfolded my birth certificate, which had been folded into quarters, and shoving it right under the policeman's nose, she read, "Daniil Fayvlovich

Rayev, born 1936. Father—Fayvl Borukhovich Rayev. Nationality—Jew. Mother—Shayna Wolfovna Kogan. Nationality—Jew."

The policeman Dodonov walked away silently. Surrounded by
frosty fog, a figure separated itself from the onlookers. It was Maria
Osipovna, our distant relative. She put her arms around mama, patted my cheek, and said in her deep voice, "I waited and waited for
you, dear ones. The soup's getting cold. So I decided to come
meet you along the way. And you, Stellochka, have created a riot
here."

"I just can't let these anti-Semites spit in our faces, Maria
Osipovna."

"That's right, my sunshine. But each protest will return to us
like a boomerang. And I really doubt that this *shiker* understands
what anti-Semitism is and who the Semites are."

Toward evening, we returned home. I crawled onto the *polati* to
get warmed up. In the *izba,* they had already heard of the scene on
the market square. Baba Lena, kind soul, came to ask mama to join
her for tea with honey. Mama didn't come out right away. She was
sullen. Ded Andrey came home while they were drinking tea
brewed with dried raspberries and topped off with sweet honey. He
had no days off. Every day he harnessed Starlet to a wagon or to a
sleigh, and went off on business for the grain production department. Ded Andrey washed up. Baba Lena fed him and poured him
a glass of tea. Ded Andrey was visibly concerned about something.

After wishing everyone good night, mama was about to leave
the kitchen when Ded Andrey said, "Wait, Stella Vladimirovna, we
must talk."

I was lying on the *polati* thinking about the day's events. Maybe I
shouldn't have put on the uniform, I thought. It all started with the
uniform. But papa sent me the uniform. My papa, he knows everything. And this Dodonov is a real fool. And why did the miserable
Babukh have to turn up?

It was right at that moment that Ded Andrey said to mama, "Wait, Stella Vladimirovna, we must talk."

"Fine, Andrey Mikheich, I'll stay, if we must talk. Of course, Andrey Mikheich. I wanted to ask you for advice myself."

I lay quietly on the *polati,* which were covered with orange, silky onions that rustled with every movement. Each onion was the head of a little yellow person. These wondrous little people hid their faces and were silent. Maybe they took me for the policeman Dodonov. I was afraid to budge and miss even one word. Ded Andrey finished his tea and lit his rolled-up cigarette from the pine sliver burning in its holder.

Ded Andrey exhaled an entire cloud of tobacco smoke. "Dodonov came to see me in my office," he said. "He complained about you, Vladimirovna. He says you're making a big fuss . . ."

"What am I making a big fuss about, Andrey Mikheich?"

"You're making a big fuss about your nationality, Vladimirovna."

"And what, I should hide my nationality when the likes of Dodonov, only in German uniforms, murder Jews?"

"It's not only the Jews who are perishing, Vladimirovna. As the Bible says, nation rose against nation. And death did not pass by our *izba.* But that's not what I wanted to say. Vladimirovna, you need to look at everything more clearly."

"How can I look more clearly, Andrey Mikheich?"

"Why did you come here to the Urals?"

"To save my son."

"Then go on saving him. Just don't stick your neck out. These here are faraway, quiet places. And you need to live here quietly."

"I should quietly swallow the fascist Dodonov's speeches?"

"He's no fascist, Vladimirovna. He's a wounded veteran. A war invalid. And he's got a little power over people." Mama didn't say anything. Ded Andrey continued, "You're quiet, Vladimirovna, which means you don't agree. So you're thinking Mikheich is a double-dealer. I'll tell you my story. I, Vladimirovna, was not so quiet and agreeable in my youth. I was for the Second International, not for the Third. At that time, they would see me more often in Perm and Vereshchagino than in our village. I was an activist. They strangled us. Some of the Socialist-Revolutionaries were executed, others got scared away. I turned quiet, went to the bottom, like a fish in the winter. I moved back to Siva. Got married. Had children. And I didn't stick my neck out. I don't enter into arguments with the likes of Dodonov on the market square. Pray to God that all this will just end with that one conversation."

But it didn't end there. The postal carrier brought mama a notice to appear at the local military enlistment office. In the notice it said that mama was to bring me, too. Mama took off from school. It was a long way to walk. All the important buildings in Siva stood on a hill behind the market square. It was so cold that mama made me tie down the flaps of my military hat. Mama was wearing a wool scarf over her short sheepskin coat. She wound a warm scarf around the collar of my coat. We both wore our felt boots and clumsy, knitted mittens, so that when we tumbled in from the outside, the head of the military enlistment office took one look at us and burst out laughing. As he laughed, his black, curly hair jumped up and down like shiny springs. He was a cheerful major, sent to Siva from the hospital, where they had amputated his right leg. Laughing and limping and leaning on his cane, he hurried to help Mama unwind her scarf and to take off her fur jacket. I stood by the door in my hat and coat and didn't undress. Right away, I disliked this major because of his boisterous laughter and his unrelenting insistence on helping mama.

"I'm Kogan," she said. "Stella Vladimirovna Kogan. You told me to come with my son."

"And what's your name, little boy?" asked the major.

"Danya," I answered.

"Very good, Danya. Now, take off your military coat and your hat with the crab. We'll have a little chat. My name is Aleksandr Semyonovich."

"What will we talk about, Aleksandr Semyonovich?" I asked the major.

"Danik!" scolded mama. I scowled and turned away toward the window, which looked out onto the market square, empty since it was a normal weekday. "Please, excuse him, Aleksandr Semyonovich. Living in the country, he's become uncivilized," mama said, looking at me angrily.

"Don't give it another thought. I also have two such ruffians," said the major and laughed. It was his habit to laugh in order to show his friendliness.

"You have two sons?" mama smiled.

"Borya and Marik," the major answered, "seven and nine years old. And my wife's name is Masha. You know what happened? I was teaching Marxism-Leninism at the Kharkov Pedagogical Institute. Summer vacation had begun. We went to Moscow with the whole family. We stayed with my cousin Sima, who lived near the Losinoostrovskaya railroad station. Not far from the Agricultural Expo. It was the best vacation ever. And suddenly, the war. I rushed to the Moscow military commandant's office. I was a political officer in the reserves. They immediately ordered me to the front with a unit that was just being formed. I was able to get just one day's leave to decide what to do with my family. I knew that they couldn't go back to Kharkov. In the event of German occupation, they faced certain death. You know what the Germans are doing with the Jews."

"So you see! That's why I got upset when Dodonov started to insult Babukh," mama joined in.

"First of all, Karaites are not quite Jews. And second, the market square is no place to discuss policy on nationalities," the major laughed again.

"Particularly since the policy of our Party is full equality for all Soviet nationalities. There's nothing to discuss!" he added. Without saying anything, mama nodded her head. I was still looking out the window.

The major continued. "I evacuated my family to Tashkent, and I set off as the political officer to the front lines. And here. . . ," he pointed to his cane.

"My husband was also wounded. And my sister got frostbite. What's important, though, is that you will return to your family alive," said mama, and she smiled. She had tears in her eyes.

"Thank you for your compassion, Stella Vladimirovna. May I call you Stellochka? I would really like that," said the major and looked at me, as if seeking support. But I sensed something bad in his words, although, at that time, I was not able to analyze what was happening to mama and me. I saw that it was not papa, but a stranger in a uniform, who was dressed like papa, laughing boisterously and saying such words to mama that she is obliged to smile in return. I think at that time I was most upset by mama's helpless smile. Had I been older and smarter I would have said, "Mama, I won't wear this uniform. We'll hide this greatcoat and hat until we get back to papa. I don't want you to have to smile for this laughing stranger in a military uniform just because of me. Let's get out of here, mama!" If only I had been older and smarter. If only I had just been different. But, at that time, I was a seven-year-old boy, devoted to papa and mama. Again, I turned away from the major.

"Well, all right," he said. "I'll think about what to do. You just can't wear a uniform if you didn't take the military pledge, can you, Danya? That's against the rules. I'll give it some thought. And you, Danya, don't wear the uniform until I've made a decision."

I continued to wear the uniform. Mama objected. I was stubborn and made references to papa. "If only papa . . . He would have stood up for me . . . papa isn't afraid of anyone. . . ." Mama gave in to me. A week later, we got another notice to appear at the military enlistment office. This time the major summoned mama alone.

I see her dress half-heartedly. She looks in the little mirror that she had brought from Leningrad. She kept the mirror with the lipstick, with the box of pink cheek powder and with a little bottle of perfume, all in a purse shaped like a half-moon, with a strap and a handle. She looks in the mirror. Fixes her hair. Puts lipstick on. Powder. She twists off the cap of the perfume bottle, touches the opening with her index finger. And then touches her neck, cheeks, and dress. Mama has not worn lipstick or powder or perfume since we left Leningrad.

At first, I didn't even understand what she was doing with her lips, which were acquiring a foreign, not mama's, color, and why she was sprinkling her cheeks with pink flour. Mama was almost ready to leave, but, for some reason, she dawdled, looking for something. She was different, indecisive. Finally, I walked her to the kitchen doors and stepped out with her into the entryway.

"Go back, Danik. You'll catch a cold," mama said. I heard her voice shaking.

"Mama, mama! Can I go with you? I won't come inside to the office of that disgusting major. I'll wait for you outside, in the entryway."

It's as if she were waiting for these words, and she laughed, "My little protector! Of course, you may come with me!"

He was standing on the porch, leaning on his cane. His greatcoat was thrown over his shoulder. He was smoking. He wasn't wearing a hat. His black curls were sprinkled with snow. He saw that mama had brought me again and that, as before, I was wearing the uniform.

Flinging his cigarette into a snowbank, he said angrily, "It seems that I asked you to come alone, Citizen Kogan! But you came together, and you continue this masquerade!"

"We're always together, Aleksandr Semyonovich! For my son, the uniform is not a masquerade. It's a gift from his father. You, yourself, have boys!"

Here the major lost control of himself completely. He started to bang his cane on the stoop. He was yelling as if mama had said something insulting or nasty. It was as if I was not a seven-year-old boy who was wearing a military uniform sent to him by his father, but a real enemy, who had to be, if not destroyed, then at least frightened and punished. I became hysterical. Until then, I had been growing up a smiling, peaceful, and agreeable boy. Now I yelled back at this man who dared to flout my father's will and, on top of that, had tried to entice my mother.

"I'm not afraid of you, you evil villain!" I yelled. "You act so brave but only because my father is far away. But my mother isn't afraid of you either. She's not afraid of you, and she doesn't love you! She's not afraid of you, and she doesn't love you! She's not afraid of you and she doesn't love you!" I kept on repeating, "She's not afraid of you and she doesn't love you!" Tears were pouring out of my eyes. The major had long ago left the porch. I kept on yelling after the one who had insulted me. I was yelling my first words of justice, devotion, and protest.

"Let's go home, my little one," mama kept on repeating as she wiped my face. "Let's go home, my wonderful protector."

I fell ill with a serious form of tuberculosis of the lymph nodes in the neck called scrofula. It was caused by a deep shock that had revealed the savage world of adults to me, a shock that had been particularly severe because I didn't have a full understanding of what had transpired, although, like a small animal, I felt an instinctive danger. I didn't go outside. I sat in the kitchen or lay on the *polati*. My neck was wrapped in a bandage with a smelly ointment. From time to time, I would run a fever. I didn't feel like eating. I didn't feel like playing. My only entertainment was books. Mama started to bring me the classics and also modern books she considered worthy. I reread Pushkin endlessly. Particularly his short story "The Shot." In general, the theme of revenge became some sort of a compass, an unspoken guide for any book I was reading. That is, in my imagination, events in the story or novella would be charged with a certain overriding aim, which at that time I did not call revenge," but which today is exactly what I interpret revenge to be. Therefore, Gogol's tales "Viy," "Taras Bulba," "The Fair at Sorochinsk" were for me, foremost, narratives about stages of achieving revenge for deceit, treachery, mockery, and such. Of course I also read other prose with pleasure: Kuprin's lovely story "The Wonderful Doctor," Kassil's autobiographical tale *The Black Book and Schwambrania* or the wonderful book by Volkov, *The Magician of the Emerald City.* But, at that time, tales of deadly dangers, which had to be braved in a struggle with evil, were much dearer to me. Therefore my choices were very broad: Olesha's *Three Fat Men,* Arsenyev's *Dersu Uzala,* Furmanov's *Chapayev,* Gaydar's *School.* But the book that especially struck me was Tynyanov's *Kyukhlya.* What bitter fate had befallen this boy with the strange last name Kyukhelbeker. Kind, talented, and unloved by all. First a strange boy, then a young man, an adult poet, writing poems, which didn't appeal to many. Except maybe Pushkin liked them. But even Pushkin would occasionally tease Kyukhelbeker. Not about his poems but about his eccentricity. It seemed to me that I also was not like the rest. I was strange like Vilya Kyukhelbeker. Strange Danya Rayev. I lay in bed or on the *polati,* or sat by the window behind the kitchen table. I read and reread *Kyukhlya,* and I imagined how, when I grew up, I would defend all the strange ones, the ones with hooked noses, the alien ones, who are not the same as everybody else because of the way they look, the way they act, and their different last names. I would avenge their tears, their insults, and their anguish. I would cure their illnesses.

It was probably then that I started on the path to becoming a physician.

We heard on the radio that our troops had defeated the Germans at Stalingrad. Mama and Baba Lena wept. In the *izba,* the doors kept swinging open and slamming shut. The neighborhood women were coming and going. They would cross themselves in front of the icon of Nicholas the Wonder Worker. For the first time, I heard them not only pining for those who had gone to the front, but also dreaming aloud of their return. Until Stalingrad, until the year

1943, there was total darkness and despondency. Now there was a glimmer of hope.

I also started to feel better. I would pull on my felt boots and go out into the yard into the early spring sun. And sometimes in the evening I would go next door to visit with Mitya the hunter, grandson of Ded Andrey and Baba Lena. Mitya read a lot. He wanted to go to flight school. He would talk about books. He was the one who gave me the tale about the taiga hunter Dersu Uzala. Our relatives, Uncle Buzya and Madame Bekman, lived in Mitya's *izba*. One evening, I stopped by there. The Bekmans were drinking tea. Usually everybody there drank tea with dried raspberries. Sometimes with honey. They were drinking tea with something white that looked like salt.

"Why are you drinking tea with salt?" I asked the Bekmans.

"We like to drink tea with salt," Madame Bekman answered.

"Want to try some?" asked Uncle Buzya. No, I did not.

At home, I asked mama why they were drinking tea with salt.

"They were joking. It was sugar," Mama said. I had forgotten what sugar was.

I forgot a lot about city life. Much of what I used to know in Leningrad: sugar, water pipes, streetcars, apples.

Apples appeared in our *izba* when Vanya, the youngest of Baba Lena's sons sent to the front, brought them from Kazan. One March evening, he walked into the *izba*. He threw open the doors and stood silently in the middle of the kitchen. On his back there was a backpack. The flaps on the hat he wore were crooked. His coat was cinched with a thick belt. He was smiling. The left sleeve of his coat was tucked into his pocket. "Vanechka!" Baba Lena shouted out, throwing herself at her son and kissing him. He embraced her with his right arm. "See, mama, see how I've returned." Ivan had lost his left arm at Stalingrad. After his injury and surgery, he was at a military hospital in Kazan.

To celebrate the safe return of Ivan Teryokhin, there was drinking and festivities in the *izba*. Many people came by. Mainly unmarried girls and wives of those soldiers fighting at the front. Or old women whose sons were fighting. Ivan was a real, live example of a soldier's return. Without an arm, but alive. He had returned alive from the war. It was the possibility of a miracle, a possibility in which they had now come to believe. Young widows also came. Girls came. To sit, to listen to Vanya's stories of the war, of all the acts of heroism and all the horrors he had witnessed.

Strange details float up in my memory. I remember that wine appeared in the *izba*. Not only the heady home brew that was so familiar. But an unfamiliar red wine. From some tap Ivan would bring red wine in a teapot. I remember how he poured the wine from the teapot into teacups.

"Drink, Stella Vladimirovna! Drink to my return! To the return of all of our people from this cursed war. To your husband, Vladimirovna!"

"Thank you, Vanya," mama said as she took a sip of the wine.

The home brew was something familiar. Until Vanya's return, in our *izba* they drank home brew for Easter and for Trinity Sunday at the cemetery when they remembered with home brew those who had passed away. And now red wine! And mama, sipping this red wine with slow sips from a teacup decorated with roosters, also became different.

She had long talks with Ivan. She told him all about the Forestry Technology Academy, about working with such famous professors as Krestinsky and Tishchenko. Ivan had just finished two years at the Forestry Institute in Molotov (or was it Sverdlovsk?) when the war started. He was called up into the army right after finishing his second year, when he had come to Siva for his summer vacation. He was fascinated by the way trees grew in the forest, by the shrubs, by the grasses and the moss, by the biology and the chemistry of forest plants. Mama enjoyed telling him what she knew and having such a worthy listener as Ivan. I watched all this with a vague, incomprehensible sense of fear.

What was I afraid of? What was I alarmed by? From what did I want to protect mama?

Mama became a little different. I wanted mama always to be just with me, which probably, subconsciously, meant only with papa and me.

Baba Lena, with her compassionate heart, understood the undefined awakenings of jealousy in my heart. She would store something away for me, something she knew I loved: steamed rutabagas, a pancake with honey, a mug of milk fresh from the cow. Or she'd call me to go and play with the young calf, born to our cow, Manka, after Shrovetide.

Pashka, no matter how much of a prankster he was, did not venture any jokes or insinuations regarding my mama's long conversations with Ivan. He started to look after me even more than usual. Pashka liked to read books about animals, all sorts of books, from ones on ancient methods of taming wild animals and birds to ones on training animals in a modern circus. I remember how, from somewhere, Pashka had dragged in a tattered, very old book about falcon hunting. He had never been to a circus or a menagerie. I told him what I could remember. About the Leningrad Zoo, with its very tall, as tall as two *izbas*, elephants and very wide, as wide as three cows, hippos. We decided that when the war ends, and mama and I return to Leningrad, Pashka will come to visit. Papa will get tickets, and Pashka and I will go by streetcar to the circus, where the famous trainer Yury Durov performs. And the next day we'll go to the Leningrad Zoo to see the Indian elephants and African hippos.

It was the end of May. The snows were swiftly melting. School was ending. Mama said that she was going to the village club to see a movie called *Wait for Me*. "Ivan is also going to the movies," mama said.

I stayed up a long time, waiting for Mama. I was reading *Dersu Uzala*. I was imagining that when I grew up, I'd go to the Far East to the taiga on the Amur River. Where brave hunters live and catch the Amur tigers for the circus and zoos. I was reading and dreaming and waiting for mama to come home from the club, but she didn't come back. Neither did Ivan. I kept reading and dreaming and waiting for mama. Until I finally fell asleep over the book in the kitchen. Mama returned late and took me, half-asleep, to my bed.

The next day, mama told me that we were going to visit Aunt Musya and Borya (the wife and son of mama's brother, Uncle Mitya) in the town of Nizhnie Mully, which was on the Kama River, like the city of Molotov. Aunt Musya worked as an accountant in a military hospital. Borya had just finished first grade. Uncle Mitya fought in a tank division. Memory is so selective! I remember very well how, going into evacuation, we had made our way to Siva on a cart, but about our trip from Siva to the train station in Vereshchagino on the way to Nizhnie Mully, I remember nothing, not a single detail, image, or conversation (either with mama or with the old driver). By that time, I had seen and probably gotten used to such things as roads through the forest, horses and carts, roadside *izbas*, fields and hills, all so common to a village boy.

We took the train from Vereshchagino to the city of Molotov (formerly—and now again—called Perm). Mama had a friend in Molotov, a ballerina from the Kirov Theater. The Leningrad Theater of Opera and Ballet named after Kirov (the former Mariinsky Theater) was evacuated to Molotov during the war. The city had helped me rediscover those forgotten and half-forgotten objects and concepts. For example, I was most amazed by the plumbing system. The water ran out of the faucet all by itself. You didn't have to bring it from a well. I was also amazed by the streetcars and motorcars, which had reappeared from my dreams.

From Molotov we took a ferry along the Kama River to Nizhnie Mully. When we stepped onto the dock, there was no one there to meet us. Mother started to get nervous. She had forewarned Aunt Musya by sending her a telegram. I was standing next to our bag with the presents. We were bringing honey, dried raspberries, and some salted foods for Aunt Musya and Borya. We even had the loaf of village rye bread Baba Lena had given us for the trip. Mama went into the ticket office, and came right back out again. No one knew anything.

Finally, we saw a boy, about eight or nine years old, who had climbed out of a boat a short distance away from the dock. In the boat, holding oars in his hands, an old man sat unperturbed, smoking a hand-rolled cigarette. The boy ran up to us. His eyes were blue like mama's. He was smiling, and when he smiled, you could see dimples in his cheeks. And he had a dimple on his chin, just like mama's and mine. He wore a gray derby and a brown coat.

"Borenka! That's our Borenka!" cried mama, rushing over to kiss him. This was Borya Kogan, the son of mama's brother, Mitya. My first cousin.

"Aunt Stella! Danik! I knew you right away from the photographs. You know, we have some pictures from before the war. I'm sorry I'm a little late. We had a hard time rowing against the current. Aunt Stella, you'll go in the boat, and Danik and I will run along the shore. It's only two versts to the hospital."

Borya was capable and mature, like a little adult. Immediately, I remembered everything: his serious manner of talking, his slightly misrolled r's, his precise recommendations, almost commands, when he woke me up in Akulovka during the German Junker air raid. The way Borya had gotten the other children out of bed, ever so carefully and firmly, and then how he had led us all to the basement of the house, to the bomb shelter.

Mama greeted the old boatman. He threw his cigarette overboard. Mama handed him our bag with the gifts. He put the bag close to the bow. Then he helped mama get into the boat and settle on the bench. The boatman swung the oars from the boat into the water and began to row. The boat went along the shore.

Borya ran with confidence, keeping up with the boat. I tried not to lag behind. Mama was watching us intently. As soon as mama would see that we were lagging, she'd ask the boatman to row more slowly. From time to time, he would stop rowing altogether, lift the oars out of the water, and put them on the bottom of the boat. Taking out a piece of newspaper, he would fold over the edges, pour some tobacco from his pouch into the little hollow, and roll it into a little cigarette, gluing the edges with his saliva. Then he would strike two flints together to light a little wick, and light his rolled cigarette from the wick.

We stopped to rest. I looked over the banks sprinkled with the yellow dandelions. The Kama River was wide. Passenger and freight boats, motor barges and freight barges towed by strong and sturdy tugboats, all went down the Kama toward the Volga River and back. The barges were loaded all the way to the top.

"What are they carrying?" I asked Borya during one of our rest stops.

Borya answered, "They're carrying grain and arms to the front."

"And from the front?"

"Trophies!" said Borya.

Actually, Borya knew a lot about things to which I paid little attention. He was an honor student. He had finished the first grade with all A pluses. Later, I came to understand him much better. That is, I watched my cousin Borya all my life. And everything I knew (or thought I knew about him) was the result of my observing and pondering our lifelong relationship as close relatives.

Borya Kogan was one of those people who have been blessed with a rational mind. Because I do think that there is an irrational logic of artists (writers, musicians, and others)—the nonrealists. He drew each subject well and rationally, just like it was supposed to be drawn. It looked just like a pretty *izba*,—or a fence, a dog, a well. His *izba* looked like an *izba* that had already been drawn by somebody, that is, like one that had become the standard for a drawing of an *izba,* a picture-postcard *izba*. For me, an *izba* was, first of all, a home, a place to be lived in, made of logs that had their own patterns of wood left over from the time when the logs were still tree trunks, where beetles and caterpillars crawled under the bark.

Maybe just the opposite was true, and I was the realist?

Borya solved problems easily. He understood boat schedules, geographical maps, the blueprints of instruments. All that was beyond me. The goddess of technology had passed me by. At the same time, I noticed details of life that bypassed Borya's attention: waves splashing, birds singing, floorboards creaking, feet shuffling, raindrops splashing, the lowering of voices during mama's and Auntie Musya's conversations. I told Borya about our vegetable patch, about our pig, Fifer, named after the one who was slaughtered in the fall, or how I would go fishing with Pashka as soon as I returned home to Siva. Borya was a polite boy, and I was the younger cousin and a guest. He listened politely to my stories. And right away, he would suggest we play checkers, dominos, or battleship. He practically always won.

Mama was anxious about something, as she always was before an event or a conversation so important it demanded all of her strength or a total baring of her soul. We had stayed with Aunt Musya and Borya for almost a week, and it was the eve of our departure. We talked about papa, Uncle Mitya, mama's sisters, Pesya and Fanya, about Uncle Eyno and his family living in Lithuania, who had disappeared (as was later confirmed, forever), about Musya's brother Nikolay and his friend Yura—it seemed we covered everything there was to talk about. But not everything, apparently.

Borya and I played to our hearts' content in the yard by their house. They lived in a dormitory of a military hospital. It was a wooden barracks with a long corridor with doors leading to many rooms. Nurses, orderlies, accountants, cooks, stokers, and other service personnel all lived there. All of those who fit into the category of non-conscripts. Seriously wounded officers and rank and file soldiers were being treated in the hospital. Borya told me all about that. A large part of the medical personnel, excluding army doctors (mostly women), lived in the same barracks as Aunt Musya and Borya. There were many children. The evening before we left, Borya and I played as much as we wanted to and returned home just before supper. Auntie Musya and mama fed us and sent us off to bed. Of course there was only the one room. Borya and I slept head to foot on Aunt Musya's bed. Mama slept on Borya's bed. And Aunt Musya made her bed on the floor.

Mama and Aunt Musya sat over tea for a long time. Borya fell asleep. I heard his sniffling. Ever since we were little, almost from infancy, when we would go to visit Uncle Mitya in Nevskaya Zastava or when they would come to see us on the Vyborg Side in Lesnoye, they would had me sleep with Borya. There was no spare bed. Borya would fall asleep right away, and I would spend a long time thinking about the day's events, or dreaming about something while listening to the gentle breathing of my cousin, before dozing off. This time, too, I couldn't fall asleep. I knew it wasn't nice to listen to grown-ups' conversations. But I couldn't help hearing mama and Auntie Musya. I wrapped my head in the blanket, but mama's words reached me anyway. "Pavel is at the front . . . faithfulness . . . Ivan . . . I can't explain it . . . a good and unhappy young man, an invalid . . ." And Auntie Musya's words in reply, "You're young . . . life makes its own demands . . . at the front—do you think they're all saints? . . . you should see what goes on in the hospital!"

We returned to Siva. Mama went to the Village Council. I don't know what she said there, but she managed to convince the officials. They gave us a separate room in a two-story red brick building that stuck out on the edge of the market square. Before the Revolution, it had been a wayside inn, where merchants and rich peasants stayed when they brought their goods to market. To this day, memories of the building evoke negative color associations for me: red bricks, red flags during the November holidays, red meat called horsemeat that mama received on her worker's ration card.

Even though we had moved from the Teryokhins' to a new apartment, they convinced mama to plant potatoes, cabbages, and the rest of the vegetables, like the year before. In the summer, mama worked on the collective farm, and whenever I got the chance, I would run away to my old *izba*, to Baba Lena, to Ded Andrey, and to Pashka. Ivan left for the city to continue his studies in forestry. I didn't like our new place. It was a single room you entered directly from the street. The walls were plastered and whitewashed to a regulation hospital color. There were two metal frame cots. On the walls mama hung pictures of papa, grandpa, and grandma, Uncle Mitya, and other relatives.

In the fall, I entered first grade. We would go to school together when mama had her classes. Or I would make my way alone along the wooden sidewalks thrown down along the fences. Otherwise, you could get stuck in the clay for a long time and lose your rubber boots or bast shoes.

I can't remember my first teacher. But I do remember how unbearably bored I was in school. I had read the alphabet book long before. I read books with ease. I helped the teacher with my classmates' reading, although I did have trouble with penmanship. I knew how to write words. Which letters to use. It was boring to draw out the straight lines and curves with the different levels of pen pressure. I would break the famous "Number 86" pens (copper with stars) without giving it a second thought. I wrote quickly and was a good speller. The teacher gave me Bs, although I probably deserved Fs for my penmanship. Once the teacher said, "Judging by how quickly and illegibly you write, you'll probably be a doctor, Rayev."

She wasn't mistaken.

Winter had come. I could ski well. Many of us made their way

to school on skis. It was much easier and faster. I wasn't any different from the village kids. Pashka took care of me, as before. He'd
come by to get me and we would rush to ski down the mountains.
We would leave the ski poles at the bottom of the mountain. It
wasn't considered fitting to use ski poles when skiing downhill.
Maybe there was a reason for that: if you fell, you could jab yourself
with their sharp points. It was a particularly dashing thing to ski
down a hill that ended in a ski jump. In addition, boys stood at the
bottom of the hill, just before the ski jump, and threw their poles in
front of the skiers who were flying down the hill. You had to jump
up and first fly over the poles and then over the ski jump.

I lost my sense of fear.

Mama was teaching German and singing to the village children.
The winter was flying toward New Year's. In January of 1944, they
announced on the radio that our troops had broken the Germans'
three-year siege of Leningrad. Then Tallinn was liberated. Papa's
unit of torpedo boats took part in the battle for Königsberg. Papa
was awarded the Order of the Great Patriotic War. At the end of
April 1944, papa sent us an affidavit authorizing us to come back.
We could go home to Leningrad.

Mama took the affidavit and her passport to the Village Council
and began preparations for our departure. We sold a lot of our
things in order to stock up on food supplies. Then, one day, mama
and I departed for distant villages with funny names: Bochenyata
and Prokhoryata—which meant Barrel's Babies and Prokhor's Babies. We left early in the morning. The road led past the cemetery,
through the forest and over the fields, which were just losing their
snow cover. In one of the villages we exchanged mama's dress for a
few kilograms of honey. In Siva we still had one of papa's suits, but
mama wouldn't part with it for anything. "We'll return to
Leningrad, the war will end, papa will be discharged, and we will
have a Victory celebration. And papa will put on his favorite gray
suit!" Toward evening, we were on our way back. The honey was

heavy. The road was bumpy: potholes on the country road, puddles, barely dried clay. It got dark. It was particularly scary to go past the cemetery at night. The dark silhouettes of the crosses reached out toward us from behind the fence.

Baba Lena gave us a tall, sturdy, old-fashioned jar. The word MONTPENSIER was stamped on the jar. Mama said that *montpensier* was a kind of sugar candy. This old jar had, at one time, contained sugar candy. She had melted the honey with butter and filled this sugar candy jar with the aromatic paste. We also prepared dried berries, dried and finely chopped carrots, dried mushrooms, peas, and some other staples to take with us.

Finally, at the end of May, the Village Council gave us permission to leave. Mama started to work on getting train tickets from Vereshchagino to Leningrad.

About a week before our departure, when all of our things were packed and a cart had been ordered to take us from our house on the market square to the train station in Vereshchagino, a terrible thing happened. Tanya, Moysha Grinberg's wife, died. She had had a very serious case of rheumatic heart disease. As often happens to the chronically ill in the spring, the health of our Tanya had declined, leading to her death. The evening before the funeral, there was a thunderstorm, a deluge. The sticky mud, which had filled the road, made it impossible to get to the cemetery on foot. Aunt Enya hired two wagons. The first one carried the casket with Tanya's body. Around the casket sat Aunt Enya, the old gravedigger, the watchman at the cemetery, Malvina, and I. The rest of our relatives, Madame Bekman, Uncle Buzya, Aunt Tsilya, Uncle Yanya, Maria Osipovna, and my mother, all traveled to the cemetery in the other wagon. The day was cold and windy. The pine trees over the crosses on the graves were swaying like old Jews in a synagogue. The grave had been dug earlier. I peeked into it. There was water at the bottom, like in a well. They lowered the casket into the grave. Each of us threw in a handful of dirt. The cemetery watchman filled the grave with dirt. Uncle Buzya began to read the prayer for the dead—the Kaddish. When he finished, something happened that, in my mind completely, metaphysically separated our family from the surrounding Russian world. We lifted our heads and saw that the cemetery watchman was dragging a cross in our direction. Malvina and I didn't understand what was going on. We saw that something terrible had happened, something more terrible than Tanya's death because all our family were standing there, frozen, staring at the watchman. He walked up to the grave, dropped the cross in the middle of the mound, and was about to shove it in deeper, when old, stooped-over Aunt Enya seemed to straighten up and to regain her strength and stature.

Steadfastly, she said to the watchman, "Please take it away! Get this thing out of here!"

The watchman was surprised. He wasn't insulted, or angry, just surprised. And owing to his genuine surprise, he smirked, stroked his gray beard, and said simply from the heart, "How will she be? How can the dearly departed Tatyana be among all of them without a cross?" He pointed to all the other graves. "Was she a Party member? Then I'll put up a marker with a red star."

Our Aunt Enya looked the watchman straight in the face and said firmly, "Thank you, my dear man, for your good intentions. But please understand us and don't take offense. We are Jews. We bury our dead without crosses or red stars."

At the Vereshchagino station they loaded us up in a heated freight car that had been outfitted for transporting soldiers to the front, and the wounded back from the front to hospitals. There were wooden bunk beds in the car. I took the top bunk. From living in the village, I'd learned how to climb up onto the *polati* easily and quickly. Mama slept on the lower bunk. The air in the train car was thick and stuffy. During the day, the passengers would mostly gather in the middle of the car. The majority were women, old men, and children. They were all being recalled to Leningrad. We had a distant and long road ahead of us, from Vereshchagino to Kirov, through Vologda, to Leningrad. We were crossing the northern part of Russia with its many slow rivers and streams, which flow out of the boundless turf bogs and stretch to the Barents Sea and White Sea in the north or to the Volga River and later to the Caspian Sea in the south. We were nearing Kirov. The group of boys in our car, my age and older, included the fifteen-year-old Volodya we called Captain after the hero of Jules Verne's novel *A Fifteen-Year-Old Captain*. Between battles of dominos, cards, checkers, and chess, our whole group discussed a book that was very popular at that time, *A Boy from Urzhum*. The main character in this book, Seryozha Kostrikov, who later became the leader Kirov, was born in the small town of Urzhum, not far from the provincial capital Vyatka. Vyatka was renamed Kirov in honor of that slain leader. The book told how Seryozha had huddled on a trunk, under the light of an oil lamp, devouring one book after another. We all liked him a lot, this Seryozha Kostrikov. The book told how he grew up poor, how he read a lot, how he dreamed of freeing the working people from the oppression of the capitalists and landowners. Combining Dick Sand from *A Fifteen-Year-Old Captain* by Jules Verne, Borya Gorikov from *School* by Arkady Gaydar, Vanya Solntsev from *The Son of a Regiment* by Valentin Kataev, we were forging our image of a young brave hero. We all would have liked to run away to the front, to the real army or to the partisans. Of course we dreamed of deeds of valor and of glory.

As it happens, Lady Luck found us. Our train consisted of a smoking engine, which blasted its whistle at each stop, and of a long row of freight cars outfitted to transport passengers. Our car was the last in the train. At one of the stops, when our group of boys jumped out to run around in the field that surrounded the railroad tracks, a soldier came up to us. He and a fellow horsebreeder were escorting horses to the front. Today, in an age of supermodern military technology, when even tanks seem like dinosaurs, it's hard to imagine that each army had cavalry subunits. In addition, horses were used as transport for mobile hospital units, for field kitchens, and for other everyday purposes. The cavalry grooms asked if we boys would like to sleep in their train car, on the hay. We were all to eager to. Our mothers finally let us, though with fear in their eyes. There was no way they could fight a united front of boys.

Our whole gang moved over to the train car with the army horses. The cavalry grooms treated us to canned pork, square city bread, and strong, sweet tea. Trained as veterinary technicians in the horse brigade, the cavalry grooms were bringing the horses to reinforce those on active duty in the army. We heard unbelievable stories of raids by our cavalry against the German rear guard. We imagined how we would have attacked enemy fortifications riding in Cossack saddles, with glistening blades bared and rifles slung over our shoulders. The horses were peacefully chewing hay in the stalls, munching and crunching oats, shifting from foot to foot, and happily neighing to one another.

In the morning, the cavalry grooms again gave us their simple soldiers' food and tea. We kept waiting for the train to stop so we could freshen up and see our mothers. But it didn't stop. It sped on and on into the unknown. Finally, the engine tooted triumphantly and the clanked the whole length of the train. Our train car jerked like a horse that had been suddenly reined in and, rocking back and forth, came to a standstill. One of the soldiers threw the sliding car doors open. The train car was the last in the train. The car with our mothers was nowhere to be seen. The oldest in our group, Volodya Levin, told us to wait for him on the platform. He went to the stationmaster. It turned out that our train was heading southwest. Our mothers' train car had been added the night before to a train going toward Vologda, to the northwest.

"We have to decide where we're going," our Captain said. "Are we going to the front or are we going to look for the train car with our mothers?"

We became pensive. Of course it would be great to go to the front to join the army or the partisans. But what about our mothers?

I imagined my mother's teary eyes and said, "First of all, let's find the train car with our mothers, and then we can go wherever we want. I, for one, want to go to the Baltic Sea, to my papa, to serve as a cadet trainee on a torpedo boat!"

And so we decided. Volodya went to see the stationmaster again. I don't know what he told him, but when they both came out onto the platform, the stationmaster pulled his peaked hat with the red top over his forehead, scratched the back of his head, and said, "What have you little bastards done! And now I have to get you out of this mess. Your papas are fighting for all of us at the front." Using the telegraph, the stationmaster located the train car with our mothers and asked them to detach it and put it on the emergency tracks. He took us to his office and showed us on the map the station where their train car would wait for us on the emergency tracks. Then he traced our way on the map and showed us at which stations other stationmasters would transfer us, until we met up with our mothers. I watched intently and tried to remember the names of all the transfer stations. And Volodya wrote all this down in his notebook. Then the stationmaster took us to the food stand at the station, where they gave us each a piece of bread, a bowl of soup, a plate of pasta, and a glass of tea. The tea was unsweetened, though.

And we went off along the transfer stations toward our mothers. We made our way to them in all kinds of different train cars. Mostly, they were freight cars outfitted to transport passengers. Sometimes passenger trains, sleepers, or regional trains. Once, we got to ride in a first-class train car. But not for long. Only two or three hours. How did it happen that we were so far away from our mothers? Volodya Levin had finished the eight grade. He drew a right triangle. "Here," he pointed to one side of the triangle, "is where the train car with our mothers went during the night. And here,"

Volodya pointed to another side of the triangle, "is where we sped off to the southwest with our cavalry horses." The third side of the triangle was left, the one that joined the other two. "This is a hypotenuse," said Volodya. "It's longer than either of the other sides. We are now going along the hypotenuse to our mothers." When they finally brought us to the station, where our old train car stood on the emergency tracks, our mothers kissed us and cried and laughed with joy, but the other passengers of the car, who hadn't temporarily lost their boys only said, "Well, thank God! Finally we can move on." At this point, we felt like real heroes . . .

For a long time, we rode along streets lined with burned-out buildings. There were almost no houses that remained untouched by the German bombing or artillery shelling. Burned-out walls. Empty rectangles of windows where once light had shown through. Invalid buildings without one or two walls. Staircase jaws spilled right onto the pavement. Leningrad was in ruins. From the train station we crossed the entire city to the Vyborg Side, to Lesnoye, where our house had stood. I don't remember who, if anyone, met us at the station. We crossed the entire city, which was totally changed. All that was left of many buildings were the burned-out walls. Sometimes, where one or two walls had collapsed, the jaws of staircases rolled out onto the pavement. Windows were boarded up with plywood or crisscrossed with glued strips of paper or left to glar with empty eyes. Sidewalks were covered with plaster, broken bricks, shattered glass, with fragments of what, before the war, had been a wall, a staircase, a railing, a balcony, a door, an arch, a window frame. We rode in silence, crushed by the sight of this catastrophe.

Our house was across from the park of the Forestry Technology Academy on the outskirts of the city. It was untouched by the bombing and shelling. A two-story brick house, with yellow stucco on three sides. And, on the other side of our courtyard, Iodko's house with the communal laundry also stood as before the war. Everyone in our apartment house made it through the siege, except the old lady, Aunt Dusya Krylova's mother. Aunt Dusya was now as big as a blimp. Mama said that Aunt Dusya swelled up from hunger during the siege.

I remember my first day back. I ran out into the courtyard. I wanted to see the other kids. I thought about them all through the evacuation. It was an early July morning. The sun was bright. I stood in the middle of the courtyard. But no one was there. In front of the sheds there were green vegetable patches. The potato plants had blossoms. Little globes of apples were starting to swell in both of the Iodko orchards. I remembered that Slavik lived in apartment number 11, off the same landing as ours. Slavik was the one who'd fallen into the manhole. The one the yardkeeper Uncle Vasya had pulled out of there. Mishka Shushpanov also lived in apartment number 11. I would even have been happy to see him. The doors to number 11 were not closed. I recalled that Slavik lived in the second to the last room. To the right of the outside wall. And Mishka—in the last one, straight ahead. I knocked on the door of the room on the right. No one answered. I knocked again. The door opened slightly, and a boy's head appeared. It was blond, green-eyed, with thick lips.

"And who are you?" the head asked.

"Danya Rayev," I answered.

"And what are you doing here?" the head asked.

"I'm looking for Slavik," I answered.

The head thought for a while, rocked from side to side, rolled its eyes, looked through its white eyelashes, and said, "You know, Danka, you head out into the courtyard. I'll lock the door and come out."

In five minutes a blond, stocky boy came out into the yard. He said, "My name is Borka Smorodin. They call me Smoroda. You're looking for Slavik?"

"Yes," I answered, "Slavik and Mishka Shushpanov."

"The thing is, Slavka and his mother both died of hunger during the siege. We got assigned their room. My mother and me. We used to live over there." He pointed to a vacant lot with garbage piled on it. "In a wooden house. They took the house apart for firewood. My stepfather, Konstantin Konstantinovich Biserkin, also died from hunger. It was when we were still living in the wooden house. Mother and I almost died, too. I swelled up, and my mother wasted away till she was just a skeleton. Osip Osipovich Smilgevich saved us from hunger. He's Polish. He has a draft deferment as an optics specialist. He got my mother a job at the Svetlana Factory. Osip Osipovich now lives with us."

"And how about Mishka Shushpanov?" I asked.

"Mishka is in a reform school for stealing," Borka explained without beating around the bush. And then he added, "Mishka's mother, Lizka, got together with Romka the Supplier. He knocked her up."

"What's knocked her up?" I asked.

"She's gonna have a baby, and soon, that's what it is! And you, where did you come from, Danka?" Borka asked.

"We were evacuated to the Urals," I answered.

"That's why you talk funny. Like you got a hot potato in your mouth," said Borka.

"What do you mean?" I said in surprise.

"Say *korova!*"

"*Korova,*" I repeated.

"I told you, you got potatoes in your mouth. You say all your o's." Rounding his lips, he copied me, "*Korova.*"

"How do *you* say it?" I asked.

"We say it *karova.*"

"But you write it *korova,*" I insisted, quite sure how the word for "cow" was spelled.

"Who cares how it's written!" Borka brushed it aside, and then he asked, "Where's your father, Danka?"

"On the Baltic Sea. He commands the torpedo boats," I answered.

"You're lucky, Danka!" Borka said. "You have a father."

In a few days, I saw papa. Mama was just making dinner. The door flew open. Papa came in and hugged us both at once. That's how big he was, my papa. He flew from the Baltic on a navy plane. A friend of his, a pilot, was dispatched to Leningrad for a day. He was flying back in the morning. Papa had to go back with him. I have almost no recollection of that evening. I don't even remember what papa looked like then. His pictures have merged with real memories of him. He was kissing mama and me. He was smiling. He was pouring champagne for mama and himself. And cream soda for me. We were sitting at the table. Papa brought chocolate, cookies, and canned goods. I remember the canned crabmeat, the champagne, and the cream soda. We were sitting at the table. From time to time, neighbors would come knocking at the door. Mama would open the door. She'd invite them in to sit with us. She'd offer them food. "Pavel Borisovich!" one of the neighbors would call out, "Your Stellochka is a real beauty, and that's not all. Look what a fine lad your son has grown to be!" Mama would tell them about the evacuation, papa about all sorts of things that happened at the front. I was amazed by papa's story about the capture of Königsberg. How the sailors from his boats landed on the narrow strip of land recaptured from the Germans and fought them in hand-to-hand combat. Then they put me to bed. When I woke up, papa had already left for the military airport. Mama had to go to the factory.

A week after I returned to Leningrad, mama went to work at SRF, which stood for the Streetcar Repair Factory. It turned out that papa had managed to get the affidavit for us to return to Leningrad from the Streetcar Repair Factory, under the stipulation that mama would work there. She was appointed plan economist to the assembly shop. They assembled totally reconditioned streetcars and trolleybuses there. Mama would leave at half past six in the morning and return no earlier than seven at night. Sometimes later. There was so much work there. It's a good thing I made friends with

Borka Smorodin. We spent entire days together. His mother, Auntie Lyuba, also worked in a factory from morning till night. Mama would leave me food for the day, as Auntie Lyuba would for Borka. We heated up the food on hot plates or on kerosene stoves. First we would eat at my place, then at his.

We were always hungry. Maybe because of Borka's stories about the siege hunger. They were given only a little piece of bread per day. Borka knew many ways to get hold of food. First of all—the legal way. We had to wait in long lines to fill our bread ration cards. Everybody knew how to do that. You had to take your place in line, and, arming yourself with patience, wait your turn. Then there were things to eat in the parks, the Forestry Technology Academy park or the Udelny Park. A sour, but edible plant called rabbit cabbage grew there. We picked nettles or sorrel for soup our mothers would cook. When birdcherries ripened, we'd climb up on the black, twisted branches and pick juicy bunches of black, shiny berries with green pits, which made our mouths pucker. On the sly, we'd take sour apples from both the Iodkos' orchards, puckering up as we ate them, out of respect for our own bravery and out of contempt for the concept of private property.

Day and night, smoke billowed out of the bread factory, which was across the street from our house on the corner of Karl Marx Prospekt and Lanskoy Road. The rich aroma of bread intoxicated us. All day long, we thought about bread. Borka got a metal rod and made me a hook like the one he had. It was hot in the bread factory. We knew this because the women bakers worked just in smocks over their bare bodies. When the smocks would open up, the pink, well-fed bodies of the female employees teased us, just like the golden bodies of the breads. It was hot, and the women opened the windows. On the side of the street where Borka and I and the other neighborhood kids would hang around, on the outside of the windows, there were metal grates made of the same wire as our hooks. The workers would put the freshly baked loaves on the windowsills.

Probably not for us, but for themselves, because you couldn't eat the bread when it was steaming hot. They were cooling the bread by the open windows protected by the metal grates. Often they would cut or break the bread into chunks. And this was when one of us, whose turn it was to procure our daily bread, would saunter up to one of the open windows and shove the hook through the square opening of the grates. He'd push the hook into the chunk of bread, pull the loot out in a shot, and, hiding the bread under his jacket, dash across the road to the Forestry Technology Academy park. There, we'd divide up the spoils. Like the other guys, I stole the bread when it was my turn. We were always successful, and it was starting to look like the women bakers were opening up the windows and intentionally putting the bread out there for us. But once, when I dropped the hook in through the bars and was poking a chunk of bread, I felt a tug. Someone had gotten a hold of the hook and was dragging me to the window. I looked inside. A full-figured young woman was standing by the windowsill. Tucked under a gauze kerchief, her fiery red hair had managed to escape in a glowing golden halo around the kerchief. The redhead was dressed in a white sleeveless smock. The right side of the smock had slipped down from the strain of the struggle for my hook. And one of her breasts peeked out through the gap. The redhead's armpits were on fire with burning red hair. I dropped the hook, and my eyes opened wide and bugged out at this wonderful sight. Too bad Borka couldn't see it, too. He was waiting for me in the park with the other boys.

"What do you think you're doing?" asked the redhead. "Our Russian people, you know, are always hungry. But you kikes, don't you have enough to buy your bread?"

I was silent, dispirited.

"Here, little Jew, eat. I don't care. It's government bread."

The redhead let go of my hook together with the bread on the end. I was eight years old then. Probably I still hadn't learned to make the right decision on the spot. I grabbed the bread, hid it under my jacket, just in case a policeman came by, and dashed to the park. In a clearing at the foot of an old oak tree, Borka and the other boys from our courtyard were waiting for me to return. We divided up the bread and started to eat. Suddenly, I felt nauseated. A heaviness descended into my chest and my stomach. My temples were pounding. I ran into the hawthorn bushes and vomited.

Sometimes we would hide behind the sheds next to the corner of Novoseltsevskaya Street and Engels Prospekt. We would wait for a slow-moving truck filled with cabbages to come by, so we could roll some off with a hook. Sometimes we were lucky. There were crucians and perch in Lanskoy Pond, which was located on the corner of Karl Marx Prospekt and Lanskoy Road. It was here that Natalia Nikolaevna Pushkina (Goncharova), Pushkin's widow, had moved with her children after she married General Lanskoy. We were very lucky to get two or three little fish a day. We would fry the crucians and the perch in a frying pan. Borka was masterful at frying fish, potatoes, and finely chopped cabbage.

I was totally happy with this new life that had opened up for me in Leningrad. There was still the entire month of August before school started. Borka and I spent our whole days cruising Lesnoye, looking for food and adventure. It was true freedom. We did what we wanted. I learned to jump onto steps of the streetcar as it slowly climbed uphill from Serdobolskaya Street along the fence of the Forestry Technology Academy park. You could ride on the steps until the conductor made you get inside and buy a ticket. At that point, you had to push off with enough force to offset the speed of the streetcar. The most agile ones would jump off in such a way as to come to a halt on the ground. Even if the streetcar was speeding up. The neatest thing was to ride the "sausage" on the bumper of the last streetcar. Here and there, you could find unused cartridges, filled with gunpowder—some with brand-new caps and bullets. Sometimes these were tracer bullets. We would put the cartridge on the tracks before an oncoming streetcar and watch how the cartridge blew up. At night, you could see the bluish-green golden light of the tracer bullets. Many kids got maimed. Their nickname was demolitioners.

Suddenly, our freedom came to an end. Some representatives of the District Department of People's Education appeared in our courtyard to register all school-age persons left without supervision while their parents worked. Borka Smorodin and I belonged to this group. Our mothers got a summons from the Education Department, in which they were expressly instructed to bring us to school number 117 on the first of August. From there, they would send us off to the Udelnaya train stop to go to the Young Pioneer camp of the Vyborg District of Leningrad. Neither Borka nor I wanted to go to any camp, including Young Pioneer camp. Hounded by the Education Department representatives, our mothers caved in. I distinctly remember that we both hated the Young Pioneer camp. I also clearly remember that it was in the summer camp that I was persecuted for being Jewish. When I went to the bathroom, the boys noticed that I was different. That I was circumcised. They made fun of me, and I didn't know what to do. I grew despondent over all of them taunting me for something I was totally innocent of and couldn't possibly change. In addition (and this had been my curse since childhood after the pneumonia) I was cross-eyed. So the boys had more than enough reasons to make fun of me. Borka fiercely defended me. Little by little, the taunting and deriding quieted down. My memory saved me. Since I had read a lot, I could retell any book I had ever read. There were about twenty beds in our bunkhouse. At nine in the evening the camp bugler played taps. "Time to sleep, to your bunks, Pioneers, October children . . ." We were too young to be Young Pioneers—we were October children. The troop leader put us to bed and went to his own room. We would start to talk quietly. Finally somebody would suggest, "Hey, guys, let Danka tell us the rest of yesterday's story." And I'd continue telling them the rest of the book I had started the night before. The boys particularly liked to listen to Grimm Brothers' fairy tales. Almost all of them had survived the hunger of the siege. That's probably why they wanted to hear wondrous tales of life during peacetime, which maybe their grandparents had known. I remember they liked the tale about the "The Wonderful Porridge Pot" so much I had to tell it several times. Yes, it was hard to feel satisfied on the meager camp grub. Mostly, we got soup made of *khryapa*. That's what we called the green outer cabbage leaves. First, we would filter out the liquid part of the soup mixing it with little pieces of bread, and then, we'd mash the *khryapa* with potatoes or barley with potatoes (if it happened to be barley soup). It turned into mush. An extra main course. And then we got the real main course. We put the stools under the table and hid extra servings we would snatch away, later to share them with all our tablemates.

We came back home at the end of August 1944. I was assigned to the second grade, group 2A, in boys' school number 117, which was located on the Second Murmansk Prospekt, across from Bolotnaya Street. During the Revolution, the People's Duma of the Lesnoye-Udelnoye District of Petrograd was located on Bolotnaya. Future Soviet President M. I. Kalinin was the leader of the District Duma. Borka had already gone to this school for a year. Now he was also in the second grade, but in 2B. Cool autumn weather had set in. Before going to the factory, mama dressed me up in a navy blue jacket (which was quite acceptable) and (to my detriment) in a gray cap, prewar civilian type, with a button in the middle. Borka and I arrived at the schoolyard. He went off to see his classmates. I went to look for my 2A group. There were still no teachers in the schoolyard. I looked here and there until I bumped into a group of boys my age. One of them, with pink cheeks and curly hair, was waving a little flag with "2A" on it. A short hunchback, wearing a patched jacket that couldn't be buttoned because of his unusually bulging chest, walked up to the pink-cheeked flagbearer. A protruding square hump split down the back of his jacket.

The hunchback shot a thin stream of spit right at the feet of the boy with the flag and announced with self-importance, "Hey, you, Gagarin, mama's boy, give me your ass-kissin' flag!"

"I will not, Hunchy! Valentina Nikiforovna asked me to carry the flag!" mama's boy Gagarin answered, waving his flag.

"If you don't give it to me, I'll take your brownnoser's flag and cut it up with my wand," said Hunchy. He ripped the flag away from Gagarin and cut it up with a razor, which he held adroitly between the index and the middle fingers of his right hand. Hunchy's eyes were bugging out and turning blue, like blocks of ice. His huge mouth was twisted into a mocking smile. And his short nose was impudently stuck way up in the air, above the schoolyard, somewhere beyond the low autumn clouds. I was flabbergasted by the injustice of this situation and by Hunchy's brazenness. I couldn't stop staring at him.

"And what are you staring at, you parasite?" Hunchy said, sending a stream of spit my way. By that time, I'd already had some experience in defending myself and in fighting. For a month, Borka Smorodin and I had hung around Lesnoye and then spent another month in the Young Pioneer camp. I'd become part of a group of peers who had survived the siege. On top of that, injustice always aroused a feeling of protest in me.

I answered steadfastly, "I'm not a parasite at all. I have a name: Danka Rayev. Why did you take away the little flag and cut it up with a razor?"

Hunch screwed up his eyes in surprise, "I cut it up because it's a brownnoser's flag. Because he's a mama's boy, and you're a parasite!"

"Why am I a parasite?" I asked.

"Because you have a parasite's cap, with a button," Hunchy answered. Whipping the cap off my head, he cut off the button with his razor and threw it into the burdocks. He tossed the cap at my feet and followed it with a stream of spit.

I could not tolerate such an insult. I tripped him and smashed him hard in his bulging chest. He rocked and slammed down like a heavy cupboard onto his sharp hump, howling from pain and anger. He was like a turtle turned over on its back. He flailed his arms and legs trying to get up. The razor fell from his hand. Mama's boy Gargarin ran to pick up the razor and rushed over to the excessively heavyset lady with a high hairdo and a heavy bead neckless and heavy earrings, who was making her way toward us.

"Valentina Nikiforovna, Hunchy cut up the flag with his razor and cut the button off the new kid's cap!" Valentina Nikiforovna (he was our teacher) picked up my dismembered cap. Bending over Hunchy and grabbing him by his ear, which looked as big as a bat's wing, she lifted the vanquished offender from the ground. Hunchy just stood there, screwing up his face.

"Answer me, you cutthroat," Valentina Nikiforovna declared, holding him by the ear and rattling her beads and earrings, "did you cut up the 2A class flag?" Hunchy was panting hard and saying nothing.

"It was him, Valentina Nikiforovna! He's the one who cut up the flag! And he ruined the new kid's cap!" mama's boy Gagarin kept on repeating as he circled around the teacher.

Valentina Nikiforovna turned to me, "And you, Rayev, why did you throw Nikitin to the ground?"

I was silent.

"Nikitin called him a parasite and ruined his cap!" cried Gagarin, butting in again.

"I wasn't asking you, Gagarin," the teacher cut him off. "When I ask you, then you may tell me!" And again she turned to me, "Rayev, answer me! Was it Nikitin who ruined your cap with a razor?"

I looked at Hunchy as he stood in the grip of the teacher's tenacious fingers. It seemed to me that the ice and the mocking scorn in his eyes had been replaced by a question or maybe even a request. Or by hope. But hope for what?

Valentina Nikiforovna repeated her question, "Was he the one who ruined your cap, Rayev?"

I answered, "That's how it was!"

Valentina Nikiforovna let go of Hunchy's ear and went off to the other students. Mama's boy Gagarin followed her.

We were left alone. I with my ruined cap. And Hunchy with his smarting ear. "You, Danka, are an okay guy. Let's stick up for each other!" said Hunchy.

"Let's!" I said.

"And don't worry about the cap. After school, we'll stop by my mother's. She'll sew it up."

Soon I made friends with other boys. Dimka Boch was a brilliant freak with a huge pinecone of a head, covered with thin red curls. He stuttered, fought like a pro with his head, and knew many poems by heart, including some in English. Dimka Boch's father was a professor of geology and his mother a teacher of Russian language and literature in high school. Kolya Khrustalyov was the top student in our class. Mama's boy Gagarin, who was not friends with anyone, was also on the honor roll. An elderly aunt would bring him to school. Gagarin's father was a colonel and taught something or other at the Military Communications Academy. Kolya Khrustalyov, on the other hand, came from a very poor family. His father had been killed in action. His mother could barely provide for Kolya and her other two children. Kolya was a quiet, skinny boy. He wore wire-rimmed glasses. He was the best in the class at writing dictations and solving math problems. I was also friends with the Greek boy Lyalka Kalafati. Lyalka was an almost girlish derivative of his proper name, Leonard. He lived with his grandfather. His grandfather called him Lyalik, and the boys called him Lyalka. Lyalka's parents had either perished or lived somewhere far away. So far that even letters didn't come from there. Lyalka was recklessly brave. He would climb out of our classroom window on the third floor and shimmy down the gutter pipe.

I only had one sworn enemy in the class. His name was Minchyonok, but they called him Mincha. He was everybody's enemy. But mine in particular. All the boys in the class tried to steer clear of him. Even Hunchy didn't mess with him. He had recently been released from reform school, where he'd started first grade. They said that Mincha was the spotter for a gang that robbed apartments. You could find him smoking with the upperclassmen in the bathroom. And Mincha himself had nothing to do with anybody in our class. He was just marking time in school. Or not showing up at all. Valentina Nikiforovna tolerated his presence as her duty and punishment. In general, she was very strict with all of us. Anyone who transgressed was hit on the head or on the hands with her long wooden ruler. And she would loudly bang her ring on the teacher's or students' desks. And sometimes we would get it on the head with her heavy signet ring. Being hit on the head or on my hands with her ruler stayed in my memory for a long time. She didn't touch Minchyonok. It's as if he hovered above our class, touching no one, except me. Yes, he treated me differently from the first day. I felt his unfriendly gaze. One day, Mincha could no longer bear to hide his hatred, and he acted on it. Hunchy and I were standing by the window in the classroom, planning some dashing adventure. Probably going to the movie theater Miniature, which was just a half a streetcar stop from the school. You had to wait by the outside door until the end of a showing and slip in against the stream of people leaving the theater. You'd hide between the rows and wait for the lights to go out and the movie to start. Most of all, we liked to go to see *Jolly Fellows* and *Chapayev*.

Hunchy and I had just decided to stop by 2B and take Borka Smorodin with us, when Mincha walked up to us and said, "I look at you, Hunchy, and I can't believe it. You're one of us. You're a hood. You smoke. You steal. You kid around with your wand. Why are you ruining your reputation?"

"And what is it that I'm ruining my reputation with, Mincha?"

"Sticking up for this little kike, Hunchy!"

"You, Mincha, are a fool, even though you're a thief. Danka and I are friends. We stick up for each other!"

"He's a wimp. How could he stick up for you?" Up till then, I just took it, because we were in a classroom, and Valentina Niki-forovna could come in at any moment. But when Mincha called me a wimp," I said, "Mincha, you're a wimp yourself! Let's fight after school!"

"You and me?" Mincha asked.

"Yes, you and me!" I answered.

"Okay, Mincha," Hunchy said, "only no steel pens, and no wands. If I see any, I'll poke your headlights out myself!"

After classes, Mincha and I fought behind the school. It was a real boxing match. Before the fight, Hunch searched us both for razors, switchblades, brass knuckles, and files—all of these instruments were used in fights at that time. The fight was rough. I defeated Mincha by giving him a bloody nose and a black eye and making him "eat dirt." This was at the end of the fight, to show my total superiority over him. I straddled Mincha and shoved his face into the wet autumn soil.

From that day on, Minchyonok grew quiet. Soon, he completely disappeared. First to reform school, then, they said, to the prisons and the camps.

One day, right out of the blue, our teacher, Valentina Nikiforovna Levchenko, started to tell the class about her childhood. She was born into a poor Ukrainian family. Became an orphan early on. A childless couple took her in, both of them schoolteachers. They were both Jews. I remember how Valentina Nikiforovna said, looking sternly at the class, "I was treated only with kindness by my foster parents. All of us, Russians, Ukrainians, Belarusians, we've known—and continue to know—nothing but kindness from Jews. You, Daniil Rayev," she gave me a forbidding look. "You must be worthy of your Jewish nationality!"

Valentina Nikiforovna followed her principles all her life. Stern and totally honest, she helped each and every one of us. Fedya Prokhorov's father was killed in action. His mother worked as a cook in the factory cafeteria. One day, she was stopped and searched at the gate. In her bag she was carrying a pot of leftover wheat cereal from the cafeteria. Fedya's mother was put in jail. Valentina Nikiforovna took Fedya in. He lived with her until they let his mother out.

Valentina Nikiforovna started a puppet theater in our class. The whole class took part in the puppet theater. Some moved the puppet strings, some made the sets, others made the puppets, still others put together and took apart the stage or played in the percussion band. The only thing we didn't have was a prompter. Valentina Nikiforovna hated prompters. We started to rehearse for a play called *A Forest Tale*. I played an eagle owl named Pucci. For a long time after that, they called me Pucci the Owl. We put on our show for different classes and even for other schools in the Vyborg District of Leningrad.

Many of the boys' fathers had been killed in action. People called them the fatherless ones. My father was fighting on the Baltic Sea. The fall of 1944 was approaching. The war was moving toward Berlin. I never had any doubt that the war would end and that my father would return home. Now, looking back, it seems that mama was worried about something. She was afraid for my father, as she had been before. She was afraid that he would be wounded again, that the injury would be serious. She had been afraid of that during the evacuation. Now a new type of fear developed: a fearful anxiety. Sometimes mama would even say, "It would have been better to wait out the war in Siva." Mother had a bad feeling about something. She had that gypsy gift. She even passed it on to me.

That my paternal grandparents had returned from Sverdlovsk, where they had been evacuated, only added to her anxiety. Grandpa was terminally ill. He had cancer of the stomach, and it was too late to operate. I remember how he patted me and kissed me, as if to soften the sorrow that his death would bring. Or was it that grandpa and grandma and the other relatives weren't telling the whole story?

One Sunday at the end of October 1944, mama and I went to the movies. The Union was at the end of the route, where streetcar number 18 made a circle. The movie theaters still had cosmopolitan names (Union, Miniature) from before the war. The movie theater Union was across the street from the Polytechnical Institute. We bought our tickets for the next show and sat on a park bench. I was reading a book and didn't notice when a woman in a black hat and coat sat next to mama, although I did see her later. Totally engrossed in my book, I didn't listen to their conversation. Suddenly, it seemed to me that mama was crying. Yes. Mama was crying, clutching her mouth, rocking back and forth, and repeating, "It can't be true, it can't be, it can't be, it can't be, it can't be, it can't be, it can't be . . ."

We got onto streetcar number 18 and went back home. We didn't get off on the Serdobolskaya stop, which was close to our house. We went past our stop. The streetcar was going on to the Petrograd Side, where grandpa and grandma lived. Uncle Yanya, Aunt Tsilya, and Malvina, who had recently returned from Siva, were living with them. The streetcar was moving, ringing its bell, clickity-clacking, its metal contact shoes crackling overhead and spewing electric sparks. We were sitting in silence. Mama's face was like stone. At Geslerovsky Prospekt, we got off the streetcar and went past the small public garden on Zelenin Street, where grandma would take ailing grandpa to get some fresh air. We went to the corner entrance of the eight-story brick apartment building. We climbed the wide marble staircase to the third floor. We rang the doorbell.

Grandma opened the door, "Stellochka! Danik! What wonderful guests! Look what wonderful guests! Take off your coats, and I'll get you something to eat!"

Mama went inside without taking her coat off. Grandpa was sitting in his chair. His hair was colorless. His face like wax, his eyelids heavy. Grandma followed us into the room and closed the door.

Mama turned to grandma and cried out, "Mama, you knew?"

"I knew, Stellochka," grandma answered, crying.

"And you, papa, you also knew?"

Grandpa said nothing. He covered his face with his hands and began to mumble something in Hebrew, probably a prayer.

My life changed completely. I used to dream about the war ending. About papa coming home to stay. It would be like it was before the war: Sunday walks with papa, while mama is still sleeping. Hot rolls. Grapes called ladyfingers. Mama calling us home from the courtyard, "Boys, breakfast is ready!" Sunday breakfast. Morning sun and eggs sunny-side up in the cast-iron frying pan. Trips to the zoo. To the theaters and to the circus. Many, many things we can do when papa comes home from the war. But now we had crossed over to the category of the abandoned ones. Mama said that papa had a second wife. That's what they called frontline wives. And a daughter, born six months before we returned from the evacuation.

I'd been abandoned. Just like Borka Smorodin, my dearest friend. His father left him even before the war, when Borka was two years old. Borka's mama, Lyuba, was eighteen years old when she was hired from a village as a maid to a Jewish family in Leningrad. She'd been born in a village on the Luga River. These were the years of famine for the peasants. The Lokshins, who took Lyuba in as a maid, lived in prosperity. Their son, Sasha, was studying to be an engineer. Sasha liked the maid Lyuba. She was pretty and cheerful.

They would go to the movies together, ride the roller coaster, eat brown cows. Borka was born. Lyuba registered him with her own last name. Six months later, the older Lokshins said that they no longer needed a maid. They got Lyuba a job in a candy factory named after Mikoyan. Borka went to day care. Lyuba worked hard and became a shock worker. She received a room in a wood house on Novoseltsevskaya Street. Sasha Lokshin came to see her every week for a year or year and a half. He would bring sweets and some money. Then he came less and less often, until he stopped coming altogether. Sometimes he would mail her some money. Lyuba never filed for child support. Then she got married to an elderly bachelor accountant, Konstantin Konstantinovich Biserkin, and took his last name. But Borka kept his mother's maiden name and stayed a Smorodin. And Sasha Lokshin married Riva Steinman, a medical student.

Grandpa was dying. When mama and I came to visit, he would almost always be lying on the couch or in bed. Last time, we came for Hanukkah. Grandpa was very weak. When he spoke, his voice was just a rustling whisper. He kissed me, put his hand under the pillow, and pulled out a brand-new hundred-ruble note. "Danik, that's your Hanukkah gelt!" grandpa said. He died before New Year's 1945. Papa flew in for the funeral. He came to see us, when mama was still at the factory. Papa was unshaven. He told me about grandpa. About their life in Ukraine. The Rayev family owned mills. Grandpa and his brothers, Azril and Yakov, worked all week from morning till night. They would come home only for dinner on Fridays. They observed the Sabbath. And on Sunday mornings they would go back to the mills. Grandpa loved Ukrainian songs and horses and dogs. Papa and I sat on the couch in the living room. The black birdcherry branches were coated with snow. The inside walls of our corner room were coated with frost. It was freezing. Usually mama would stoke up the stove when she came home from work. This time, papa went to the shed, brought in an armful of firewood, made kindling, and started the stove. Mama came back and saw papa. He got up and went to embrace her, but mama pulled back. "It's a great sorrow for us all," she told him. "I understand how you feel, Pavel, but, nevertheless, get out! Get out and don't ever come back!"

Grandpa was buried in the Jewish Preobrazhenskoe cemetery beyond Nevskaya Zastava. Papa went back to the Baltic. The war was approaching Berlin. All anybody talked about in class or in the courtyard was the upcoming victory. Of course, we boys were excited about that. Although most of us had lost our fathers at the front, and there was no hope of a return. Only perhaps if the father was "missing in action." There was much talk of revenge. How they'd exact revenge on the fascists when they captured them. Particularly Hitler. We decided that Hitler would be put in a metal cage and taken to all the destroyed cities and villages in the world. Of course they would bring him to Leningrad. Let him die from fear and shame!

Borka Smorodin and I talked about all these things. It was good to have such a friend. We went to school together and came home together after school. We walked past vacant lots with their skeletons of houses, burned out or picked apart for firewood. Past vegetable gardens with blackened potato plant tops. In winter, they all turned into dead fields of snow. We talked about the siege and about the evacuation. About hunger and food. About our mothers and fathers. Borka and I talked with brutal frankness, like I'd never talked with anyone before.

Victory came in May of 1945. We went with the crowds to Palace Square. We were happy that the war was over, that no more people would be killed. The music thundered. Fireworks shot off into the sky. Balloons were flying over people's heads.

In early June, we tilled the vegetable garden and planted potatoes. I begged and finally convinced mama not to send me off to Young Pioneer camp, as Borka did Auntie Lyuba. We ran around the Forestry Technology Academy park, played soccer, and went to visit my grandma. Borka became a part of the family. We made friends with children from the orphanage. Particularly with Vaska Akhmetov. Vaska's father had been killed, and his mother had died from starvation. His orphanage was on the former Lanskoy property. Because Vaska was an avid fisherman, like Borka and me, we became especially good friends. The pond was next to the orphanage. One day, when we were fishing in the pond, we heard a heavy tramping sound. It grew ever louder and was coming toward us. We ran out onto the street. An endless column of German prisoners of war was streaming in our direction, coming north from downtown Leningrad toward Karelia. First came the officers in swamp-colored uniforms. No epaulets and no belts. Their caps were missing cockades. Their boots dusty and worn out. Thousands of officers. Behind them came tens of thousands of soldiers in faded, earth-colored field shirts. Also without insignia and belts. Wearing dirty, worn-out boots. The visors of their ski hats were pulled down over their eyes. Their heads were down. Our submachine gunners walked on both sides of the column. We stood with our fists tight and watched the defeated enemies. Vaska, Borka, and I. The Germans came, and came, and came for several hours. We stood and watched them with hatred and with triumph.

2001

Translated, from the Russian, by Arna B. Bronstein
and Aleksandra I. Fleszar

# Autumn in Yalta

A STORY

Every time I had met her during the fifteen years of our—well, I fail to find
the precise term for our kind of relationship—she had not seemed to
recognize me at once . . .
—Vladimir Nabokov, "Spring in Fialta"

Samoylovich smokes through the lowered driver's side window of
his ramshackle Volga. He bought the Volga right after Kolyma.
Bought it with the savings from his previous life. After Kolyma,
where he did time. Full term. Ten years. Luckily, not in the ura-
nium mines but above ground. As a physician's assistant in the camp
infirmary. From reveille to lights-out. Full term. And he returned
to Moscow, not St. Petersburg. "If it were still Leningrad, that
would be a different story!" he joked. "You know, I'd gotten used to
the leader's name." But it was all because he both feared and longed
to see her, because of her . . . Because of her, he earned his tenner.

And all of this for one night. One crazy autumn night in Yalta.

Sticky March snow is falling down. Big flakes stumble into the an-
tenna, into the bare branches, like a drunk—into another's open
hand. Ah, no use remembering and tormenting yourself for nothing. You must live. Survive says it better. Ten years down the drain.
You must catch up with life. And so, by night, he chases the rabid
ruble.
     Samoylovich is waiting for customers outside the Sofia Restau-

rant. Late-night customers are the most generous ones. Though who knows where they'll want to be taken. Still a long way until morning. You come across all kinds here.

"Hey, chief! Going to Strogino," the liveried doorman yells through the half-open doors of the restaurant.

"How many?" responds Samoylovich.

"How many what?" the doorman snaps.

"Passengers—how many?" Samoylovich clarifies. He has his own reasons. In a group, revelers are always more generous, and also safer.

"Four. Enough for your money?" the doorman is losing patience. "Call 'em."

A gentleman in a lacquered leather overcoat plops onto the front seat. Two ladies seat themselves in the back. Samoylovich knows they are classy ladies without looking. The scents of their perfumes intertwine, like silk lace ribbons, over their heads. Intertwine and travel from each of the two ladies to the men, and to Samoylovich. A second gentleman occupies the backseat, along with the classy ladies. Samoylovich makes out the gentleman with just a sideways glance, even though the silk ribbons of perfume are suffocating as they slither inside his memory. No, it can't be, the one Samoylovich tells himself, having resolved to put all that hurt and anguish behind him. Still back at Kolyma, how many times had he resolved to cut it off, once and for all? But the other Samoylovich . . . gently strokes the jacket pocket where he keeps his revolver.

"Okay, chief, you just go down Tverskaya, then straight down Leningradsky Prospekt. Turn onto the Volokolamskoe Highway and take it all the way to Strogino. Well, I'd better show you the way." The gentleman in lacquered leather, the one sitting next to Samoylovich, takes charge. Leaning over, as though Samoylovich were his accomplice, he adds, "Will a fifty do it?"

"Sure thing," nods Samoylovich.

"Wait, wait, Misha, why to your place? Last night it was your place and tonight again your place? Alyosha, say something, don't just sit there like a sphinx!"

Samoylovich waits patiently. The usual after-restaurant negotiations: where and how to finish off the party.

"You, Polechka, you've got it all wrong. We have an Alazan Valley already chilled and an *abunditry* of spicy Georgian snacks to go with it . . .

(*Polechka,* Samoylovich shudders, and not from the lady's unusual pun conjoining abundance and banditry.)

. . . just arrived from Tbilisi on yesterday's flight. Misha, say something!"

"I've said it already and I stand by it. Okay, chief, let's head over to Strogino, and then we'll figure it out. Nina, you're in charge of convincing Alyosha."

Samoylovich drives down Tverskaya Street, both believing and refusing to believe this total coincidence—Polechka-Nina-Misha-Alyosha. Like in a game of solitaire. He hears the sounds of backseat horseplay between the good-looking affluent ladies and the aristocratic gentleman they call Alyosha the Sphinx.

It was a luxurious September day. After the scorching Crimean summer, the autumnal resort town of Simeiz breathed without effort. The sanatorium was perched atop a steep rocky seashore with a meandering lizard of pebbles and shells for a beach. It was a TB sanatorium where patients could stay for a time. Because the tuberculosis infection progressed slowly, the courses of treatment ended up lasting a few months, sometimes as many as six. At a regular health resort, the arrival or departure of a guest, and especially a young woman or a vigorous young man would stir up interest or a desire for their company, if only for a while, or cause regret at having to say good-bye. But here at the san, given the languid pace of life, any arrival or departure became a significant event. And yet, the leaving of a certain young actress had gone completely unnoticed.

Later, it became known that she'd been hurried off to the shooting of a new picture. Everybody at the san was still distressed after what had happened on the eve of the actress's departure.

The day before, it had also been lovely outdoors. Not too hot, the air filled with the fresh breath of the Black Sea, the scent of cypresses, junipers, and Italian pines, and the faint aroma of the last, honeysweet peaches ripening in the surrounding orchards. The inhabitants of the sanatorium had scattered all over the grounds. Except the ones resting in their rooms after a pneumothorax or other burdensome procedure. Many patients languished on the beach under the shadow of blue-red-and-yellow umbrellas or even in the open sun, their straw Vietnamese mats or san-issued blankets thrown right over the hot pebbles.

Samoylovich was at the clinic, sitting through the three daily hours he was expected to spend in his office, just in case one of the patients might need his care. Those three hours after breakfast and one, sometimes two hours before supper were the price Samoylovich paid for the freedom of pursuing his research in a small cottage outfitted as his lab.

His office door opened, and Polechka came inside.

Love had started in the autumn of a faraway year, and for Samoylovich it had never ended. It was an exceptional love. One could even call it love aiming for the absolute zero. After all, we know cases of being burned by dry ice—frozen carbon dioxide. Samoylovich experienced something very like that with Polechka. That is, he clung to her love with a heart perfectly ablaze. While she . . .

Samoylovich saw Polechka for the very first time on a bright September afternoon (autumn again). She was sitting on a bench in a public garden that encircled a monument to the Russian destroyer *Guarding,* which the Japanese had failed to capture during a war in the early twentieth century. Polechka was sitting on the bench, smoking a Northern Palmyra. A box of these *papirosy* lay on top of her rusty-red leather purse. On the box was the view of the *strelka*—the spit—of Vasilievsky Island and the Rostral Columns that had made Northern Palmyra a signature souvenir product of Leningrad's tobacco industry. The girl was enchanting. With her huge, sparkling blue eyes, she stared up at the turquoise dome of the Mosque of Bukhara's Emir. Sparkling blue eyes, hair the color of ripe acorns, chin jutting slightly forward—all harmonized with dark-cherry lips that betrayed an admixture of hot southern blood. But her face was matte pale. And, through its dewy paleness, now and again a flush would appear, signaling a persistent ailment. Yet Samoylovich didn't notice the febrile flush, and only much later did he learn about her illness. During his first encounter with Polechka, her illness was obscured and, one might say, in retreat. Even Polechka had forgotten about it and taken to smoking again.

Samoylovich sat down beside the blue-eyed girl.

"Where I come from," he said, joking around like a bumpkin, "even mice and guinea pigs are forbidden to smoke, and especially on such a beautiful day."

"And where I come from, it's permitted. And what's more, it's even encouraged, to entice Black Hens, Little Red Riding Hoods, and Three Little Pigs into the smoking den," the blue-eyed one said and laughed so disarmingly that Samoylovich lit up one of her *papirosy*. Taking a puff, he coughed as he inhaled the smoke, practically for the first time in his life. He felt his head spin blissfully. The turquoise hat of the mosque was taking elaborate contredanse steps in time with its lanky suitors, the two minarets. Samoylovich felt like a happy child, like he'd never felt before around girls.

"Nice, very nice," he mumbled, pulling in one puff after another. "Sort of sweet, it envelops you somehow, but nice!"

She glanced at him, as though for the first time. What an odd specimen had installed himself beside her, and what silliness he was talking! She peered closer and, using her ironic grin as a magic magnifying glass, saw it. Samoylovich looked like a treasure. His was a particular type that an artist, especially an art film maker or a painter of compassionate genius like Toulouse-Lautrec, yearns for. Samoylovich was endowed with a square head and a spade-like face: square with a chin that looked like it was flying off a cliff. He only cut his hair once every six months because it was thin. Like lichens, it grew with reluctance. And, also like lichens, it tended to wind itself into coarse, wiry twists. His eyelashes were blond and his eyebrows red. His ears, in places here and there covered over with hairs, seemed like an outlandish cross between pink burdocks and bicycle wheels of the sort that racers use for training: without spokes and all filled in with plastic.

Nevertheless, our heroine Polechka—they'd introduced themselves ("Samoylovich." "Polechka.") in between the little bluish turbans rising above their *papirosy*—possessed a God-given ability, a talent she'd had been anointed with. She could leaf through a new acquaintance and immediately latch on to his or her most essential feature. Thus she'd leafed though Samoylovich and, ignoring the spade of his face, the burdocks of his ears, the barrel of his torso, instantly focused on his eyes. And from that time onward, she would always concentrate on them. He was intelligent and sensitive. He quickly appreciated this remarkable talent of Polechka's, which helped the budding of his love for her. They started chatting. At first, they sat on the bench, gazing at the sculpture of the Russian sailors who had elected to kill themselves by opening the Kingston valves and scuttling their ship—rather than surrender to the Japanese and betray Russia.

Then Polechka and Samoylovich crossed Kirov Prospekt and approached the mosque.

"My father is descended from the Crimean khans," Polechka said with a little sigh.

Samoylovich didn't feel right asking her why she sighed. But she told him anyway (their walk had already lasted over one and a half hours, bringing them to the beach at the St. Peter-and-Paul's

Fortress). Kicking pebbles into the dark waters of the Neva, she said that her father had died in battle. And that, if he hadn't, then their entire family would've been exiled to Siberia, as the other Crimean Tatars were. All the while, her mother was a pure Russian. To which Samoylovich graciously responded, that it looked like times were changing and, little by little, the Tatars were being allowed to return to the Crimea. Most likely, these Tatar matters didn't interest Polechka. She was whimsical, and afterward, Samoylovich couldn't recall her mentioning either the mosque or her father ever again.

Polechka's union of the erratic and the practical made their relations delectable—but also created a fretful tension between them. She was perfectly capable of calling him the next day, after having said no to their dating—an irrevocable no for a month, a year, forever—and asking, did he have any herring? as if nothing at all was the matter. It would turn out he did have herring. Samoylovich's grandmother had purchased a mind-boggling supply of it, from which she made chopped herring for her grandson. He lived alone in a squalid room that opened directly onto the staircase landing, which made it a separate apartment of a sort. His cramped quarters were located in a gigantic prerevolutionary apartment building on Sennaya Square, not far from where Dostoevsky spent his last days, and had their own tiny bathroom, and also a kitchenette with a miniature gas stove. Friends of Samoylovich's had dubbed his place the "gas chamber." Polechka would arrive by taxi, with Samoylovich waiting for her at the front entrance to pay the fare. This always happened at night, after performances at the Comedy Theater, where Polechka was employed as an actress who "showed promise." Someone else in Samoylovich's place would've asked, after a year of their friendship, even if jokingly: "And by the way, pretty darling, why don't you pick up a can of sprats or Baltic anchovies or whatever else they have at Eliseyev's (the grand food store next door to the theater)?" But that sort of assertiveness never took hold of Samoylovich. He felt blessed by Polechka's visits. He was simply happy, that's all. She would sometimes leave a guest pass for him at the theater, and from his added chair, he would observe her onstage. "You, Samoylovich, cannot go uninvited when I'm in a new play. I'll sense your look when I'm not quite in top form. You have a *special* way of looking."

We've already mentioned Samoylovich's eyes. It was his eyes that lured Polechka to cast aside the structural incongruities of his head and torso. They were a soft brown. They'd follow you, or rather the emotions crossing your mind, with a rhythm and a brightness or dimness that exactly suited your conversation with him. "You have such intelligent eyes, Samoylovich," some people would say to him. "You have such kind eyes, Samoylovich," others would say. "You have such unusual eyes," still others would say. Polechka rarely said anything about his eyes. But he could feel that she needed his gaze, that she used it almost as a cure.

Sometimes she would disappear. For just a few days or for months on end. He never tried to find her, although it was sheer torture for him not to. Unable to sleep, he'd wander aimlessly in her neighborhood on the Petrograd Side of town, near her building at Bolshoy Prospekt and Vvedensky Street.

Then, she would resurface.

"So, Samoylovich, how was it without me?" she would say, hugging him.

"Bad," he would reply.

"I know it wasn't very good," Polechka would say. "Well, I've had all sorts of things happen, good and bad. Now let yourself look at me."

And then she would tell him something or other about the theater, her male admirers, a crazy female devotee ("You have no idea what she comes up with!"), about one Aleksey Petrovich, a Moscow astrophysicist who had proposed to her . . . Samoylovich would listen and gaze at her, and she at him—into his gentle, understanding eyes—and this would bring her back to norm.

"I'm serious, Samoylovich, you're a psychic. Why do you even care about your mice and guinea pigs? To hell with the experiments! You should cure people with hypnosis."

During that happy period, her illness had retreated so far back Polechka forgot she even had it.

Those meetings of theirs, they were so strange. Now frequent, now rare. And under no circumstances could Samoylovich and Polechka be called lovers. He loved her madly, only living for their rendezvous and his work at the Institute of Tuberculosis, where he saw patients and conducted experiments. Sometimes at night, sitting at her feet on the bed in his dilapidated room while they smoked Northern Palmyra and talked unhurriedly, Samoylovich would ask Polechka: "Why do you even *need* me, if you're like that?"

Despite his medical education and the sophistication of his scientific vocabulary, he was hesitant to label "that" with any commonly accepted term. Something got jammed in his head when he thought about it. Most often, Polechka would lie motionless, her head tilted back at the pillow, eyes shut, until he roared like a wounded beast, pouring onto her the rain of his uninhibited openness. She would kiss him tenderly on the forehead and say, "Well, now it's good" or "Now you'll calm down." She would take a shower and later they would fall asleep or Samoylovich would take her home in a cab.

Meanwhile, even though things hadn't gotten all that serious with the Moscow astrophysicist or that crazy female devotee of hers, a different kind of adventure turned up in their path. New Year's was approaching. The annual New Year's celebration in the company of friends. Usually, Samoylovich spent the holiday with his classmates from medical school. And, this time, too, he thought about going to Grisha Libov's, a couple of champagne bottles in hand, and chatting with his old pals until about two or three in the morning. When all the guests would be exhausted and would fall into their hosts' bedroom and force themselves to watch the rest of the *Little Blue Light* holiday special, while Samoylovich would head back home to Sennaya Square. Thank goodness, it was only a five-minute stroll from the Libovs', who lived at Gorokhovaya Street and Fontanka Embankment, to Samoylovich's. He didn't ask Polechka about celebrating New Year's together. In years past, she'd acted in the skits the actors put on for the annual theater party, which sometimes lasted till midnight, and, later, she would ring in the New Year with the other thespians. But, suddenly, just two days before New Year's Eve—on the 29th of December it was—Polechka phoned Samoylovich and invited him to the actors' skits and party. "But what about the Libovs?" Samoylovich asked, terrified by the suddenness of her knight's move. "The Libovs will get over it!" said Polechka, slicing off the phrase. Samoylovich didn't object. In fact, he was so happy he went to the Leningrad House of Commerce and bought himself a new suit.

In the New Year's skits, Polechka got nowhere near a lead part. She sang in the chorus—to use the term chorus in the sense of Greek drama. Or you could call it the corps de ballet of the skits. The place was chock full of actors and actresses from other theaters and from the Lenfilm Studios, and of students from the theater schools and other guests and other guests' guests. There she was, Polechka, performing with all the celebrities onstage. Samoylovich was terribly proud of her. Well, and what if it's actually true? he thought, perhaps for the first time. Would Polechka have invited me to her New Year's party otherwise?

But Samoylovich instantly chased away this brash idea, the way you chase off a pesky fly. And he kept staring at the stage, where the skits were so unbelievably amusing. Through the years, Samoylovich had seen almost the entire repertory of the Comedy Theater, and he now took pleasure in being able to catch a double entendre hinting at such-and-such an actor and get a joke about actress so-and-so. Even a very subtle allusion to the Soviet Minister of Culture wasn't lost on Samoylovich. He was happy, immeasurably happy, and he completely forgot about the Libovs. And when the

Libovs' name did cross his mind, as he was marveling at Polechka onstage, he thought to himself: They're so boring!

The skits ended. The actors and guests made their way to the foyer, where long tables had been set with hors d'oeuvres and wine. Samoylovich saw all of this as if in a dream. Which is to say, he followed the crowd to the tables, sat himself down, introduced himself to those sitting next to him and across the table, and even made jokes as he saved a seat for Polechka—but, all the while, he thought anxiously, Where is she?

Barely a minute before the chiming of the Kremlin bells and the opening of champagne, Polechka descended to the foyer. She looked spellbound. The cause of her spell walked by her side, the famous comedy actor Mikhail Kaftanov, all the while doing an impression of someone they both probably knew. Kaftanov's imitation must've been vivid and hilarious. Polechka laughed unabashedly, as though she were the only one there. Kaftanov escorted Polechka over to Samoylovich, who sat there waving at her. Kaftanov escorted her and walked to the arthritic section of a long table, where the theater's artistic director sat with elite members of the troupe.

After the New Year champagne toast, it was time for *vodochka* and herring, smoked fish, and other appetizers to go along with the theatrical gossip delivered in a loud voice or whispered in ones's ear. Colleagues stewing in the same artistic pots occasionally like to enjoy this kind of revelry. Polechka was terribly agitated, her cheeks burning like sunset on Maundy Thursday. She hardly ate a thing and kept asking for refills of champagne. Samoylovich had to hunt down bottles from all over the tables, and later, when all the bottles at their potluck feast had been emptied, he rushed to the cash bar in the theater cafeteria to buy more.

Now and then, Kaftanov would cast a patronizing glance at Polechka, tearing himself away from a conversation with a famous actor or playwright. Quite understandably, Samoylovich didn't notice Kaftanov's glances. He had Polechka sitting next to him, her cheeks ablaze and her blue eyes radiant. But she simply couldn't stay put. She fidgeted in her chair, ran to the ladies' room a hundred times to fix her dress or hair, opened the bottom of her dress so wide it was as if she were in a bicycle race, not a New Year's celebration at her theater. Samoylovich lovingly tolerated her behavior the way a parent indulges a child's moods. The main thing was that the beloved child was right there next to him, and he could touch her, stroke her, press his lips to her shoulder, as she danced in her seat to the festive tunes.

At last, Kaftanov stopped sending Polechka his telegraphic glances. He'd had one drink too many and was engrossed in a conversation with Sazonova, an aging but still very popular and influential stage and film actress. The actress Sazonova was famous, not only for her popularity with theatergoers and film buffs, but also because, every year, she would put together a troupe of four or five good actors (distinguished as "Actors of Merit" or even "People's Actors"), all a generation younger than herself. She would take the little troupe on a late summer-early autumn tour (usually to the southern coast of the Crimea), performing two or three vaudeville pieces per evening. The famed Sazonova would herself appear in each of the pieces with one of her younger partners. In theatrical circles, being asked by Sazonova to join her makeshift troupe was considered a high honor, an unofficial distinction in and of itself, and a step toward a high-caliber career. It was also known that, in addition to the rehearsals, Sazonova held seminars of a kind after the performances. In her hotel suite. Accounts of these seminars varied, but everyone dreamed of being asked.

"Well, Kaftanov is just like the rest of them," Polechka suddenly said with much bitterness. Samoylovich tore himself away from a discussion he'd been having with the person to his right about the merits and medical dangers of luminescent makeup.

"Do you need help, Polechka?" he asked.

"Yes, help, I need help! Take a note over to him."

"Sure. Go ahead, write it."

And she wrote Kaftanov a note: "You have completely forgotten our agreement to go for a smoke when we're both bored. I'll be waiting over at the dressing room in ten minutes. P."

Of course Samoylovich didn't read the note. He apologized to the circus entertainer Astaurov for having to interrupt their discussion of luminescence and delivered Polechka's note to Kaftanov.

Kaftanov read the note. His conversation with the famous actress had ended more than successfully. All that remained was to decide on the vaudeville pieces. The famous actress had been interested in staging an excerpt from Fyodor Sologub's novel *The Petty Demon*. Something like the scene of a scandal, when Peredonov, after breakfasting on jam-filled doughnuts, starts spitting on the walls. Kaftanov didn't reject the Sologub idea outright, but calculated that, besides Sazonova and himself, the scene would require at least one more actor—for the part of Peredonov's young crony, Pavel Vasilievich Volodin. In light of this, Kaftanov proposed that, instead of Sologub, they put on Aksyonov's short story "The Local Hooligan Abramashvili." He nominated himself for the part of the young Georgian Gogi—and for the actress Sazonova, he proposed the part of Alina the painter, paying an obvious compliment to the stage longevity of the one to be cast in the role of a young Moscow society lady.

In short, Kaftanov read the note with improved interest and thanked Samoylovich. Seeking out Polechka's flaming eyes, he nodded alluringly.

Samoylovich returned to his seat next to the circus man Astaurov. Together, they resolved that skin cells were capable of imbibing chemicals that glowed in the dark. And since the internal medium was and always had been dark, the cells would therefore glow in the darkness of one's body, which violated evolutionary harmony, which in turn traced its origins to the depths of the world's oceans. To the tune of this most engrossing of discussions, Samoylovich and

Astaurov polished off a bottle of vodka. Clearly, Samoylovich had taken no more notice of the moment when Polechka stepped out to rendezvous with Kaftanov than he had of the comings and goings of the others around him.

Polechka's return was not at all triumphant. In fact, it was pitiful. Her lowcut, silver-gray dress, fringed in Vologda lace, was ripped at the shoulder, in the very place where a little boat might be tied to the river bank—if we imagine a woman's body to be a river. Beneath the delicate spot where it flowed into a triangular lagoon, Polechka's neck was crimson with a bruise left by the sucker of a greedy octopus—if we now let our imagination follow the river to the sea. Polechka had hastily slipped her featherlight, black patent leather shoes onto her bare feet, without stockings. Which was very careless, considering both the winter season and her unsteady health, and which, more than anything, gave away what had happened.

Of course it wasn't the absence of Kaftanov but Polechka's unseemly state—completely undone, messed-up, *tseshoybert,* if we may resort to the Yiddish of Samoylovich's grandmother—that momentarily shook our nature-philosopher to his senses.

"Polechka!" Samoylovich trumpeted in a tragic voice. "Did something terrible happen to you?"

"I don't know if it was happy or terrible, but please get me out of here right now," Polechka whispered hoarsely, smearing the watercolors of her makeup on her swollen cheeks.

"You've been insulted . . . law enforcement . . . arrest him . . . punishment," Samoylovich muttered, seizing Polechka and seized by her, as always, and running down the Comedy Theater's front steps.

Over at Samoylovich's after a hot shower, a mug of strong tea with rum, swathed in his loving care, Polechka, like a teenager finally rescued from a gang, told him what had happened, getting lost now and then in her own words because she was still drunk.

"You realize, don't you, Samoylovich, *what* exactly Kaftanov means to me? To me and my entire theater generation. He is a genius. A star. He is a role model for all of us. Do you know that I've spent many nights awake, or half-awake, if you like, envisioning myself as Kaftanov's stage partner—and his mistress. My God! Maybe my own exalted imagination or how much I was actually driven to him stood in the way of my normal sensations? You know what I mean, don't you, Samoylovich? You doctors call it frigidity. I would call it waiting for a miracle. I've been waiting for it my whole life. I wanted him all my life, and so I asked him. Samoylovich, forgive me, my good old Samoylovich, but he knew some sort of a secret. Just for me—a secret. He made me suffer, he hurt me, he humiliated me, but my desire for him didn't weaken. It only grew stronger. I begged him, but he kept putting it off, deferring it, teasing me until I . . . I don't remember what happened . . ."

"And Kaftanov?" asked Samoylovich.

"He vanished. But that's not the point. I know that one needs a secret. Do you love me? Say you love me?"

"Of course I love you, Polechka."

"If you love me, and I know you love me, will you do as I want? Promise? You won't get scared?"

"Yes . . . no," replied Samoylovich.

Two months later Samoylovich found out that Polechka was at a TB clinic outside Moscow, near the Yauza train stop. On a Friday that fell on March 7th, Samoylovich bought a ticket for the Red Arrow and went to Moscow. He had a colleague in Moscow who had done graduate work at the very same research institute where Samoylovich labored at the time. Sytin had married a young Muscovite lady and settled with her on Chernyshevsky Street. Wet from the night rain, the Red Arrow slid under the glass dome of the Leningrad Station. Samoylovich rushed to a pay phone to call Sytin, forgetting it was early Saturday morning. Coughing and bellowing about being woken up, Sytin persuaded Samoylovich that it made no sense first to come over to his place on Chernyshevskaya Street near the city center, but that it made perfect sense to walk just around the corner to the Yaroslavl Station, hop on a commuter train, and ride straight to the Yauza stop.

"And after you visit your friend, I'll be expecting you here. We're hosting a dinner party," Sytin concluded, finally waking up.

Samoylovich remembered it was March 8th, International Women's Day, and rushed to find mimosas. Searching around the station flower stalls for at least a tiny bouquet of the fluffy, golden touch-me-nots, shaving in the bathroom of the waiting hall, having coffee with some unidentified pastry, and suchlike silly distractions had eased the grip of his road-trip anxiety. By the time Samoylovich glided toward his commuter train over frozen puddles set in mosaics of broken black ice, it was already ten o'clock.

With the help of his medical license, the white coat he had brought along, and his knowledge of how to address the on-call medical staff, Samoylovich managed to find the right ward.

Polechka had the room all to herself. She was exasperated by his visit. The frail mimosa sprigs he'd brought looked like a scrawny little chicken next to luxurious greenhouse carnations on her bedside table.

"Why did you show up?" Polechka asked in a frosty voice.

He didn't recognize her voice, or anything about her. He had never seen Polechka in a hospital robe. He now recalled bitterly that he'd never seen her wearing a house dress. Not even a nightie. Always in a rush, after a performance: a hastily cast-off sweater, a snapped-off bra, the soaring blimps of her tights, and the mocking rollers of her panties. Which meant that all of the spectral happiness of his love for her could fit in one picture of that maple-and-turquoise autumn day of their first meeting and in the chiaroscuro prints of their nighttime rendezvous. And all those flashes of his otherworldly flights, flashes that could never get her frozen shutters to open. And that New Year's night, when he'd been lacerated by

her wild urges and wails. And Polechka's subsequent disappearance
. . . For this most gentle Samoylovich, it was unthinkable even to
have lived through that ordeal, and it had ended with a total fiasco.
Those thoughts tormented him as he stood at the bedside of his
beloved. She was just as beautiful as before, perhaps even more
beautiful now, when her beauty had assumed its final shape, turning
from an epithet into a metaphor of completeness. And her mean-
spirited anger had catalyzed this transformation. Polechka's blue
eyes, the chestnut forelocks of her hair now cut short, her cheeks
flaming with sickness and her lips, lusterless, like fading rose petals,
all expressed her disgust with him.

"Why did you come, Samoylovich?" Polechka asked ven-
omously.

"I love you, Polechka, you know that. You disappeared . . . I
didn't know what to think after you'd vanished for a week, then a
month, two."

"You want to know, don't you, Samoylovich," Polechka answered him, heaving with agitation, anger, and her lung ailment.
"You want to know, so I'll tell you. My present acute condition is all
on your conscience. Whatever happened—it's all your fault."

He was silent.

"Because of your unbridled behavior, I became pregnant, and
this led to the recurrence of my illness."

He was still silent. What she said could've been true, but how
utterly unfair (lopsided?) was her cruel truth.

"You saw that I was drunk and beside myself. You took advantage of my helplessness and humiliation. I opened up to you—a
doctor. And you, Samoylovich . . . How could you!"

He could no longer contain himself. "And Kaftanov? Why do
you only blame me?"

"Because Kaftanov is a genius, and you are nothing, Samoylovich. Because I love him, and you I hate and detest. I knew right
off it was your baby—because I was being turned inside out. The

pain didn't let up even for a moment, until I was rid of it. It couldn't have been Kaftanov's baby. I know, I could feel it. And now you have the nerve to commit this blasphemy. You drag yourself down here with a pitiful little bunch of twigs on the idiotic women's holiday."

Convulsed with sobs, Samoylovich rushed out of the room without uttering another word. He could see nothing before him: not the road, not the visitors trudging from the railroad platform with bouquets of flowers, many with sprigs of mimosa.

It was almost high noon. The usual crowd milled around the square outside the train stop. Through a film of tears, Samoy-lovich made out the sign "Liquors." He added himself to the queue that was squeezing through the entryway. At the counter, he pointed to a goodly-sized flask of brandy. The saleswoman, wearing a swollen robe over her sleeveless sheepskin jacket, asked:

"Care for a chocolate bar, too, or just the brandy?"

"Just the brandy," he answered. "Actually . . . why don't you ring up the chocolate, too."

He left the liquor store feeling some relief. He'd given his soul a new space in which to come back to life, after it had nearly died half an hour ago in Polechka's ward. He was about to immerse himself in a buffer solution, where he could now cleanse himself of the inconceivable sorrow and longing he felt. Snow started coming down, still unsoiled by the passing trains' exhaust. I must give myself a boost, thought Samoylovich. He kept fondling the flask of brandy, which snuggled his chest like a kitten under his coat. He wanted to find a nook where he could drink this nourishing solvent. Sooner or later, he told himself, one needs to replace the buffer with genuine nutrients for the soul. Otherwise, the brain cells will suffocate from memories. His anguish had receded, and the main thing now was to stop the medusa of memory from filling the vacant spaces in his brain with its jellylike tentacles.

From time to time, as he looked around, he asked himself, Why is she like that? What did I do to her, and if I did something, wasn't it her own wish—so why does she hate me so? Why am I so unhappy? But much more frequently (relative to the frequency of his self-questionings per unit of that snow-powdered March afternoon outside Moscow), Samoylovich cast sober glances at the dachas on a side street lined with treacherous ditches. Rickety wooden walkways stretched across them to clenched gates. Only one gate was ajar. A little onion dome of a gazebo painted green showed itself from behind the house. The house itself looked empty, closed up for the season. The seeming absence of the owners and the mysterious gazebo, a chapel of a kind, beckoned Samoylovich (considering the antireligious thrust of those Soviet years). He wanted to avoid other people. The blue glow of TV screens, the smoke above the roofs, the barking of dogs and their fox-like tracks on the walkways and around the gates—all this repelled him. Samoylovich entered the property and ambled toward the gazebo. No one accosted him, nothing fended him off. A red-breasted bullfinch hopped from the little dome of the gazebo onto a rowan branch with a cluster of blackened berries. Samoylovich didn't know what to offer the bullfinch, and he smiled guiltily, slouching on the bench and opening the flask. The burning brandy thawed the last bit of his icy longing, which had already started to melt on its own. It's all her cursed illness, he comforted himself, pressing his lips to the bottle. Polechka has a right to detest me. Unfortunately, I'm a doctor. And then the whole story with Kaftanov and her pregnancy. Samoylovich was absolutely sure it couldn't possibly have been his baby. Polechka was awfully drunk. He'd always been careful, and after the violence to her body she herself had invited that night, he was a thousand times more careful. Such sane reasoning, coupled with the beneficence of the brandy and the bullfinch's fussing in the rowan tree, helped Samoylovich to relax. After a while, he made up his mind to urinate somewhere in the corner of the property. For instance, behind the shed that stood next to the fence separating the property from an apple orchard. Samoylovich trudged to the shed, incising watery marks of his tracks in the icy snow. He flung open his thick wool navy overcoat. Resting his gaze on the rusty sheet-metal wall of the shed, he started picking a random tune on the buttons of his fly, when he suddenly heard laughter. It had been forever since he had last heard such a trilling laugh as this one, coming from behind him. Samoylovich closed the flap of his coat and stuffed the black bone buttons back into their holes. He thought he heard laughter behind him, but he could also be hallucinating. With the sober parts of his brain, he knew this feminine laughter, bright and trilling, to be real. But with the part of his brain that the brandy had tranquillized—the part adjacent to the sober ones—Samoylovich regarded reality as a hallucination, and his romance with Polechka as both real and hallucinatory. Turning around, he saw wet footprints on the porch, short boots lined on top with shearling, the brazen nudity of a woman's leg clad in a silk stocking, a pink kneecap, an overturned shot glass of a short skirt, a long sweater draped over it, the amber blots of a necklace, the laughing mouth above a chin dimple and between cheek dimples, and finally, a rick of straw-colored hair, below which lake-green of eyes, large and impish, darted to and fro.

"Now, do come inside, you silly man!" the giggling monkey mouth called out.

Samoylovich silently ogled the teaser as she continued to amuse herself: "You'll freeze your bottom off! Oh, come inside, I don't charge for using the bathroom!"

Realizing he was back to reality, he ran into the gazebo (had he left a mess and was there any brandy left?), then approached the front porch.

"I wouldn't mind taking advantage . . . if I might."

"Only if you might," said the owner of the dacha, smiling hospitably. "Straight ahead and first door on the left," she pointed while leading him through the dim entryway (shovel, bucket, and skis) into the kitchen with a Likhachev Factory refrigerator and glazed blue-and-gold crockery inside an ornate cupboard.

"Samoylovich," said the unexpected guest, presenting himself after emerging from the bathroom, There, in a state of utter weariness and dissatisfaction, he had examined the hand towels, a scented potpourri in a wicker bowl, and a small library for light reading. The bathroom library consisted of a set of issues of *Theater Life* and a few coffee table books of actors' and actresses' photos.

"Samoylovich," he repeated. "The unbidden guest who brings unrest." He decided to make a joke of it because the hostess had ignored his first introduction. Actually, he hadn't even noticed she wasn't in the kitchen when he stepped in there after relieving himself. By the time he made his second self-introduction, she'd come back, introducing herself as "Nina." She had changed into a lacy negligée, although she kept on her shearling-top boots.

"Would you mind if we had something to eat?" she asked.

He didn't mind. Fishing the flask out of his inside pocket, he placed it on the table.

"Some leftover brandy, I had no idea. . . ," he apologized.

"Leftover brandy comes in handy," Nina accepted his apologies and took a bottle of champagne out of the refrigerator. "And would you please take off your coat. It's hot in here, and why be uncomfortable."

But he knew what led to what. He was hot, but continued to sit in his overcoat, pressing between his knees his heavy three-flap hat lined with what was commonly known as "dog fur."

"I think I'll be going, Nina," Samoylovich finally said, after they'd finished the brandy and each had had a little champagne.

"As you wish. But I thought we would watch a movie on the tube."

"What's on?" Samoylovich asked.

"I can't believe you don't know, it's *The First Vacation Day* with Kaftanov in the lead part!"

"Then I certainly won't stay," said Samoylovich, pulling on his hat.

"What a funny fellow you are," Nina said with a chortle of disappointment. "And I thought we could sit around and chat."

"But we're barely acquainted," said Samoylovich.

"It's more fun that way. You know, I've had it with all my casual friends. I live by myself. So they think that when I invite them, serve them a meal, and that sort of thing, then what—it's off to bed with me?"

"And what do you think?" he asked.

"I want something else. I just want to have a heart-to-heart talk, even if I don't know the guy. Heart-to-heart. Like in the movies. Well, of course, what they say is scripted. I sometimes get on a commuter train and just sit there, waiting."

"For what?"

"Waiting for somebody to sit next to me and start pouring their soul out."

"And then?"

"And when it's their stop or we arrive in Moscow, then it's all thanks and good-bye."

"But we're not on the train," Samoylovich remarked.

His head spun from the alcohol and from the heat, which pressed in on his body under the warm wool overcoat. His aching for reality had passed, and in the new irreality, Nina played the role of Polechka, except there wasn't the oppressive longing. Even Kaftanov, appearing on the screen as a sign of pain, couldn't cause him pain. Irreality had freed Samoylovich of Kaftanov the way mirage lets go of us after the angle of refraction has changed.

"Very well, Nina. Very well, I'll take off my coat and gladly chat with you. But what about?"

"Are you married?" she asked.

"No, not really, no," Samoylovich groused, following Nina into the living room, where they both sat on a sofa across from the TV set.

"I'm not married either," Nina sighed with sympathy. "Tell me something about yourself."

Samoylovich told her about his native city on the Neva. How as a child he lived through the siege. How his mother died and his father was killed in battle. He told her about his grandmother and his medical work. What illnesses he treats.

"You're a lung specialist?" Nina said happily. "Now I see, of course. You're here on a scientific assignment. The central TB research facility is just nearby."

Samoylovich didn't dispute what she said since it gave him a chance to postpone, at least for a time, having to confess about Polechka.

"And you, Nina?" asked Samoylovich, out of politeness. He utterly didn't care to know what the young woman did for a living. He only thanked God she'd invited him in and distracted him from his thoughts.

"I'm in the appraisal business," she answered.

"???"

"Oh, yes," she went on. "That isn't something you encounter as an academic."

"???"

"I appraise merchandise in a consignment store."

"Uh-huh," Samoylovich imagined Nina looking all spiffy amid piles of goods: shearling coats, blue jeans, sneakers, bathing suits, tape recorders, and other foreign-made things, brought into the country by Soviets privileged to travel abroad and by foreign tourists. He visualized all this and frowned.

"What, you don't approve?" Nina guessed.

"No. I mean, it's perfectly fine," Samoylovich politely muttered, his eyes telling Nina something else. He pulled his spadelike head into his shirt collar, and his big round ears became scarlet red, ready to spin out of control, from shame. I've never sunk so low before, the thought rushed through his head.

He'd had his own experience with a consignment store. The experience had left a residue of loathing and shame. Polechka had been to Holland on a tour with the Comedy Theater. She brought back a Sharp stereo sound system: a combination tuner, tape deck, and turntable. She needed to sell this machine to pay off a pile of debts she owed. No sooner had Samoylovich arrived in a cab than various shady types started calling him to one side, away from the entrance to the store, trying to wrest from him, by secret manipulations of their fingers and lips, the brand name of the sound system and then gesturing what they could offer him for it. He waved off the pushy middlemen, elbowing his way inside the store, toward the appraisers' counter. He waited in line until his turn came to show the merchandise to a brash woman with a astonishingly thick, greasy layer of blue-red-and-black makeup, which made her look like a flag of some anarchist navy. Aiming her circus eyelashes at the Sharp system, the appraiser summoned with her finger some guy wearing an ocher suede jacket with tassels and straps on the sleeves and around the bottom. She talked to him in a whisper, then addressed Samoylovich, smelling of Sen-Sen and musk.

"How do you wish to handle this: a thousand minus seven percent or cash plus one hundred right now, no paperwork?"

"What do you mean no paperwork"? Samoylovich asked in bewilderment.

The tricolored appraiser rewarded him with a glare of contemptuous pity and started doing the paperwork. When Samoylovich gave Polechka an account of the whole affair, she looked at him with bitter disappointment and never again asked for such favors.

Nina understood his expression and laughed, "I just knew you wouldn't approve of my line of work."

Agitated for the first time since Samoylovich had met her, Nina suddenly jumped up and turned on the TV. The film with Kaftanov had reached the point where the author of well-known detective novels arrives in a university town in one of the Baltic republics, hoping to collect materials about collaboration of the local academics with the Nazis during the occupation. He rents a room from a daughter of a former collaborator. Of course she knows nothing about the activities of her father, who had been sent to Siberia after the end of the war, and who died in one of the Gulag camps. The writer and the young Baltic woman start a love affair.

While Samoylovich stared at the screen like a mopey bull, Nina followed Kaftanov's every word with adoration, forgetting her guest.

At last, Samoylovich got up. "I'll be going now, Nina,"

Entranced by the film, she didn't respond.

He walked out of the little house, making footprints in the fresh snow. Night had fallen. Samoylovich stepped outside the gate, turning around to glance at the little dome of the gazebo, now powdered over with snow. Weighed down by heavy sleet, the rowan tree pressed itself to the gazebo like a pauper to the steps of a cathedral. Samoylovich felt pangs of sadness as he headed for the train stop. The commuter train pulled in. He was about to elbow his way into the train car when he felt with his chest muscles a hollowness in his inside jacket pocket. His wallet wasn't there, and in it were the return ticket to Moscow and all his papers and money. Makes total sense, Samoylovich thought and chuckled. What else can you expect from a woman who works on commission! He thought of Dostoevsky's old lady pawnbroker. Well, what am I supposed to do now, murder her? I'll go back and demand my wallet.

He trekked back to Nina's dacha.

She was waiting for him on the porch, a shearling coat thrown on top of her negligée. "Goodness, I didn't know what to do! You dropped your wallet in the bathroom."

He remembered, yes, he took of his jacket and counted his money after locking himself in the bathroom with the small library. He felt it was time to lighten up and make a joke of it.

"I left it there on purpose, so I could come back."

"So why did you run away?"

"I couldn't bear watching that . . . sensualist," Samoylovich replied with such fervor that Nina glanced at him with amazement and realized that his reaction to Kaftanov was not accidental.

They had tea and talked for a while. Step by step, word by word, Nina learned everything that had happened between Samoylovich and Polechka. She kept asking her guest more and more questions, wanting to give him empathy, consolation. But as happens in such circumstances to people who have been around the block (and Nina certainly had), she found out so many things that mattered only to her that this newly gained information acquired a life of its own. A life outside the Samoylovich-Polechka-Kaftanov triangle. It's like a manuscript of an unknown genius. Found amid worthless junk stored away in the attic, it can make the finder a fortune.

And it happened to Nina.

But Samoylovich couldn't possibly imagine any of this on the snowy March day he spent in the Moscow countryside. Soon after that, he forgot about Nina. On his own, he mastered the craft of getting on without his turned-inside-out love. And later, to rule out even a small chance of running into Polechka in Leningrad, he got a job as a staff physician at one of the sanatoria in Simeiz, on the Crimea's blessed shores.

But he hadn't completely ruled it out.

"You know, Samoylovich, I'm not angry with you," said Polechka, swaying her shoulders.

"Well, that's good," Samoylovich said lamely.

"Rage, according to my calculations, dissipates after three years. And it's been three and a half. Therefore I'm absolutely not angry with you, Samoylovich. But admit that you did it back then, didn't you?" she babbled on, still swaying her shoulders.

"Well, I don't know," Samoylovich answered vaguely, afraid of breaking the crystal ball, which was now happily returned to him.

They were sitting in a cozy café facing the waterfront. They were drinking Red Stone Muscat. A crowd of vacationers strolled along the embankment, reading playbills that announced the titles of vaudeville pieces to be performed. In one of the pieces, the famous actress Sazonova was to appear together with Kaftanov. Samoylovich had seen the playbill at the bus stop after arriving in Yalta from Simeiz, but, in his hurry to meet Polechka, he'd immediately forgotten about it. They snuck into the café separately. They had to be discreet. All because she was a patient, and he—he was her doctor.

"Besides, I'm married."

"???"

"Yes, yes, Samoylovich. I'm a married lady."

"And who is he?"

"You don't remember, of course. Aleksey Petrovich Murov, a Corresponding Member of the Academy of Sciences, a State Prize laureate and so on and so forth. I actually once spoke to you about him. But you wouldn't—"

"—Polechka, I do remember. Aleksey Petrovich, the astrophysicist from Moscow."

"That's correct! You have such a fabulous memory, Samoylovich. You were made to recite miles of Shakespeare."

"Are you happy?"

"Yes and no," she answered vaguely, just the way she used to answer in the past.

Samoylovich said nothing.

"Make what you will of it. A three-bedroom apartment on Kutuzovsky Prospekt. A dacha in Opalikha. A Mercedes."

"So what else is there?"

"Still the same problems, my dear Same-ol'-love-itch."

"With him also?"

"And what is he, made of different clay?"

"So why did you marry him?"

"An excellent match—that's reason one. Moscow—that's reason two. And we're getting old, Samoylovich—that's three!"

"I understand," he took a gulp of the sweet aromatic wine as tormenting suspicions entered his mind: Had our Tatar princess followed Kaftanov to Moscow? And now here to the Crimea?

"Thank God, you understand. And now let's get roaring drunk so we can forget this conversation neither of us wants."

"Of course, Polechka. We'll get drunk and forget all about it."

They ordered more wine and coffee. And little cherry-filled tarts to go with coffee. Polechka recalled that, once in Leningrad, Samoylovich had treated her to such tartlets at the Nord Bakery-Café. They had them in the downstairs café, their coffee cups lined up on the edge of a marble counter. Outside, a blizzard lashed at the windows. Snow was falling down, sticky and russet-colored, as if it had been mixed with chocolate. On that day, Samoylovich received a cash prize for a paper he'd given at a conference. He got so emboldened he phoned Polechka at the Comedy Theater and invited her to the Nord. He had never phoned her at the theater before.

And only then, as he followed with his eyes the pendulum of Polechka's matte-white shoulders swaying between the liana vines of her tropical sleeveless (sleepless?) dress, only then did he tie together that chocolate December snow, her light merriment of the twilight hour when they still had a little time left to catch up before her performance, and her startling invitation to be her date for the New Year skits and party at the Comedy Theater. At that point, their entire life might've turned out so differently. There might not have been all those forsaken years without her. But there she was before him. He needed to forget what had happened like a misfortune, like an infectious disease after which you're immune for all your remaining years. But he didn't want this immunity, thrust upon him by chance. As though deciphering the verbal pattern of his thoughts, Polechka asked,

"And tell me, Samoylovich. Is my illness dangerous?"

Jolted upright in his black lacquered Viennese chair, he was ready to surrender to her hypnotic swaying. Ready to respond and to cure, but only the ailment of her soul. With love and hope. She then asked again, most specifically, about the bodily ailment for which she was spending time at this resort of a TB sanatorium.

"No, Polechka, it's not dangerous. As I see it, it's not even real tuberculosis, although it progresses in a similar way. It's a mask that fools your immune system into thinking you have TB. It's even believed microbes have nothing to do with it. Well, at least not TB bacilli. You'll get some treatment here—and then go back home."

"So I couldn't be contagious, could I?"

"I love you, Polechka."

"Did you miss me, Samoylovich?"

"Dreadfully!"

"So take me away somewhere. Remember your dingy room at Sennaya?"

He paid the waiter. On a side street, they hailed a taxi.

"Faster, faster, faster, Samoylovich," she hurried him, as if not gasoline, but her impatience were fueling the engine, winding the automobile along the serpentine mountain road. The phosphorescent September waves on the Black Sea lit their headlong rush. Polechka clung to Samoylovich so tightly her body filled the hollow below his muscular torso, which jutted out like a rocky ledge above the soft backseat of the taxi. She kissed his hair, wiry like lichens, and whispered, "Faster, faster, faster . . ."

He asked the driver to stop near a stone wall that stretched some two hundred yards outside the gates of the san. They'd agreed that she would return to her room and later, when the patients had retired, she would steal into his cottage.

The cottage was at the edge of the sanatorium grounds, in an overgrown corner of a park. It stood over a wild beach where nobody swam, and where only two or three old motorboats rocked and swayed on their chains like forgotten convicts. The cottage housed a research lab that Samoylovich had bargained out of the chief physician as part of his employment package. In his lab there was an incubator, a refrigerator, a fireproof safe, a bunsen burner, and a microscope. White mice skittered in their cages. Rabbits scratched the walls. His living quarters consisted of one room and a kitchenette with a gas stove. The gas stove was the same brand as the ancient one in his "gas chamber" at Sennaya Square, and Samoylovich, like most physicians, believed in the magic law of pairs.

He put the kettle on. The water boiled. He sought out, somewhere on the upper shelf of his cupboard, where it had been preserved as a relic, a tin containing Polechka's old favorite, Chinese jasmine tea. He set the table with cups and sliced the pound cake he'd bought to go at the Yalta café. He closed the curtains made of old blankets, so that even the saucer of the moon couldn't be the third dish and his rival at the evening table.

Two hours later, Samoylovich was finally ready to believe Polechka had deceived him. He went out onto the porch. The whole sanatorium was sleeping. Beneath his feet, the Black Sea rolled onto the wild beach. A path dropped down from where he stood. He started to follow it, but then turned around and went back to the cottage. In the lab, inside the brown, fireproof safe, he kept acids, alcohol, and ether. He filled a vial halfway with pure alcohol and locked the safe. In the kitchenette, Samoylovich mixed the alcohol with an equal amount of tepid jasmine tea. He downed the drink and felt better. He ripped the curtain from the window facing the sea. The moon had gone over the cottage roof. He had no reason to fear anybody. He thought of the ridiculousness of the whole thing. And he burst out laughing. Polechka was surely asleep in her remote building and couldn't hear his cascading laughter. In all honesty, Samoylovich wasn't even thinking about her. He thought of himself. Of what a fool he was.

A fool from childhood. From first grade, when, in '43, grandmother took him to school. Other kids who had lived through the siege surrounded Samoylovich and started asking for food. He had nothing with him. There was a kid by the name of Zinchyonok who kept pestering him. Samoylovich still remembered his name after so many years. Zynchyonok had eyes that fired glances like bullets. Samoylovich brought him home and showed him where they kept the bread ration coupons. He wasn't afraid of Zinchyonok. He simply couldn't bear those bullet eyes. In medical school, Samoylovich would read from the anatomy textbook for anyone who asked. It was easier for the other students to memorize that way. He was always available to read from the textbook and never said no. At parties, he would always be saving somebody a seat, running out to buy vodka for someone, lending money to this or that person. But for whom and to whom—he would instantly forget.

As he walked down the path to the wild beach, he laughed at his own foolishness. He seemed to be sobering up under the impact of this fiery cocktail concocted of pure alcohol, strong tea, laughter, and the green rays of the moon sliding across the waves. He was sobering up and freeing himself. Stars were falling. They touched down near the yellow lights of the coastguard boats, which zigzagged along the coastline. From time to time, the coast guard boats would stretch out the tentacles of their ubiquitous searchlights to snatch up a falling star. Several times the searchlight beams of the coastguard boats whipped across his eyes. Samoylovich screwed up his eyes as he had back in childhood, when the yardkeeper Uncle Vanya would splash the other boys and him with water from a distended fire hose. He screwed up his eyes but continued to shake with laughter.

Samoylovich climbed into a little motorboat tied to an old chain no thicker than a dog chain. More than anything, Samoylovich thought, the little boat resembled an old yard dog. It kept tugging away at the chain, trying to escape from the shore. There was also another motorboat, a newer one. Apparently, the chief physician had his eye set on this boat and was planning to fix it up. That's why the newer boat had been pulled out of the water and placed on a wooden platform. The newer boat was of no interest to Samoylovich, who had no intention of helping it slip off the platform onto the pebble beach and into the free element of the sea, which rolled big waves onto the shore.

Samoylovich yanked at the rattly chain of the older boat, which was drawn through a thick cast-iron ring. The ring was cemented into what had remained of an old stone jetty. "I'm coming, old fellow, I'm coming. I'll let you loose," Samoylovich kept saying to the older boat, which pushed its nose into his open hands, like a dog abandoned by refugees. But the chain was fixed to the ring with a lock. Samoylovich got into the little boat, looking to see if there was any way of taking off the chain. The chain was fastened to a bracket. And the bracket was fastened to the boat with two screws. He needed a screwdriver. Samoylovich went back to get one. The path was steep. Its pebbles slipped under his feet, and two or three times, he tripped and fell. "You just hold on, old fellow, just hold on," he said, turning to the boat, impatiently rattling its chain.

Polechka sat on the stoop of his cottage. He let her in and turned on the light.

"What happened to you, Samoylovich?" asked Polechka, visibly frightened. He had blood on his clothes from falling down on the steep, rocky path. He seemed not to hear her question and answered with a non sequitur: "I'll go set him free and come back. You just wait here, Polechka. Have a cup of tea. Eat some cake."

She had on a Chinese quilted silk robe. The shiny scarlet flowers with emerald leaves were embroidered with silk moulinet thread. Seeing Polechka's embroidered robe made Samoylovich remember the lyrics of a racy song, performed to the tune of "Can-Can."

He burst out laughing. He was laughing at the innuendo of the song:

> I was a merry seamstress,
> I couldn't ask for more,
> And now at the nightclub
> I work as a . . . waitress.

Stupefied, Polechka watched Samoylovich go outside, singing "The Merry Seamstress" and conducting it with a screwdriver. She ran over to the window facing the sea and, still in a stupor, continued to watch after him. At first, there was no one on the beach. Only the tentacles of searchlights as coastguard boats shot out onto the dark waters and, groping for something but failing to find it, dashed in a different direction. Then she saw a figure of a man— Samoylovich—approach a little motorboat.

Samoylovich came up to the little boat and climbed inside. "Bear with me, old fellow, and you'll have your freedom," Samoylovich muttered as he unscrewed the first, then the second screw from the stern. The bracket came loose and, with it, the chain broke free, dropping onto the pebbles with a merry jingling. Feeling its freedom, the boat rocked from one side to the other and then raced after a fleeting wave. Samoylovich laughed with happiness, gulping in the autumn breeze of the Black Sea, sharp and urgent, like the leap of dolphins. He remembered having been this happy in the starry hour when he kicked the winning goal right beneath the bar guarded by the illustrious goalie Khavkin. Samoylovich had played on his college team and "showed great promise."

Samoylovich laughed with happiness. He doubled up, laughing at himself—the former fool having seen the light and freed himself. Back in his cottage, Polechka was having jasmine tea with pound cake. She was sitting there in her seductive silk robe with its shiny little flowers, waiting for him, Samoylovich. But he couldn't care less about that. He had set himself free, *was* free. The blithe boat rocked on the waves as they carried it farther and farther into the black hole of the night.

Suddenly, the tentacles of two searchlights got ahold of the little boat, their beams growing ever thicker and brighter. Samoylovich heard the roar of approaching engines. Two coastguard vessels drew near and seized his boat. Samoylovich was arrested.

The KGB investigator pressured Samoylovich to confess he was attempting an escape to Turkey. Samoylovich told an idiotic story, in which an old boat turned into an old dog, a mutt. The chief physician, hoping to help Samoylovich and also rescue the honor of the TB sanatorium, gave the KGB the idea to have Samoylovich's health evaluated. They requisitioned the files from a local clinic and a military enlistment center near Sennaya Square in Leningrad, Samoylovich's hometown. The results weren't encouraging: Samoylovich was healthy. Then the chief physician started looking for eyewitnesses, even if chance ones. Perhaps somebody could verify that Samoylovich was drunk that evening. The coastguard officers testified that the intercepted man was in a state of severe alcohol intoxication. The KGB investigator insisted on his own version: Samoylovich had first hijacked the boat to escape abroad, and later, as he was committing a high treason, he drank vodka to keep himself warm. The chief physician affirmed that the boat was old and unfit for fast travel: the engine didn't work, there was no fuel on board. The investigator stuck to his version, which the District Attorney's office backed, that in ninety percent of all attempts to escape abroad the fugitives resorted to the most absurdly dilettantish methods, which were doomed to fail. But that didn't vindicate their betrayal of the Motherland. A weak link in the investigation (in trying to prove Samoylovich's guilt) was his heavy inebriation, which the coastguard officers verified. But they had found no liquor bottles on board. "Disposed of the bottle," the KGB investigator insisted. The chief physician didn't believe in Samoylovich's guilt. He interviewed every patient. Had anyone seen Samoylovich that evening—perhaps in an unusual state or at an unusual place? No one had seen anything out of the ordinary.

Samoylovich was sentenced to ten years at a high-security labor camp.

The car speeds along Leningradsky Prospekt. The linden trees on the island separating the two sides of the traffic are coated with yellow snow. Why's the snow yellow? Samoylovich wonders, letting out tendrils of smoke through the side window. And sometimes there's chocolate snow. The rich folks in his car don't mind his smoking. They've dozed off. The snow is yellow from the street lights. It's all so simple, Samoylovich thinks. He throws out an unfinished Northern Palmyra *papirosa* and stares point blank, in the rearview mirror, at her, to whom he said good-bye ten years ago, one crazy autumn night in Yalta. He stares at her point blank and gently strokes the jacket pocket where he keeps his revolver.

1992

Translated, from the Russian, by Maxim D. Shrayer

# The Love of Akira Watanabe

A STORY

In the story there's a he and a she.
        —Boris Pilnyak

In "The Story about the Writing of Stories" by Boris Pilnyak, there's love and death. The love of a young Russian woman and a Japanese writer. The birth of love and the death of love.

I witnessed the love of a young Japanese man for an American woman. And the death of his love. This story is about the love that my protagonist could not get over.

When the story began, I was working in one of the oldest universities in New England. I worked in a lab and had to communicate in English with technicians and researchers at the Cancer Center. I also had to read numerous articles from journals on immunology and molecular biology of tumors. Two or three times a year, I wrote papers and reports on the results of my research. And I had to write them in English. And talk, talk, talk. All in English. No one understood Russian—not even the laboratory animals we used for our experiments. One day, while looking through my daily mail, most of which was junk, I came across a letter inviting "foreign professionals" to sign up for an evening course of "English as a Second Language."

I passed the interview and placement test and became a student in a very diverse group. As in Noah's Ark, there were creatures of every kind, both male and female. I must point out here that, even in such matters, the University had very high standards. The partners within our group were matched, not in accordance with the biblical principle (opposite sex, same kind), but in keeping with the liberal principle of encouraging all sorts of contacts: interracial, international, intersexual. A Serbian man who was a basketball coach was matched with a Croatian woman who worked at the office of the University Vice President. Two women from the Basque country came into the classroom holding hands, straight from the laboratory of neurostimulants, where both were working on their PhDs. An Ethiopian man who was the art director of an African music ensemble sat side by side with an Italian woman who was a pediatric resident at a children's hospital. A Chinese poet-dissident softly giggled and traded jokes with a French expert on international terrorism. I was matched up with a sluggish, yet fastidious Baltic Jewish woman who studied Letto-Lithuanian languages and, as it turned out, also Gothic. But the two of us could still exchange a word or two of Russian when one of us was hopelessly sinking in English.

Akira Watanabe didn't have a partner in our class. Such was his luck. Akira had come from Japan, where he had earned a doctorate at Kyoto University. His thesis dealt with the application of probability theory to information exchanges between viruses and animal cells. While telling our class about this (we were each supposed to introduce ourselves), he dropped his head and stared at the barren yellow surface of the long table around which we were all sitting. As Akira spoke, I looked up and began to take him in. He was skinny and not very tall. His Asian features were offset by the whiteness of his complexion and by his straight nose, which had a slight Semitic curve to it. I'd heard that Jewish blood runs in some of the Samurai clans. I'd long been intrigued by the possibility of genetic exchange within the human species (a horizontal model of exchange of genetic information), as well as between species, families, and classes of plants or animals (a vertical model). Exchange of genes by means of viruses?

That, in addition to the traditional sexual model?

And what if. . . ?

The name of our teacher was Margaret Brown. I believe Margaret was about thirty-five or thirty-six. She was at that happy age when a woman's attractiveness reaches its peak before it begins to retreat to the foggy lanes of an autumnal park. Which is not to say that autumnal parks lack their beauty; theirs is the beauty of waning and parting. Having gone back to school, Margaret was finishing a master's degree in art history, writing a thesis on the art of glassmaking. She sometimes exhibited her own designs and compositions of colored glass in local art galleries. What else? Oh, yes—what did she look like? She was slender, with brown hair. Her forehead, nose, lips—everything about her was quite up to the standards of feminine beauty. Remember the Italian movie star of the '60s, Silvana Pompanini? Well, nowadays the standards are a bit different. Different proportions of body and face are admired today. Sharper, more angular. Not as gentle. More athletic. One wouldn't call Margaret tall. No. Think of quality bronze—a large casting, perhaps, or a miniature statuette. The full play of bends, twists, and curves of alluring femininity expressed itself in her figure. All in all, Margaret was a cheerful and sweet-natured teacher who was very much in love with her native English language. And who really wanted us to love it, too.

There was no curriculum to speak of. Instead, Margaret decided to teach us the craft of story writing. Perhaps not quite the same way as it was taught in my native Russia: dramatic opening, culmination, and stormy finale. At the end of a Russian story, the protagonist, exhausted by the marathon of the plot, drops dead at the feet of his beloved (or else, is killed by a Chechen bullet, stabbed by a traitor's knife, or murdered by a jealous husband and so forth). Margaret's goal was to teach us how to write, in clear, grammatical English, an account of an incident that happened in real life. "A true story." Her idea was that, if we could learn how to do this, then we would be able to describe correctly and truthfully any of our scientific experiments. With such training, she believed, we would then be able to write a paper—or an academic report if needed. All based on true facts. She wanted to teach us the craft of factography.

In class, we read out loud the texts Margaret would bring for us. We sang songs and watched video clips. And then we would recount what we'd seen or heard by first retelling it to our partners (working in pairs), and then discussing it as a group. But the cornerstone of Margaret's system was homework. We were supposed to make up stories and write them in English. Usually we'd type our compositions on the computer and record them on tape. Then we would bring both printed stories and tapes back to class to hand them in. Lugging our texts and tapes in a huge tote bag, Margaret would read and listen to our opuses, and return them with comments. It seemed that half of Margaret's belongings were housed in that bag. Besides tapes and folders with papers and books, there was also a thermos, little packages of hard candies (she liked to suck on them herself and to offer them to others), and her cell phone, which would often tumble out of her bag. Occasionally, during class breaks, Margaret would unfold her cell phone and call someone by the name of "Les."

At such times, Akira's face would freeze into a mask of suffering. Like those masks in the Kabuki theater: facial muscles tightly pulled toward petrified mouth, eyebrows drawn to bridge of nose, eyelids blocking passage of welled-up, burning tears.

Each of us had a partner for the drills. The Chinese poet-dissident had his Frenchman. The graduate student from Basque country had her own girlfriend. I had the sleepy Jewish woman from Lithuania. Everyone had a partner! And, well, perhaps for the first time, the lonely star of our Japanese colleague turned out to be lucky. He didn't have a partner, so our teacher Margaret had to be it. Paired up with Akira, she tried to animate him with her jokes and anecdotes, which she then readily repeated for the whole class. And she succeeded. I noticed that he no longer stared at the table. His eyes would now wander across Margaret's face. When she got up to see how things were with the other pairs, Akira's eyes followed her like compass needles. No, not like compass needles, but rather, like the pilot lights of oil burners, shimmering on their wicks and trembling from the slightest breeze, whisper, or sigh. Akira followed every breath of our English teacher Margaret Brown. I had no doubt the young Japanese man was in love!

Occasionally, a sweet ringing would emerge from Margaret's bag. She'd take out her folding phone and smile, listening, sometimes repeating the same words: "Yes, darling. Sure, Les." At such times, Akira, who was Margaret's drill partner, turned into a stone idol, staring, as before, into the middle of the table. I wondered whether Margaret noticed these changes in the mood of the young Japanese man. Most likely, she did. As soon as she'd said her last "I love you, too" to the invisible Les on the other end of the phone line, Margaret would fervently resume the language drill with Akira.

Words give birth to motion. Motion gives birth to a story.

Akira finished writing his account. The story of his life. "A true story." As a matter of fact, by the end of the second month of our lessons with Margaret, we had all learned how to describe, logically and with proper English grammar and syntax, specific episodes of our lives. Margaret's method of rigorously correcting our initially very timid essays had not been wasted on us. It's amazing how sincere and open we all were in relating the facts of our lives.

One of the two Basque girlfriends described a horror story that happened to her while she was in college. She was driving on a mountain road when, suddenly, two policemen stopped her and demanded to search her car, claiming that some explosives were being transported by Basque separatists. Finding no explosives, they forced the girl into their van and, one after the other, raped her there.

The story of the Ethiopian student was an account of an expedition to the land of the Pygmies, where he bought a unique flute made from an ostrich's hip.

The Lithuanian Jewish woman from Kaunas wrote a story about her father's search for the grave of a Catholic priest who hid Jewish children during the Shoah. The Nazis shot the old priest. The Jewish community of Kaunas built a monument to him.

I described something terrible that happened in June 1941, when I was five years old. I was spending that summer in a Young Pioneer summer camp near Novgorod, when the Nazis invaded the Soviet Union. Of course the children didn't know anything about it. For some reason, we weren't sent back to Leningrad, to our parents, right away. Or maybe it all happened so suddenly and unfolded so rapidly that there was no time to evacuate the children, even though the Nazis were advancing. I was asleep when, suddenly, a rattling sound awakened me. The other children also woke up. It was pitch-black outside, and the crisscrossed searchlight beams looked like lightning bolts against the dark sky. At first, we all thought it was a storm: thunder and lightning. But, in fact, it was antiaircraft fire, planes roaring, bombs exploding, and searchlight beams reaching everywhere. Suddenly, right above our window, I saw an airplane with black crosses on its wings, all illuminated by yellow lightning. Since then, every evil invading my life has been marked with the black crosses I saw on the wings of that Nazi airplane.

When Akira Watanabe finished writing his story, he tape-recorded it for Margaret Brown, printed it out, made copies for each of us, and then read it out loud in class. The story told by the young Japanese mathematician was bizarre, short, and tragic, too tragic to be simply a true story. Rather, it was a confession. The title of Akira's story was "How and Why I Left My Home for Good." He began with something like this: "When I was twenty years old, I finally realized that I didn't love either my mother or my sister. And that I hated my father. I couldn't bear to stay in the same house with them any longer. And I left for good. Here's why . . ." What followed was a doleful account of Akira's life. How he was born, an unwanted child in a family that belonged to an ancient Samurai clan. How all the boys in his clan were prepared for military service from the day they were born. For a male Samurai, it was the only dignified occupation. But the war ended with defeat for Japan, and so it made no sense to think about a military career. Given that, a boy born into the family would be useless, thought Akira's father as he looked at his pregnant wife. Out of spite and against his father's will, a boy was born. The father ignored him. The older sister never played with him, and when his family sat down to eat, the mother always filled Akira's bowl last. This is how it was, all through his childhood. Nothing changed when he was a teenager or, later, a college student. Akira would come home after school. Nobody at home paid any attention to him. Nobody ever asked him how he was doing or what was new in his life. Did he get drenched in the downpour? Did he get chilled to the bone in that freezing ocean wind? Was he hungry after a long day of classes? His father would be reading the paper. His mother would be cooking. His sister would be getting ready to go to a girlfriend's house. So Akira heated up his own supper. He fed the goldfish in the aquarium. He watched TV, no matter what was on, just to ease the burden of loneliness. Later, he would go to his room to study. He finished college and was accepted to graduate school at Kyoto University. In the fall, when he was leaving for Kyoto, he said good-bye to his parents and sister, telling them he was leaving for good . . .

It was springtime, the beginning of May. On the campus cherry trees were in blossom. Akira and I went for a cup of coffee.

"A cherry tree in blossom is a symbol of a man's life. Branches cut off from a cherry tree are a symbol of a man's death. Like harakiri. You know, don't you, that Samurai were the military aristocracy of Japan? Cherry trees grew around their castles," said Akira.

"Like in Chekhov's *The Cherry Orchard,*" I said, jokingly.

"Oh, that is very true!" said Akira. "The Japanese love *The Cherry Orchard.*"

I walked Akira back to the mathematics department. We exchanged business cards and promised to stay in touch now that our ESL course was over.

"Are you going to the graduation party at Margaret's?" Akira asked.

"Sure, if nothing. . . ," I replied a bit vaguely. In general, I don't like farewells. Getting sentimental in my old age? Or maybe there've been so many farewells in my life that I now tend to leave without turning back and prolonging the ache of parting. That's the way one leaves Jewish graves: without looking back.

"Of course you should come," insisted Akira. "We can talk some more about the drift of human genes."

"Okay. I promise, I'll be there!"

"Do you think Margaret will invite her Les?" asked Akira.

"Leslie? Oh, him! I've no idea." I'd completely forgotten about the mythical Leslie Margaret used to talk to on her cell phone with such tender endearments. Or rather, I didn't care. Akira, however, was thinking about him.

By a strange coincidence, we both pulled up to Margaret's house at the same time, Akira in his Toyota, I in my Ford. Margaret lived in a townhouse. The outside was painted green. Near the entrance there was a cherry tree, its branches like big wings, all in white and pink blossoms. Akira was holding a bunch of purple roses in his hand. A dozen roses whose long stems looked like heron's legs. I felt as if no time had passed since our last conversation. A cherry tree in blossom. And once again, I was drawn to the topic so dear to my heart—the drift of Jewish genes. We should've hurried up the steps to the house of our teacher, Margaret Brown. But we did nothing of the kind. Instead, we stood there under the frozen waterfall of a cherry tree, chatting about problems that could never be solved.

"They say Jewish blood runs in the veins of some of the Samurai," Akira said pensively, somehow retracing the same spiral of thought I had followed when we'd met and spoken for the first time.

I remembered being intrigued by the Semitic nose of the young Japanese man and the fairness of his skin. "I think I once saw what looked like a Samurai sword and armor in a museum of Karaites in Trakai, in Lithuania," I said.

"Those could've been Khazar swords and armor," said Akira.

"Fabulous. What a scenario!" said I, getting excited and speaking rather loudly. "Some of Khazars from the Volga basin return to the Far East, moving farther and farther east, until they reach the Isles of Japan. "Who was I mocking? Akira? Myself?

"Quite possibly," agreed Akira. And then he added: "If we assume that, by that time, Turkic Khazars had merged with the Jews of Persia and become Judaic Khazars. Well, it's not impossible."

"This is why the Japanese are drawn to cherry orchards," I said. It all comes from the lower basin of the great Russian Volga, where the Khazars once lived."

Akira seemed not to notice the irony in my voice and remained pensive and serious. Our conversation was just some background murmur for him. A background against which Akira envisioned very different pictures.

Margaret opened the door with a welcoming smile, leading us inside as if we were little kids who'd come to a birthday party at a house where we'd never been before. As soon as we came in, she asked us, very much in the American style: "What would you like to drink?" I asked for vodka. Since he had promised his hostess he'd be in charge of grilling the ribs, Akira asked if he could have something that wasn't as strong as vodka—red wine, perhaps? Margaret brought us our drinks and went back to the kitchen. I downed my vodka and started looking around. One of the doors from the living room opened to a bedroom with a queen-size bed. Above the bed on the wall, there was a large photo of two women. One of the women—I'd never met her before—looked older than Margaret. She had short hair, almost a crew cut. Her eyes were deeply set. The younger woman in the photo was our teacher Margaret. She was smiling happily, her left cheek pressed to her friend's. Or perhaps it was a relative? I'm quite near-sighted, so I went into the bedroom to get a closer look. No, it was what I thought it was. Margaret was pressing against the older woman as if asking for protection.

As for Akira, he was in an inexplicable (at least to me) state of euphoria. He walked from one room to another, glass in hand, sipping his wine and becoming ever more euphoric in the giddiness of his emotional nirvana.

I returned to the living room and plunked down on the couch next to the Serbian basketball player and the Lithuanian Jewish philologist. We began to discuss the problems of Bosnia-Herzegovina. The Serb argued that both their Slavic genes and their Slavic languages (it's all practically the same Serbian language, he insisted) would eventually bring the Bosnians back to a united Federation of Southern Slavs. The Lithuanian Jewish woman, for her part, maintained that religion was more important. And I stood firmly for the autonomy of both religion and language within the framework of the European Commonwealth.

I'd seen Akira go into Margaret's bedroom. I can't say for sure how long he'd stood there staring at the photo. Then he'd gone into the kitchen, empty glass in hand, poured himself some more wine, and come up to the couch where we were sitting. (I should note here that, in Turkish, *divan* (couch) means place for conducting important discussions. This is a propos of the Bosnians, who, as the Balkan Christians believe, are actually Serbs forcibly converted to Islam by the Turks . . . )

The Japanese are known to be extremely polite. Sipping his Chianti with a glint of triumph in his eyes, Akira waited patiently for a pause in our discussion. It was now the turn of the Lithuanian

Jewish woman to speak. After every phrase, she would take a sip of mineral water as if it were her source of inspiration. And she tried, once again, to persuade the Serbian basketball coach that Bosnian Muslims should be left alone and granted independence.

"The same thing is going to happen to the Albanians in Kosovo," she prophesied. "It's very different in Israel, you see, where in another two-three generations all the Ashkenazic, Sephardic, and Ethiopian Jews will mix. *We* can be proud of it!"

"And why are we *here* and not there?" I asked subversively. She choked with anger at my bluntness and didn't reply, nervously sipping her mineral water.

Akira seized the opportunity to pull me by the sleeve toward Margaret's bedroom. "You see?" he pointed to the photo. *This* is Leslie! The same Leslie who had sometimes phoned Margaret. I'm such an idiot! I became jealous, I thought it was Margaret's boyfriend. Or even her fiancé!" And the happy Akira went off to start the grill and cook the ribs.

It was a lovely spring evening. A light breeze blended the smoke of the charcoal grill with the scent of cherry blossoms. Somebody put on music in the living room and people began to dance. I was watching Akira through the open door of the porch. He looked so happy. Carving knife in hand, he sliced through a section of the rack of beef that had been soaked in a special marinade, cutting the scarlet muscles of the sacrificial animal along the ribs. Scarlet meaty ribs stained rusty brown by the marinade. Then Akira put the ribs on the red-hot grill. I'm pretty sure he was humming a tune. Maybe even a Samurai song. Triumphantly he waved, now the carving knife in his right hand, now a spatula in his left, singing something joyous as he turned over the sizzling ribs.

Everything was ready. The steaming ribs occupied the center place on the table. Placed around them were platters of fiery red tomatoes, radishes that looked like downsloping eyes, circles of onion, curly bunches of parsley, piles of lettuce. There was also pizza, green beans, and various cheeses and grilled sausages. A real potluck feast! But the principal dish, the royal treat, was Akira's grilled beef ribs. And this made him so happy. Nobody was eating yet—we were all waiting for Leslie, who was due any minute.

"She's a surgeon. Just finished operating," Margaret explained. "What do you think, should we wait for her?"

"Sure," we all agreed and continued dancing.

Akira was dancing with Margaret when Leslie came in. She was in her scrubs, having come directly from the hospital. Leslie was a tall, broad-shouldered woman of forty or forty-two. Sharp, quick, strong. She kissed Margaret and waved us all a greeting as she headed for the bedroom. "I won't be a moment. Just need to change," she said. "Please start, don't wait for me!"

We froze in anticipation. Akira leaned on the carving knife as if it were a sword. He was dumbfounded. What was he expecting? It was all so clear. Margaret sensed our unease, our bewilderment. And she hurried to explain, to fill the awkward silence: "This is where we live together, Les and I. There," she pointed to the closed door, "is our bedroom." Right at that moment, Leslie came out of the bedroom. She'd changed into tight blue jeans with a wide belt and a denim shirt with chest pockets. She lit up a cigarette and took a Bloody Mary from Margaret's hand. We attacked the food, piling it on our plates, and then spread out across the living room. The beef ribs were delicious. I finished my first plate and got up for another helping. I looked for Akira among the feasting guests—I wanted to toast his talent for making ribs. He wasn't in the living room. I went to the kitchen and saw Margaret and Leslie standing there, embracing.

"Coffee will be ready soon," announced Margaret.

And Leslie added: "Like all Russians, you probably drink your vodka *straight*?"

"You're right," I nodded.

"If you ever get sick of it, let me know and I'll make you a killer Bloody Mary."

"You bet," I said, trying out an expression I'd learned in Margaret's class, and walked out of the kitchen.

I couldn't find Akira anywhere. Not among our classmates crowding around the table. Not on the porch. Not in the bedroom. When I went outside, I stumbled over some branches. They'd been cut off the cherry tree and scattered on the ground. I suddenly felt desolate standing there and staring at what was left of the cherry tree. A carving knife was thrust into the trunk of the naked tree, the same knife Akira had used to carve the ribs as he joyfully sang his Samurai songs.

Margaret came outside. "Where's Akira?" she asked. She had a book in her hands. "I wanted to give him a present—a book of Japanese poetry in English translation. Just listen, this is so beautiful:

It's only where the cherry blossoms fall,
Like snow flurries flying in the air . . .
But now it's springtime and this snow
Doesn't melt as quickly as the real."

She recited the verses and asked again: "Where's Akira?" Only then did she see the disfigured cherry tree and understand everything.

"Akira just took off," I muttered meaninglessly. "He didn't say anything,"

"I'm so sorry . . . It was all so ridiculous, so stupid!" said Margaret, almost in tears. "Oh, why did he have to leave in such a hurry?"

1999–2004

Translated, from the Russian, by Emilia Shrayer

# Carp for the Gefilte Fish

A STORY

If you take Route 44 West out of Providence, in about half an hour you'll get to the town of Greenville. There, on the outskirts, lived Raya and Fyodor Kuzmenko. Raya worked as a nurse's aide in a home for the elderly and did some cleaning and cooking, on the side, for the town's affluent families. Fyodor was a mover at Kapler's furniture store. The Kuzmenkos lived in a small, split-level house on the outskirts of Greenville. Where they lived, it was no longer Greenville proper, but the country. A tiny farm in the sticks. Fyodor and Raya had no children. Back in Borisov, in Belarus, a urologist had told them it was a result of Fyodor's "hereditary alcoholism."

They intentionally chose to settle not in Providence, where Raya had family, but in rural Rhode Island. They wanted to lie low. They had no desire to see or hear from any of their fellow immigrants. Just to live quietly, to grow cucumbers and tomatoes.

Raya also cultivated flowers, and Fyodor went fishing.

Still back in Borisov, Fyodor had the reputation of being an incredibly lucky fisherman. Raya's whole *meshpucha* made gefilte fish from the carp and bream that Fyodor would catch in the Berezina River. But even this didn't earn him much love. Fyodor's Jewish in-laws referred to him only as *shiker* or goy. Behind his back, of course. Only after immigrating to America did Raya and Fyodor finally get the chance to move away from Raya's well-wishing *meshpucha*.

Back in Borisov, Fyodor didn't have any blood relatives. His father drank himself into cirrhosis of the liver and died in great tor-

150

ment. A year after that, in the middle of the night, as she was walking back to her village from a party, Fyodor's mother fell into an ice hole and drowned. She had been widowed young and still wanted to sing and dance her fill. The local social hall was in the village across the river.

The six-year-old Fedyushka was left with Granny Alyona. He grew up and was drafted into the army. After serving in a tank division, Fyodor returned to his village. His grandmother had already passed away. As a tractor and combine operator Fyodor earned decent wages, but his loneliness drove him to drink, and to go on binges. He would probably have drunk himself to death, had it not been for Raya.

They met at the district agricultural fair, where Fyodor had been sent by his hometown collective farm. Raya was working at the cafeteria bar. There they met and fell in love "at first sight." As it happened, Raya's high school friend, Manechka Flyugershteyn, who was studying journalism by correspondence course, had been assigned to write an article about Fyodor. To make sure the article was completely accurate, the editorial office of the district newspaper *The Banner of Labor* dispatched Manechka Flyugershteyn to Shishkovichi, Fyodor Kuzmenko's village. Raya came along with her. Of course, Manechka had arranged the whole thing. She was dying to help Raya. Manecha herself was unlucky in love. All the decent Jewish men had moved away to the big cities, and Manechka wasn't interested in getting involved with a reckless drunk (be he Jew or goy). Obviously, neither Raya nor Manechka had the faintest suspicion about Fyodor's alcoholism, "hereditary" or "acquired." The girlfriends spent three days in Shishkovichi, and they stayed at Fyodor's *izba*.

A golden Belarusian September lingered in the air. While Fyodor was harvesting potatoes and Manechka was finishing her article, Raya would wander about the nearby fields and forests, dreaming of her future life with Fyodor. When he returned from the fields late in the evening, smelling of fuel oil and earth, Manechka would already be long asleep in the spare room. But Raya would be waiting for him with supper. They'd each have a glass of a fortified sweet wine called Madeira, which Fyodor had bought in the city, then go off to sleep in the hayloft. But who could even think about sleep? Every night, they loved each other. All three nights.

When Raya returned home, she told the whole story to her parents, Lyuba and Misha Khaykin, and her (maternal) grandmother, Feyga Solomonchik. They were mortified by the very idea of becoming related, through their daughter's marriage, to a tractor driver by the name Kuzmenko, shock worker though he was. A full-blown war broke out in the Khaykin household, with Raya holding the defensive line, and her parents and enormous *meshpucha* leading the offensive. Over the phone, Raya reported to Fyodor the daily digest of military operations. She'd call him from the municipal post office. At prearranged times, he'd call her on the radiophone from his collective farm.

For two straight weeks, Raya, in tears, begged her parents at least to meet her beloved. They were adamant and ruthless. They recalled all the tragic incidents of mixed marriages, from biblical times and the Great Inquisition to the Warsaw ghetto and the anti-Semitic plot of the "doctor-murderers." In short, Fyodor wasn't allowed so much as to come near the Khaykins' house, let alone court Raya.

In the meantime, the newspaper *The Banner of Labor,* in the regular section "News from the Field," had printed Manechka Flyugershteyn's article about Fyodor Kuzmenko. Complete with a photograph of him behind the steering wheel of a combine. Raya framed the article and put it up in the dining room. Her father, Misha Khaykin, begged Raya to remove the odious photograph, but she stood her ground. The newspaper clipping had magical powers. It seemed to possess diplomatic immunity. This meant that you could hate it, but undertaking any actions against it was dangerous. And so the parents, Misha and Lyuba Khaykin, together with the grandmother, Feyga Solomonchik, refused to use the dining room. Let that goy hang there all by himself! In protest, Raya continued to eat alone in the dining room, right under the framed newspaper clipping. For an entire week, Lyuba, Misha, and Feyga ate in the kitchen, where they also moved the TV. Raya could no longer bear it, so she called Fyodor and said: "Do what you like. I can't live like this any longer!"

The next day—it was a Saturday morning in early October—Fyodor drove up to the Khaykins' house in his tractor. He pressed the forehead of his metal monster to the gate, he climbed down from the cab, walked into the house, and addressed Misha, Lyuba, and the elderly Feyga Solomonchik with a speech. All the while he spoke, they continued to sit around the kitchen table, having tea with honey cakes. He addressed them rather decently, without threats, foul language, or other such things you might expect from this sort of a suitor. He said, "I love your Raya. Let her marry me. Otherwise, I will crush your anthill with my tractor. After that—prison or poverty, it's all the same to me. I can't live without Raya!"

Despite the swaggering of the war veteran Misha Khaykin, the wails of wife Lyuba, and all the curses poured over Fyodor's head by grandmother Feyga Solomonchik, in the end, they came to an understanding. Fyodor sold his house in the village, moved in with the Khaykins, and started working at a factory in Zhodino, outside Borisov.

The years flew by, one after the other, finally carrying Raya, Fyodor, Lyuba, Misha, and Grandmother Feyga to America on the wings of a Boeing. They ended up in Rhode Island, in Providence.

A year later, Raya and Fyodor moved away from Raya's family to Greenville. By that time, Raya was thirty-five and Fyodor was thirty-eight. And they had no children.

Raya found a job as a nurse's aide in the nearby home for the elderly and, on the side, cleaned and cooked for the town's affluent families, including the Kaplers, who owned the furniture store where Fyodor worked as a mover. Every now and then, Fyodor went on a drinking binge and stayed home for an entire week, sometimes two. Most often, the binges would occur in late fall, after Thanksgiving, and in early spring, after Shrovetide. Incidentally, Raya never hurt Fyodor's feelings. She celebrated all the Russian Orthodox holidays, combining them with the Jewish ones: Purim with Shrovetide, Easter with Passover, Hanukkah with Christmas. That is, it wasn't their divergent origins that caused his drinking binges. And Fyodor loved Raya just as much as ever. But they were without children. They both longed to have children, especially Fyodor: he had nobody to go fishing with, nobody to teach all kinds of manly handiwork, nobody to take a steam bath with, nobody to tell stories to about serving in the tank division, or about how a tractor runs in the fields. Raya's longing was of a different sort: she felt sorry for Fyodor, knowing how he suffered. After all, they had no children because of him. She understood this and forgave her husband his binges, his anguish, and his passion for solitude.

Mister Kapler, or "Harry," as he insisted that Raya call him, was a widower. His wife had passed on three years earlier. Kapler had a furniture store and a twenty-six-year-old daughter, Rachel. Kapler's store enjoyed a good reputation and did quite well. But his daughter, Rachel, constantly caused problems. In high school, she lived a carefree, thoughtless, empty life. She would drive around to all the beaches and restaurants in a sporty convertible in the company of various freeloaders, returning home only in the early hours of the morning, and then in total disarray. She got involved with the most unbefitting types. When Kapler or his late wife, Nancy, tried to reason with her, Rachel would lock herself in her room and stay there for days on end. People said that it was Rachel who drove her mother to an early grave. In short, Rachel didn't get into any colleges. Instead, she partied hard while all her suitable beaus left home. After his wife's death, Kapler began teaching Rachel the family business. Unexpectedly, Rachel turned out to be remarkably savvy. Starting off as a salesclerk, in three years, she became manager of her father's store. Everybody knows that, in America, you've got to be totally dedicated to your job. Moving up in the furniture business, Rachel soon abandoned her freeloader crowd. But the changes in her life didn't exactly attract any appropriate suitors. None of the eligible men wanted to date a woman who had only furniture sales on her mind. All she ever thought about were the furniture sets, armchairs, or dining tables that had to be ordered from all over the country and then delivered to customers. In truth, she had no time for suitors. It's a fact that work and sports can temporarily suppress sexual loneliness, especially in the morning, and during the day or early evening. But a single young woman spending the night all by herself?

You couldn't call Harry Kapler a completely happy man either. First of all, there was the issue of his daughter's unsettled life. Of course, Harry was rather pleased with Rachel's success in the family business. He knew that if, God forbid, something happened to him, Rachel would be left with both work and money. But he also saw how she suffered after losing all the old beaus and not finding new ones.

Harry Kapler dreamed of having a grandson or a granddaughter, which was completely natural for a Jewish man of his age and comfortable position. At his respectable age of fifty-nine, the widower Kapler ached for female companionship and dreamed of a mistress. His suffering and his dreams were as obvious to Rachel as hers were to him. We often think that we have the exclusive on reading the thoughts of our children and some God-given ability to draw accurate conclusions from our observations. There is nothing exceptional about it! They see in us what we see in them. Rachel saw how her father suffered from loneliness and how greedily he eyed the Russian woman, Raya, who came to their house to clean and cook.

Twice a week, on Mondays and Thursdays, Raya worked at the Kaplers' home. She came early in the morning so that Kapler and Rachel could both make their requests and order a menu. For instance, Kapler loved cold borscht in the summer. So, come summer, he'd tell Raya to make him cold borscht. Or Rachel would feel like having pirozhki with eggs and scallions. So she'd tell Raya to make her pirozhki with eggs and scallions. Or he'd ask for apple compote, and she—for dumplings with cherries. Both father and daughter had fallen in love with Russian cooking. Russian, Belarusian, Ukrainian, Polish, Jewish dishes—how can you separate them? Kapler and his daughter had both fallen in love with all of these dishes and, every other week, they would set about enthusiastically composing a new menu. Those were perhaps their happiest moments together, when they both felt like a real family. Every family needs such moments.

There was also a psychological aspect to all of this. Or, actually, two aspects—desire flowed in two powerful force fields from Harry and Rachel Kapler toward the Kuzmenkos. The father wanted Raya. And the daughter was crazy about Fyodor.

A bountiful New England September lingered in the air. It was a warm and sleepy Thursday morning. Outside the windows of the Kaplers' mansion, the garden was filled with radiant roses and beaming begonias. Blushing Macintosh apples hung from the branches. The roses and begonias had been planted when Kapler's wife was still alive. The apple trees had been growing here since the time Kapler's father had started the business and installed his family in Greenville. Kapler and his daughter were having coffee and bagels when Raya came in. She wanted to head downstairs to get the laundry started, but Kapler stopped her.

"Have some coffee with us, Raya."

"Thank you, Mister Kapler. I had plenty at home."

"It's Harry. Just Harry," Kapler corrected her.

"Here in America, we don't like being so formal," added Rachel.

Raya remained standing in the middle of the kitchen where the owners were having their breakfast. Ogling Raya, Kapler even stopped chewing his bagel. She looked especially attractive that morning. Raya walked to work because she and Fyodor shared one car, an old Chevrolet with 200,000 miles on it. Standing there, her face flushed from the road, a strand of black hair falling from the tight braid rolled back in a bun, in a green shirt stretched over her ripe breasts, and her blue jeans pulled daringly tight over her firm behind, she seemed to Kapler to embody the very fantasy that he had dreamed about all his life. He was a decent fellow and a good family man. He had never let his imagination run wild while his wife was still alive. Never once had he gone to those show-shmows and cabaret-shmabarets featuring naked girls. Unlike some of his friends, he would never stoop so low. God forbid! Even now he wouldn't debase himself like that. But this Raya with her lovely Jewish face, her tight braid and shapely figure, that was a different story! Of course, even looking at her lustfully was a violation of one of the Ten Commandments: "Thou shalt not covet thy neighbor's wife." Yes, he coveted Raya. The wife of a Russian man, Fyodor. The wife of a man who worked for him. Fyodor was his worker, that's right. But why should he consider Fyodor a neighbor? No, he was a stranger. As strange as it gets. A Russian who didn't even bother to convert to Judaism after marrying Raya. Maybe that's why God didn't give them any children. Surely the womb of this beautiful woman was created to receive the seed of a deserving Jewish man.

No, this Fyodor isn't a neighbor at all. And it's not a sin to covet Raya! Kapler determined, and confidently took a big sip of coffee with cream from a yellow porcelain cup.

"—beef stew with prunes . . . Dad, dad, aren't you listening?" Rachel interrupted his reverie. She'd been composing a menu for the Sabbath dinner Raya was supposed to cook for them.

"Oh, Rachel, darling, I *know* what I want! I think I've wanted it my entire life, since the time when my *bobe* used to make gefilte fish for *shabes*. Stuffed carp, *that's* what I want, Raya!"

"Nothing simpler, Mister Kapler," Raya responded with a gentle smile.

"So make us gefilte fish in honor of my late grandmother. And I'd like the fish served on that big sky blue serving platter, in aspic pink from beet juice, as succulent and desirable as . . ." Though he so wanted to say "as you, Raya," he stopped just this side of it, searching for an appropriate comparison. But, being as far removed as he was from the world of the arts, Kapler couldn't come up with anything worthy of a comparison (with Raya, of course, not the fish). Bewildered, he grew silent.

"You just ask, Mister Kapler, and I will make stuffed carp," said Raya.

"Dad, what's come over you? River fish is so *bony!*" Rachel objected. She didn't care for the Russian woman's coquettish smile and her own father's bafflement.

"I'll take the fish, add lots of beets, carrots, onions, and cook it for a long time so that the vegetable and fish juices blend together," Raya patiently explained. "Then I'll take the small bones out. And I'll arrange the ground fish around the spine. But there's only one question. Will there be carp delivery this morning to the Russian store in Providence or not?"

"Why don't you call them right now, and that's that!" Kapler said.

"Too early. They don't open until nine," Raya replied.

"What if they don't deliver today?" Kapler said impatiently. He couldn't help it, that's how much he wanted it.

"Dad, I don't recognize you," said Rachel scornfully and shook her head. "You're always so reasonable, especially when it comes to food."

He cast a quick glance at his levelheaded daughter, and repeated his question, a smirk playing across his lips.

"What if they don't deliver carp to your Russian store?"

"Well, then we can send Fyodor to the lake."

Raya's hasty words froze in the air. But it was too late to take them back.

Kapler had already clung to the idea.

After Kapler arrived at his furniture store, he gave the usual morning instructions to the salesclerks. He told Fyodor to replace a redwood bedroom set in the main showroom with a newly delivered teak set. He made phone calls to a couple of furniture factories. He performed the usual daily tasks that brought him both satisfaction and money. But, all the while, he kept glancing at the clock. It was around eleven when Kapler stepped into his office to have a cup of coffee and leaf through *The Providence Journal*. The newspaper reported a slight climb in East Coast real estate prices. He also read about the visit of the Russian president, the opening of a children's hospital in Providence, about the release of boxer Mike Tyson from prison. Kapler sipped his coffee, unsweetened and flavored with cinnamon and hazelnut, just the way he liked it, and wondered, Will she call or not? But Raya wasn't calling. So he called the house. She was still over there, cleaning. He knew that she was at his house, cleaning, walking from one room to the other. Her agile gait had none of the languor typical of American women like his late wife, a languor that isn't even true fatigue but just a habit of saying, "Oh, I'm so tired, I'm so tired, oh, I just want to sleep!" Raya's in the living room, he thought, and now she's walked into his bedroom. She's bending over, practically lying on her stomach across the bed to pull off the sheets. Her jeans are stretched so impossibly tight over her behind you want to rip them off, throw them the hell away, then lock the bedroom door, lock the entire house, and let Rachel knock all she wants, he doesn't care, if he could only just hold this Russian, this desirable young woman, press his hairy stomach and loins against her marble back and gorgeous hips, hold her so tight she becomes one with his body, and fill her beckoning womb with his Jewish seed.

He was sitting by the phone and fantasizing what would happen if he surprised her in the bedroom.

But Kapler didn't go anywhere. Instead, he summoned Fyodor and told him to drive over and ask Raya about the carp in the Russian store. If the answer was "yes" ("yes" or "no" in what sense, Kapler couldn't quite decide), if the carp were indeed to be delivered today, to go buy one and take it over to Raya at the house. And if it was "no"—regarding the delivery of the carp (and "yes" in terms of Kapler's plan), he told Fyodor to prepare for an outing, that is, to get ready to go fishing.

"I've been wanting to give you a raise for quite some time. For now, take this as a bonus," Kapler handed Fyodor a hundred-dollar bill. "Don't spend it all on booze, Fyodor!"

"How can I, Mr. Kapler! I'm getting my wife a breadmaker. I promised her one a long time ago," said Fyodor.

"And don't come back here if they don't have carp at the Russian store," Kapler instructed Fyodor. "Just telephone me and get on your way. You'll need time to pack, to get ready, right? Call me when you're leaving for the lake."

Fyodor stopped by the boss's house. Raya said that she'd called the store, and they wouldn't be getting carp today because the delivery truck had broken down.

"You know how it is, Fedya, the Russian way!" Raya said, and they both laughed at the fact that, even here in America, the Russians did everything by the rules of their old life. Fyodor decided to call his boss at the store with a report on the carp. He dialed the number and Rachel answered the phone.

"Tell Mr. Kapler that I'm on my way to the lake. Before I go, I need to buy some hooks and other tackle and also worms."

"The lake?" asked Rachel.

"Yes. Waterman Reservoir. You know it?"

"When I was younger, we used to go swimming there. It's a pretty big lake."

"I fish from the side of Route 116, behind the horse farm."

"Yes, sure, I know the spot. We used to have picnics there, off the road and to the right."

"So will you give him the message?" Fyodor asked again.

"Yes, Teddy (she called him "Teddy"), I'll give dad the message," Rachel said. "Oh, actually, he just walked in."

Fyodor repeated the whole story to his boss of how there would be no carp delivery at the Russian store and how he had to get things ready to go fishing.

"When will you be back, Fyodor?" asked Kapler. Instead, he wanted to ask, "When will Raya be making the stuffed carp?"

"I will fish until I catch enough, till late, if I have to. Raya will cook the fish tomorrow morning," said Fyodor.

"Good luck!"

"Thank you, Mr. Kapler."

While Fyodor was talking with Rachel and Kapler, Raya continued with her cleaning, but she still caught the drift of the conversation. The boss's daughter had asked where Fyodor was planning to fish. Just look at that *nekeiva,* thought Raya. Can't find herself an American guy, so she sets her sights on my husband.

"Why was Rachel asking you all those questions, Fedenka?" she asked Fyodor.

"Who knows, Rayushka. I don't care. Let her ask. My dick won't fall off from her questions."

"And what if—?"

"—you think it might?"

"What if you fall in love with her?"

"What are you talking about?" He wanted to tell her how much he loved her, that she was everything in the world to him, how he was going to buy her the breadmaker. But he restrained himself. He didn't want to spoil the surprise.

"You really won't trade me for anyone else?" she asked, embracing Fyodor.

He felt his muscle get incredibly hard and all but punch a hole through his pants. So strange. This bursting, this desire for a woman, which he felt even before his wife hugged him. Perhaps already when he came over to the Kaplers' and saw her all flushed, with a silky strand of black hair showing from under her cornflower head scarf? Or when she bent down to the vacuum cleaner brush and her green blouse slipped out of her jeans, baring her back? Or was he already hot from Rachel's voice?

"You really don't care for that moody *nekeiva*?" Raya asked again, because he was now standing in a trance, all of him turned into one blazing, unrestrainable muscle bursting to be with a woman.

Without saying a word, he pushed her onto the rug, pulling off her jeans and his own twill trousers, then rolling the skimpy panties off her hips and ripping off his own white underwear with a seamed crotch, pushing apart her hot legs and releasing all of his white postal doves, all the messengers of his love, releasing them into her heavenly expanses.

Fyodor drove back to his house. He looked over his fishing gear and set up two fishing rods. One was lighter and had a Japanese reel, the other—an American one. The American reel was bigger and had a heavier line. It was good for perch, bass, chain pickerel, sunfish. The Japanese gear was for the cautious, cunning fish—trout, carp, eel. Fyodor had to drive by the tackle shop and buy some extra hooks, weights, and floats. He also needed worms. Because he wanted the freshest possible worms, Fyodor decided he would first check out a few department stores and pick just the right breadmaker for Raya. Of course, he had a special cooler for fishing, with a freezer pack. He always took this cooler with him when he went fishing. He would pack a few sandwiches and a couple cans of soda. Handling the worms, however, was more complicated. The stupid freezer pack was liable to overcool the worms, and that would make them limp, slow, and unattractive to the fish. Even if he did store the worms in the cooler, it would only be for a short time. That's why he usually bought the bait right before fishing.

It was three in the afternoon. Fyodor took Route 44 toward Providence. Right before the bridge over Interstate 95, he stopped at the tackle shop he thought had such a cheerful name, "Canal Bait." He asked the Irishman, John, if he had fresh worms and if he could put a couple dozen aside for Fyodor. After making certain that everything would be all set, and that he didn't have to pay in advance, Fyodor went in search of a breadmaker. There were three suitable places in the area: Apex, Ann & Hope, and Sears. Of course, there were other stores where he could also shop for a breadmaker. But he didn't have much time left. The boss was counting on him, waiting for this stuffed carp as though it were manna.

What do Jews see in this gefilte fish? Fyodor wondered. He had lived among Jews for many years but could never really understand them completely. He had been eating this gefilte fish (carp, bream, pike) for many years, but he still preferred pan-fried fish. He especially liked to chase a piece of fried fish with a drink. How could one compare the soft, sweetish, bland gefilte fish with the fried fish that smelled of river and campfire, of manly conversation, and cheery vodka? No matter how much he loved Raya, no matter how much he tried to convince himself that, were it not for her, he would've never seen America, this country which never stopped, this wasn't the first time he was thinking there were still some dark corners in his soul that his wife's glance had never penetrated. Was it that she wasn't trying to look that deep? Or was it that he wouldn't let her in? What would've happened if, instead, he had married Verka, the nurse from the county hospital? He had no idea what would've happened.

A few steps away, there was a bridge over Interstate 95. Lost in thought, Fyodor walked up the overpass. The highway hummed below, the widest highway along the Atlantic coast. It was like a wide river, and in its stream cars were sliding by like fish.

He returned to his Chevrolet and drove to Apex. It took him almost an hour to buy the breadmaker. First, for twenty minutes, he walked up and down the endless aisles of the store with their countless merchandise, looking for the right department. The thing was, Fyodor didn't like asking salespeople where and how to find what he needed. He didn't for two reasons. One was because he was living in a place where people spoke a foreign language. The second reason was congenital. He didn't speak English very well and this embarrassed him the most when he had to speak with strangers. And like many Slavic males, he was pigheadedly self-confident, the type of man who prefers to make ten mistakes but, in the end, find his way, rather than humiliate himself in front of someone by begging for assistance.

He finally found the department where they sold breadmakers. There were a few different models, ranging in price from one hundred-fifty to two hundred dollars. Fyodor had stashed away another hundred—in addition to the money that Kapler had given him that day. So price wasn't the issue. The breadmakers could make anything from various types of bread to pound cake. He picked the one that had "challah bread" printed on the box. Raya liked having challah on the table for *shabes*.

It was already five or thereabouts by the time Fyodor returned to the tackle shop, bought two dozen worms, hooks of various sizes, different weights, and also a few floats, even though he usually fished without them, sensing the bite by the tug at the rod. He drove back to his house, hid the present, loaded the rods and tackle into the car, took a few slices of bread and a bottle of water, and was finally off to the lake.

He took Route 44 West out of Greenville. There, a few miles west of the town, on both sides of the highway, lay the main part of the reservoir. On weekends, fishermen congregated there. Men who had broken free of the family circle for a day or two. Men who, feeling unrestrained in each other's company, kicked back, laughed, and told jokes. Once, soon after moving to Greenville, Fyodor tried to fish in that noisy, crowded spot. He didn't catch anything except very small fish, which he gave to a couple of kids, and resolved never again to fish in such a busy place. Besides, he didn't understand American humor, and was also startled by every voice behind him, as if expecting (from nobody in particular) a gibe of some sort or else a patronizing comment. For a year, he kept trying different spots around the reservoir until he found what he wanted. That's where he was now headed, turning off Route 44 West onto 116 South. Before him was a landscape of rolling hills. Apple trees heavy with red blushing apples stood on the hills, ankle-deep in green grass. Summer was turning to fall. Fyodor rarely felt as happy as he did right then. He loved his wife Raya. He'd bought her a breadmaker and was now going to catch carp for the gefilte fish she was making. Several fish or perhaps one large carp, which would sit atop the serving platter in Mr. Kapler's dining room like a tsar on his tall throne.

Fyodor hadn't felt so good for a long time. He started singing, "There's no blossom like the apple blossom, when the apples come to life. There's no sweeter time than springtime evening, when my love will come to me . . ." This was from a song of his village youth. They now seemed happy to him, those years.

Looping around the hills, the road took him past several farms folded into the dales. Onto the gates of one of the farms a large cardboard sign was nailed, from which Fyodor gathered that they had tomatoes, corn, and apples for sale. He understood this because bas-

kets with the farm produce stood right under the sheet of cardboard
with the English words he had some trouble understanding.

Fyodor drove on, unhurriedly, remembering scraps of different
songs and singing them. He passed an intersection. On the left was
a small shopping plaza with a country store, a motel, and a saloon.
Perhaps I'll stop and have some coffee, Fyodor considered for a moment. But he didn't stop. He wanted to start fishing.

On the right side of the road, there was a stud farm. On a green
pasture, separated from the county highway and the surrounding
farms by a gray post and rail fence, Fyodor saw hobbled horses graz-
ing: two black horses, a red roan, and a white horse. After the pasture with the horses, there was a little bridge. Just over the bridge
the road turned, revealing the edge of the lake tucked behind tall
pine trees. This lake, which Fyodor had once found by himself and
kept coming back to, was part of the large Waterman Reservoir, but
it was away from all the bustle and noise. Fyodor approached the
spot where he usually left his car. On the left side of the road, there
was a solitary house surrounded by an overgrown garden. A stone
wall protected the highway from landslides. Right above the stone
wall was the lake's hilly shore. To the left, the shore gently sloped,
turning into a little sandy beach where children frolicked on summer days. By evening, it would quiet down. That's when he liked to
fish.

Fyodor parked his Chevrolet by the curb alongside the stone
wall. He took out his rods, the tackle, the pail, and the cooler,
locked the car, and headed up the path into the grove of pines,
which grew on the high shore. On one of the pine trees there hung
a metal sheet with a sign:

POSTED
Private Property
Hunting, Fishing,
Trapping or Trespassing

For Any Purpose
Is Strictly Forbidden
Violators Will Be Prosecuted

Fyodor looked at the sign and even ran his eyes over the American words. He was familiar with some of them: "fishing," "violators," "prosecuted." Everything was correct! He wasn't going to enter the little summer houses scattered over the shore or swim off the little sandy beach. He was there to fish. That word, "fishing," was on the sign. He had purchased the freshwater license and a trout button. So in no way was he a "violator" subject to being "prosecuted." And he turned right on the path that meandered over the high lakeshore, toward his cherished fishing spot.

That Thursday, Harry Kapler decided to leave the store no later than six o'clock. He made the final arrangements of the day and was getting ready to leave. Rachel had left a bit earlier. She wanted to take a drive to the ocean, to Narrangansett, she told him. "I'm meeting some friends. We'll go for a walk along the beach, have a drink . . ." So Harry Kapler was feeling very determined when he left his store. Of course, the thought of Rachel spending the evening in the company of her friends (a boyfriend, perhaps?) in itself made him happy. After all, it was practically the first time she was going out after long months of seclusion. Besides, Kapler had been contemplating a certain plan, and Rachel's absence now smoothed the way toward its execution.

He gave instructions to his salespeople, walked out through the back door, and got into his Cadillac. A package store was five minutes away by car. He picked out a chilled bottle of champagne. Not the most exquisite champagne, but still a decent one. Harry Kapler was a man of action. Untamable desire had now been added to his usual determination . . .

Flushed, with a strand of black hair falling from the tight braid rolled back into a bun, in a green blouse stretched over her ripe breasts, in blue jeans pulled daringly tight over her curvy hips, just like she was when he saw her in the morning, Raya embodied the dream Kapler had longed for his entire life.

"Where are you rushing to?" he asked her.

Raya had just walked out of the bathroom, where she was straightening herself up after a day of cleaning.

"Where are you rushing?" he asked again. "Fyodor's out fishing. Rachel went to Narranganset. Let's sit down, talk a bit. I bought champagne."

"Thank you, Mister Kapler, but—"

"—Harry. To you, I'm Harry!" he interrupted her.

"Thank you, Harry. I haven't had champagne for ages, not since my wedding. Is this *Soviet* champagne?"

"No, this bottle is from California. Let's drink it, and you can tell me which one's better."

"Probably the American one, Harry."

"Now we'll see," he turned in his hands the thick and heavy bottle dressed in golden foil. He remembered his wife. It's been three years since she passed away. And now he's about to drink champagne with a young Russian woman.

"What if Rachel comes home early? What will she think?" Raya asked.

"First of all, she won't come home early. Second, I'll lock the door from the inside. You're running late with the cooking. I'm relaxing upstairs."

"Wonderful, Mister . . . Harry!"

Raya remembered her wedding. She in a white dress. Fyodor in a formal suit of blue cheviot. Relatives and friends at the festive table. Soviet champagne bursting out of the bottles like ocean tide. She couldn't even imagine back then that one day she would fly to America, settle near the ocean. Champagne, wine, and vodka, lots of vodka. It was then, for the first time since they had met and begun dating, that Fyodor had drunk himself into oblivion. She'd patiently waited for him to sober up. Then she'd waited to get pregnant. Then she'd stopped waiting, coming to terms with the thought that, for her, Fyodor would be both husband and son.

Raya looked at Kapler. He was brawny, self-assured, with graying hair neatly combed back. The rolled-up sleeves of his light summer shirt revealed tanned forearms. The collar of his shirt was undone and the tie loosened. As she studied him, Kapler was arranging champagne flutes on a tray decorated with pictures of Las Vegas.

And what if? Raya thought.

"And what do you say if we go upstairs and listen to some good American jazz?" he suggested.

"With pleasure," Raya agreed.

He went out into the hallway and latched the front door, then bolted from the inside the other two doors—the side one and the garage door. They went up to the master bedroom connected with a huge bathroom. She knew the place well—she cleaned here every week. Sometimes, while changing his sheets after the laundry and making this wide bed, she thought of him sleeping there by himself. How did it use to be when his wife was still alive? Sometimes, to amuse herself, Raya would jump onto the bed for a second and just lie there on her back with her arms spread out. Every time she did this, she thought of the fairy tale about Goldilocks and the three bears. She wasn't a stranger in his bed.

Kapler ripped the foil off the bottle and unwrapped the wire from the bottleneck. The cork shot up to the ceiling and the champagne gushed out. He poured the frothy drink first into Raya's flute and then into his own.

"To you, Raya. To your beauty!" he said.

"Thank you, Harry," she said.

"Good champagne. Doesn't smell of yeast, not even a bit."

"Not any worse than ours," she nodded in agreement. "Sweet and goes straight to your head. I like sweet drinks."

"I have some liqueur, if you'd like," he said.

"No, let's have champagne first."

They snacked on the honeydew he had brought from the kitchen.

"Sweet melon and sweet champagne. I'm getting light-headed," she said.

"Let's dance," Kapler suggested and turned on the CD player. "This is Glenn Miller, from *Sun Valley Serenade*. Now that was a famous picture."

"Oh, I remember it! They showed it to us in the House of Culture in Borisov. It's about skiers, right?"

"And about love," he said, tugging at her arm. "Let's dance, Raya."

They danced, slowly floating around the bed, which was as wide as an orchestra pit. When they floated back to the nightstand where the tray was, Kapler poured them both more champagne. Raya felt happier than she had been in a long, long time. Maybe she'd never felt that happy. Except in her dreams. Everybody has dreams about a beautiful life. She both believed and refused to believe that this was happening to her: a luxurious bedroom, music, champagne. Like in foreign films.

"Harry, let's drink to *dreams*!" she suddenly proposed.

"You're my dream," he said and kissed her on her full, hot lips.

They drank champagne, sitting next to each other on the bed and kissing after each sip. He laid her on her back across the bed and started fumbling with his hands under her blouse. She never wore a bra in summer. Her breasts, like young affectionate animals, pushed their muzzles into his palms.

"I'm hot, Harry," she said. "Let me go change."

"You know your way around here as well as I do," he responded and suddenly realized something. How could he forget the most important thing! No, he wasn't afraid. He knew that there could be nothing the matter with a woman like her. And still, he was a man and an American, and this meant that he had to think of her first. He was raised this way.

She came back from the bathroom, wearing his red terry cloth robe.

"Let's have more champagne and drink to you, Harry. You're extraordinary. I fell in love with you the minute I saw you two years ago. You're a true gentleman."

"Thank you, darling. We'll drink to me, but a little later. Now I have to run a quick errand. I forgot, I didn't think about it. I couldn't hope this would happen."

She realized what it was. She probably guessed it because of his guilty voice.

"You don't need to go anywhere, Harry. If *that's* what you mean, you don't need to worry. I want you not to worry. I want it, you understand?"

He understood.

Fyodor was standing on a concrete dock. He'd cast from one of the rods, the Japanese one, into the middle of the lake where the water was deeper. A few perch were flopping in the plastic pail, against which he leaned the top of the rod. The sun was setting behind him, dropping into the forest that was cut off from the lakeshore by the ribbon of the country road. Fyodor was puffing on American cigarettes called Kent, slowly turning the handle of the other, lighter reel. There was nobody else besides Fyodor in this part of the lake. Every night, the water was getting a little colder. Fewer and fewer people were going swimming. The summer houses were becoming empty. The students had gone back to school. This was the best season. Nobody disrupted Fyodor's fishing with screaming and splashing. Sometimes another lover of solitude would quietly glide by in a rowboat and disappear behind the nearest bend of the shore. Here, Fyodor had time to think about life, about his place in this wondrous country. A flock of ducks descended into a little cove fringed with rushes. Where were they coming from? Were they fly-ing southward from Maine or Canada? Or were these maybe local ducks, feasting on small fish and other treats they would find at the silty bottom of the lake? How good it would be to stand on this lit-tle stone dock with a son. How old would he be by now? Five? Ten? Fifteen? These thoughts always anguished Fyodor. If this longing for a son got hold of him at home, he'd open the freezer and pour himself a glass of vodka. The hot wave would rush to his head, usu-ally driving out the bitter thoughts about a nonexistent son. And if it didn't, he'd go on a binge. Knowing that he was prone to this, Fy-odor never brought alcohol with him on his fishing trips. And this time, too, he had brought none, not vodka nor wine nor beer. Es-pecially this time, when Fyodor was on an assignment for his boss, Mr. Kapler, who had done more than simply send his worker to catch a carp. He'd entrusted to Fyodor the task of catching a carp for the gefilte fish. The carp was to be cooked by his wife, Raya, for whom Fyodor had bought a breadmaker with the bonus he'd re-ceived from Mr. Kapler. This entire bundle of circumstances—of trust and reciprocating loyalty—left no room for blunders on Fyodor's part. And what had always been his number one enemy if not booze?

And so Fyodor forced himself to drive away the bitter thoughts and the urge to drink they brought about, the urge so closely bound to his dreams of having a son. A perch started biting, violently tug-ging at the tip of the fishing rod and then slapping his tail on the water as Fyodor reeled him in. After throwing the perch into the pail, Fyodor checked the bait on the Japanese rod and decided to use his largest prize worm, sweetened with a few cooked kernels of corn. He also replaced the weight with a heavier one because the evening current was pulling the line toward the shore, away from the deep water.

After casting out a line with the heavier weight, he decided to concentrate on it, putting the American rod aside for the time being. Wanting to relieve himself quite badly, he jumped off the stone dock onto the sand and went over to lean against an aspen tree, whose warped trunk inclined to the water. The whining roar of a jet muffled the rustle of the bushes, just as someone's hand pulled them apart. He barely had time to tear his hand away and zip up his trousers when he heard Rachel's voice.

"So this is where you've been hiding from me, Teddy!"

Still standing with his back to the path and straightening out his trousers, Fyodor was about to pick out the right American words to respond to the boss's daughter, when he noticed the thin tip of the Japanese rod rapidly jerk forward, pushing the reel up against the edge of the pail. Forgetting all about Rachel, he sprang back to the stone dock, picked up the fishing rod, and began to reel in the fish. Judging by the way it fought, resisting the line Fyodor was winding onto the reel, it was a big fish. It's either a catfish or a carp, he thought cheerfully. Just please don't let it get away! And, as he pulled the fish up to the shore, he began to breathe rhythmically, his breaths keeping time with the regular turning of the reel. Carefully and freely. The way a marathon runner breathes at the end of a race. The way a lover breathes in anticipation of a final orgasm at the end of a long night of passion.

"My God, you're lucky!"

He heard Rachel's voice through a film of rapture that enveloped him as he landed a huge, two-foot carp he could barely fit in his net.

"That isn't a fish, it's a dolphin!" Rachel said. Now he could talk to her. Or, at least, his gift of speech was returned to him—that is, he was left with only his normal impediments in speaking a foreign language. With great difficulty, Fyodor began stringing words together, picking the ones that very roughly transmitted his thoughts.

"Well, yes, good fish. Good for stuffing."

Rachel didn't pay much attention to his words, knowing that he had difficulty expressing himself in English. Besides, words weren't what she wanted from him.

"I brought a few things for a picnic. Let's celebrate your luck, Teddy!"

"Good deal," he responded.

"Here, I have sandwiches, plums, and here's beer. Do you like beer?"

"I like beer," he answered.

"Except, you know, Teddy, we're actually breaking the law. There's a sign over there."

"I saw it. I have a fishing license."

She knew that the issue was not his license, that this part of the lakeshore was private property, that, even by being there, they were already violating the law, but her desire overpowered reason and she rushed on.

"Well, then, open your beer and let's toast your carp!"

"To carp!" he responded, twisting off the metal cap and taking a sip of beer from the dark-green bottle Rachel handed him. In her picnic basket, Rachel had a few more bottles of Canadian beer, sandwiches wrapped in foil, and also plums in a ziplock bag. The plums were large and brownish red. They looked like Rachel, they suited her somehow. Her red hair, reddish-green eyes, puffy eyelids. The shape of her sloping freckled nose also resembled the silhouette of a plum. Suddenly, Fyodor felt a wave of disgust. He no longer wanted to drink beer or have sandwiches with her. He wanted to throw those plums right into the lake. Maybe the ducks would eat the little brownish monsters. But she was the boss's daughter, and he forced himself to go on sipping beer from the dark-green bottle and taking small bites of the sandwich. Rachel also drank some beer. They were sitting on the wide trunk of a pine tree toppled by a hurricane that had crashed through the area just a month ago. Fyodor was smoking, staring into darkening surface of the water and hoping that Rachel would leave soon. But life in America had taught him to be courteous.

"Good beer," he said. "And good sandwich."

"Have more! Open another bottle and drink it. You're a big guy," she said and moved closer to him.

"Thank you, Rachel, maybe some other time. Today I'll fish more."

"You've already caught so much."

"But Mr. Kapler is expecting."

"Maybe afterward then?"

"When?"

"Well, you fish some more, and then we'll continue."

"It will be late."

"What are you, afraid of your wife?"

"Me?"

"Yes, you! Who else, silly? You said it'll be late."

"Rachel, you don't know me well if you think that I'm afraid of anyone."

"Then let's do this: wrap up your fishing, and I'll be waiting for you at the parking lot by the motel. You know, at the first intersection, there's small plaza with a motel and a saloon. I'm inviting you for a drink. Let's meet at ten. Okay?"

"Okay."


She went back to her car. Fyodor continued fishing, but with less enthusiasm. The joy of having caught a large carp and of knowing that the boss would be happy was tainted by the doubts and contradictions that were crawling in his brain like worms in manure. This Rachel with her beer and sandwiches! The posted sign he had read and sort of understood didn't seem to forecast any problems. But what if he had misinterpreted what it said? What if it meant trouble for him? His peasant mind told him that what was left of the fishing wasn't worth any risk, and that there was definitely a chance he had misunderstood the posted sign. Besides, his sacred faith in the decency of Americans had just been shaken. If the boss's daughter was trying to fool around with him, then there was no guarantee the boss wouldn't try the same with Raya. These thoughts made him sick. He could believe anything, but not that Raya was capable of deceiving him with anyone, especially not with that old man Kapler.

Fyodor was about to pack up and head back, but then he looked at his watch and spat with anger. It was only nine. It was all his fault. The freckled thing would be waiting for him at ten. It would be stupid to go there earlier and hang around an empty plaza in a strange town, like a total idiot. So he'd better fish for a little longer since he hadn't even gone through half of the worms. He baited his hooks and cast out both lines.

It was that time of the day when the silence and the darkness form the skein of the night. Fyodor calmed down, listening to the sounds around him the way you might take in the sounds that spring forth from the darkness of a grand piano. The splashing of fish. A frog's trilling cavil. The buzzing of a cicada. The soft rustle of a fox. Then he heard a car approach and stop.

It's probably Rachel come back, he thought, as he heard footsteps drawing near. But these were the heavy steps of men rushing toward their goal. The steps stopped suddenly, right above the stone dock where he was fishing. In the darkness, he could make out two silhouettes. The savage glare of a flashlight slashed at his eyes. "Hey, you, get up here!" someone ordered in a rough voice.

He walked up the path, squinting from the blinding light. Two policemen stood on the path. One of them was shining his flashlight. The other held his right hand on the holster.

"Your driver's license!"

Fyodor took his driving license out of his wallet and handed it to one of the policemen.

"Your fishing license!"

He took out a square of paper with his first and last name and address. The license indicated that he had paid such and such sum for the right to catch freshwater fish. And there was a small stamp confirming that he had paid extra for trout fishing.

"You'll have to come with us," said the policeman with the flashlight.

"For what"? Fyodor asked, without moving from his spot.

"We'll figure it out," answered the policeman whose right hand rested on his holster.

"Let me get my rods then," Fyodor said.

"All right," agreed the policeman with the flashlight, and went down to the water with Fyodor, continuing to shine the flashlight.

Fyodor folded his rods, closed the box with the hooks, sinkers and other tackle, took the pail with the fish, poured out the water, and returned to the path.

"Let's go," ordered the policeman with his hand on his holster.

The policeman with the flashlight went first. Fyodor followed him with his catch and fishing gear. The policeman with his hand on his holster brought up the end of the procession. They walked uphill and then down to the highway, to the spot where the sign on a metal sheet was nailed to the trunk of a pine tree. The first policeman aimed the flashlight at the sign.

"Did you see this?" he asked Fyodor.

"I saw it," answered Fyodor.

"It says here that this lake is private property, that you're not allowed to fish here, and that the violators will be prosecuted. You will be prosecuted!" said the policeman with the flashlight.

"I probably didn't understand the sign. I thought that if I had a license, everything was fine. I've been fishing here for years. Even this summer, I fished here," Fyodor said.

They were standing in front of his car.

"You can put the rods and the pail into the trunk," said the policeman whose right hand still rested on his holster.

Fyodor opened the trunk and put away the gear and his catch.

Then he turned to the policemen. The highway was better lit. The light of the moon mixed in with the light of the flashlight. The policemen saw the round broad face of a Russian *muzhik* that expressed neither fear nor anger, but only endless confusion and a preordained obedient readiness to submit to the circumstances and rely on the will of chance.

"What if the Russian didn't understand the sign?" said the policeman with the flashlight very quietly to his partner, although he might just as well have said it loudly. Stunned by the misfortune that had befallen him, Fyodor wasn't hearing a thing. More than anything else, he was afraid of screwing up in this country, of earning a bad reputation. And it was all because of the Jewish carp! Like he needed that stupid gefilte fish—along with Mr. Kapler!

"You know what, Bill, why don't you stay here with him, and I'll go check if our Russian fisherman has a record," said the policeman with the flashlight.

"You smoke?" asked the policeman with his hand on his holster.

"Uh-huh," Fyodor nodded.

"You can have a smoke," said the policeman and lit up.

"Thank you," said Fyodor and helped himself to a cigarette from his own pack.

"Married?" asked the policeman.

"Sure. We immigrants need a wife."

"Why is that?"

"We can't be without a wife. We'll get in trouble," replied Fyodor and remembered that he was supposed to meet Rachel.

The policeman with the flashlight got out of the police car. He called the other policeman to the side, and they began a conference.

"Why don't we let him go, Bill," suggested the policeman with the flashlight.

"Fine with me, Steve. Clean record. He doesn't look like the type," said the other policeman, his hand still on his holster.

"Listen up, Mr. Coosemenka," said the policeman with the

flashlight, rolling the Slavic last name around in his mouth as if its sounds were hot coals. "Here's the deal, Mr. Coosemenka. You can go home. But remember, *never* trespass on anybody's private property. If you see a sign that says PRIVATE PROPERTY, get the hell out of that place! Will you remember that?"

"I will remember," answered Fyodor.

The police car drove off.

It was almost ten o'clock, time to see Rachel.

At first, there were no doubts in Fyodor's mind. He wanted to see that redhead witch, wanted to get drunk with her. To get drunk and to spite Raya, who pulled him into this carp mess, which nearly landed him at the police station. After all, Raya was doing this to butter up her dear Mr. Kapler, not even for a moment considering how things could turn out for Fyodor. He kept working himself up, pushing aside various doubts—such as the fact that Raya couldn't have possibly suspected the outcome of his fishing expedition. A hot, stubborn anger was boiling up inside him. It was the same anger he had harbored since the time of his infamous courtship, since the day when, despairing of ever getting Raya peacefully, he was ready to smash his tractor through the Khaykins' puny fence. The age-old anger at himself and at Raya made him blind to arguments of reason, which would have stemmed from his kindness, and left him only with arguments of hatred toward everything alien that he linked to his wife's Jewishness. He swung his Chevrolet around sharply and accelerated, forgetting about the recent encounter with the policemen, about the timidity and confusion he had felt only a few minutes before. Now he only wanted one thing: to get drunk and have some crazy fun with the daughter of that damned Kapler.

She was waiting for him by the entrance to the saloon. The plaza was deserted. In the far corner, near the country store, stood a police car. All I need is to run into those policemen! thought Fyodor. Oh, to hell with them!

"Why don't you park by the motel and come back here," Rachel said.

When they walked into the saloon, a few customers were sitting on the tall stools around the bar. Two dressed-up young couples and a gray-mustached man in a plaid lumberjack's shirt. From the conversation of the two young couples, who were laughing as they recounted details of trips they'd taken last year, Fyodor gathered that both couples had been married the year before and were jointly celebrating their anniversaries. Which explained their dressy outfits. The gray-mustached drunk in a red plaid lumberjack's shirt was talking to the bartender, a sprightly bald fellow in a white polo shirt, black jeans, and a black leather apron, telling him how happy and free his life had been since his wife left him. But, judging from the bartender's sympathetic yessing, things weren't actually going so well for the gray-mustached man.

Then Fyodor remembered about the police car that was parked not far from the bar. What if they—the policemen—are waiting for me to have a drink? he wondered. A new wave of doubts came over him. And although Rachel had ordered two drinks—wine for herself and whiskey for him—Fyodor couldn't swallow even a drop.

"To your luck, Teddy!" Rachel proposed a toast, just as she had earlier, on the lake.

Reflexively, he mumbled words of appreciation and put his glass down on the bar. He had to say something to Rachel, to explain why he couldn't drink. And so he told her about the policemen and about the sign that prohibited fishing in the lake and how they finally let him go.

"So what! Forget it! They let you go, didn't they? Take it easy! Enough's enough. *Genug* already, as my grandma used to say." Rachel pushed the whiskey glass back in front of him.

"You know, Rachel, those policemen . . . I promised them I would never trespass on private property . . ."

"Oh, so that's what you're worried about . . ."

"Well, yes! I live in America now, and you have different laws here. And you and I—we, too—are somebody's private property."

"Well, you know, Teddy darling, I belong only to myself. And I can do with myself whatever I want."

"But I can't, Rachel. You have to understand. In Russia, I couldn't, either. I could never do all those things behind Raya's back. And I can't now. Please forgive me, Rachel."

She jumped off the tall barstool, tossed a ten-dollar bill onto the counter, and stormed out without a single word.

Fyodor waited until Rachel's car sped off into the darkness and then left the bar. The police car was gone. He slowly opened the door of his Chevrolet, started the car, turned up the radio, and headed home.

He hadn't felt so good in a long, long time. It was as though he had avoided some terrible, looming danger, some crippling illness after which, like after smallpox or a battlefield injury, your face has changed so much even your close relatives need a long, long time to adjust to your new state. And maybe they'll never get used to it. Somehow, he'd managed to avoid this disaster. He hadn't trespassed on what wasn't his and hadn't let any stranger capture his body and his soul.

As he drove past an apple orchard, the wind brought the strong scents of fall through the open car window: hay, apple cider, wild mushrooms. The scents of fall in Belarus were the same. He drove on, thinking what a happy guy he really was. Here he was in a new country, where he came, not like some sort of a loser, but as a married man. Both he and Raya have jobs. They have their own house and a garden. And they haven't yet hit old age. It's too bad, of course, that they don't have a boy or a girl. But who knows, maybe they'll get lucky? Here in America, even the worse kinds of ailments get cured. If it's all from his drinking, then he's practically on the wagon. And what if?

Thus dreaming, he drove until he found himself in Greenville, in front of his house. There were no lights in the windows, but the outside lantern was lit. Fyodor parked the car and came inside. He turned on the kitchen light and peeked into the bedroom. Raya was asleep. Very quietly, he closed the bedroom door. On the white kitchen table, under a tea cozy—a cotton doll with painted cheeks and huge eyelashes—stood a small casserole. A note was attached to it: "Fedenka, I made your favorite kasha. Please have some, clean the fish, and go to bed. Raya."

He put the kettle on the stove. Then he ate some of the buckwheat kasha. The water boiled. He put two teabags and a few spoons of sugar into the mug. The tea was aromatic and sweet. He loved his tea that way after fishing trips, with a slice of white bread and some butter.

He had to clean the fish. Every fisherman hates cleaning his catch as much as he loves fishing. Fyodor brought in the pail with the fish and dumped it into the sink. But, before getting busy with the knife, the scissors, and all the other kitchen utensils, he took a bottle of Smirnoff out of the freezer and poured himself half a glass. Slithering inside him like a cold snake, the vodka immediately turned into a hot ball that expanded all through his body. The world became simple and easy like a merry-go-around. He poured another half glass and, with deft motions, began to clean the fish. He started with the perch, little trout, and other small fry. And then he got to the beautiful carp that lay in the middle of the sink among the other fish, with dignity, like a general surrounded by his staff officers during a stop. Fyodor scraped off its slimy scales, tore out the pink gills that reminded him of woven seaweed and the eyes that had turned glassy, like buttons. He cut open the stomach of the huge fish and removed the intestines and the milt, which took up half of the carp's gut. What a stud! Fyodor thought to himself. Carefully rinsing the fish off, he lightly sprinkled it with salt, covered it with clear plastic wrap on a tray, and put the tray into the fridge.

Raya was sleeping and didn't hear him go to the bathroom, take a shower, and walk into the bedroom. He lifted the blanket and got in, careful not to wake her up. Remembering something, he got up and went to the basement. There stood the breadmaker, packed in a pretty cardboard box. Fyodor carried the box to the bedroom and placed it on the floor at Raya's side of the bed.

Then he settled back into the bed beside the flushed body of his sleeping wife.

1996

Translated, from the Russian, by Margarit Tadevosyan
and Maxim D. Shrayer

# Notes to the Texts

*Maxim D. Shrayer*

A significantly modified (and it is hoped reader-friendly) version of the Library of Congress system for transliterating the Russian alphabet is used throughout the entire book. Exceptions are words that have gained a common spelling in English, such as *kvass*. The dates following literary works refer to publication.

Notes to *Strange Danya Rayev*

Composed in Providence, Rhode Island, in 2001, the novel *Strange Danya Rayev (Strannyi Danya Rayev)* appeared with another novel, *Savely Ronkin,* in David Shrayer-Petrov's book *These Strange Russian Jews: Novels (Eti strannye russkie evrei: romany),* released by Moscow's Raduga Publishers in February 2004. An excerpt from *Strange Danya Rayev* was featured in *Lekhaim* (no. 36, 2003), a Moscow-based Jewish-Russian magazine.

p. 1

*Lesnoye:* Formerly a northern near suburb of St. Petersburg called "Lesnoy"; at the time of the novel and still today, a section of the Vyborg Side (Vyborgskaya storona; named after the city of Vyborg on the Karelian Isthmus), which constitutes one of the principal geographical parts ("sides") of the city of St. Petersburg (Leningrad, Petrograd). The Neva River divides St. Petersburg into three main areas: northern, southern, and eastern. The Vyborg Side, traditionally a working–class and industrial area and a Bolshevik stronghold during both 1917 revolutions, makes up the eastern portion of the northern main area of the city, along with Vasilievsky Island and the Petrograd Side, from which the Vyborg Side is separated by the Bolshaya ("Big") Nevka River. As opposed to the Vyborg Side, a geographical term, the Vyborg District (Vyborgsky rayon) as an administrative section of the city of St. Petersburg dates to 1718, and exists in its present borders since 1978; it is one of the largest districts of St. Petersburg, and presently the third most populous.

*Pavel Borisovich (Fayvl Borukhovich) Rayev . . . Stella Vladimirovna (Shayna Wolfovna) Kogan:* In Russian, a person's full name consists of a first or given name, a patronymic (derived from the father's first name), and a last name or surname. Already in the nineteenth century, the Jewish (Yiddish and Hebrew) first names of the assimilating and acculturating Jews of the Russian Empire began to be replaced with the names and forms of names common in mainstream Russian society, often chosen to correspond, etymologically, semantically, or phonetically, to the Jewish names they replaced. In the Soviet period, by the 1930s, such changes and replacements became increasingly the norm, owing to a combination of factors: the massive migration of the Soviet Jews to the cities outside the former Pale of Settlement, their rapid Russianization, popular and later state-sponsored anti-Semitism, and the suppression of Judaism and Jewish life and culture. Very often Soviet Jews born in the tsarist era would retain their old Jewish names in their papers, but assume Russian(ized) forms of their first names and patronymics in daily life; it was therefore common to encounter, especially among the generation of children born to the Jews of the former Pale in the 1930s and 1940s, a father named, for instance, "Solomon," and a son or daughter whose patronymics would be changed in the official papers to "Semyonovich" or "Semyonovna," respectively, so as to deflect at least the anti-Semitism in daily life. In the case of Danya Rayev's parents, born, as we conjecture, in the late 1900s–early 1910s, the Yiddish male name "Fayvl" assumed the common Slavic shape "Pavel," while the patronymic "Borukhovich" ("son of Borukh") was turned into "Borisovich" ("son of Boris"); the Yiddish female name "Shayna" ("beautiful") became "Stella" (from "star"), the patronymic "Wolfovna" ("daughter of Wolf") became Vladimirovna ("daughter of Vladimir").

*Daniil . . . Danya . . . Danik:* The translators and the editor have sought to preserve the richness and diversity of the forms of the characters' first names, except where it would be completely misleading for a non-Russian reader. A number of forms are commonly derived from a full Russian first name (e.g., "Daniil," a Russian equivalent of the biblical "Daniel," yields "Danya," "Danik," "Danichek," "Danka," etc.). The different suffixal derivations connote a different tone or intonation, degree of diminutiveness (e.g., for small children) or its opposite, extent of formality or intimacy, shades of sympathy or dislike, and so on.

*Forestry Technology Academy:* Lesotekhnicheskaya akademiya; formerly, the Forestry Institute, founded in 1803 and renamed "S. M. Kirov Leningrad Forest Technology Academy" in 1929; located in the Vyborg District of Leningrad and surrounded by a large old park.

p. 2

*dacha:* Russian country or vacation house and the property on which it stands, often in a suburb or a Soviet-era countryside vacation housing development *(dachnyi posyolok)* of summer cottages on small plots of land.

*kitty:* Although *kotik* literally means "kitty" or "little cat," the word also refers to seal and its pelt, a common material for coats and hats.

*Finnish War:* On November 30, 1939, Soviet troops invaded Finland in an act of aggression. Although outnumbered, the Finns heroically resisted the advance of the Soviets in what became an embarrassing winter campaign for the Soviet Union. Under the terms of a peace treaty signed on March 12, 1940, Finland ceded to the Soviet Union the Karelian Isthmus and Eastern Karelia, which still remain part of the Russian Federation.

p. 3

*Vladimir Nikolaevich Krestinsky:* Soviet organic chemist (1887–1939), professor at the Forestry Technology Academy, brother of Nikolay Krestinsky (1888–1938). An "old Bolshevik," Nikolay Krestinsky served in a number of prominent capacities in the early Bolshevik apparatus and the Soviet government, including that of the Deputy Minister of Justice, which he held in 1937, until his arrest. In March 1938, Nikolay Krestinsky was tried in a show trial of the "Right-Trotskyite Anti-Soviet Block" in Moscow; of the twenty-one defendants, he was the only one who publicly ventured to defend his innocence on the first day of the trial, subsequently recanting his testimony and pleading guilty. Vladimir Krestinsky was forced to denounce his brother. Soon after his brother's execution (March 15, 1938), Professor Krestinsky fell ill and died of cancer—but also "of grief and shame," as those close to him said sotto voce. David Shrayer-Petrov included a chapter about Krestinsky, "Orange and Conifer" ("Apel'sin i khvoya"), in his memoir-novel *Friends and Shadows (Druz'ya i teni, 1989).*

p. 4

*big, red, cancerous crawfish:* In Russian, the word for cancer (from the Latin for "crab"), *rak,* also means "crawfish"; thus, in the mind of the young Danya Rayev, cancer evokes the image of a crawfish taking away Professor Krestinsky. Crawfish are a traditional snack that Russians eat to go with their beer.

*Agricultural Expo:* The All-Union Agricultural Exhibition (VSKhV), opened in 1939 in Moscow and operated until 1941 as a propaganda theme park and popular destination for visitors. In 1954, the VSKhV was significantly expanded; in 1959, a much larger Exhibition of the Achievements of the People's Economy (VDNKh) opened in its stead.

*"Kill the kikes, save Russia":* Bey zhidov, spasay Rossiyu; Russian

anti-Semitic slogan, associated with the activities of ultranationalist organizations, known popularly as "the Black Hundreds," formed during and after the 1905 Russian revolution; historically used to incite the population to commit anti-Jewish violence, the slogan is still in use by extremist groups in post-Soviet Russia.

p. 5

*The Hunchback Pony: Konyok-gorbunok*; fairy tale in verse, first published in 1834, by Pyotr Ershov (1815–69).

*Mr. Scruba-Dub-Dub: Moydodyr* (1921); narrative poem for children by Korney Chukovsky (1882–1969).

*Mail: Pochta* (1927); long poem for children by Samuil Marshak (1887–1964).

*Uncle Styopa: Dyadya Styopa*; first published in 1935, *Uncle Styopa* is a four-part narrative poem for children, by Sergey Mikhalkov (born 1913).

*The Three Little Pigs: Tri porosyonka*; Sergey Mikhalkov's 1936 fairy tale-like adaptation of the Walt Disney animated feature (based on English folklore).

p. 9

*smoke from his* papirosa: Russian hand-rolled style cigarette with a hollow filter.

p. 11

*Caran d'Ache . . . Pencil:* "Karandash" (literally, "pencil," from the Turkic *karadash*) was the stage name of the famous circus clown Nikolay Rumyantsev (1901–83); Rumyantsev adopted his stage name after the famous French cartoonist Emmanuel Poiré (1858–1909), who used the pseudonym-pun "Caran D'Ache."

p. 12

*This is all . . . our* meshpucha: Yiddish, Hebrew for "family."

*Petrograd Side:* see note to p. 1.

*Nevskaya Zastava:* Literally, the "Neva Checkpoint"; originally, a reinforced checkpoint on the left bank of the Neva River at a southeastern entrance to St. Petersburg dating to the eighteenth century; presently, an area within the city boundaries of St. Petersburg.

p. 14

*Molotov:* Vyacheslav Molotov (1890–1986): Soviet leader, one of Stalin's closest henchmen; as Soviet Minister of Foreign Affairs, Molotov signed a nonaggression pact with Nazi Germany in August 1939.

*Novgorod:* Russian provincial capital located 113 miles to the south of St. Petersburg. The Nazi troops occupied Novgorod in August 1941.

p. 15

*Ryazan:* Provincial capital in central Russia, 123 miles to the southeast of Moscow.

*The Germans are encircling Leningrad:* Nazi Germany invaded the Soviet Union on June 22, 1941, making rapid advances in three directions and reaching Leningrad in two and a half months. Fully encircling Leningrad on September 8, 1941, the German troops laid siege to the city (the Finnish troops had regained Eastern Karelia and threatened from the north; see note to p. 2). In the course of the siege, which lasted almost 900 days, between 500,000 and one million died (in January-February 1942 alone, about 200,000 Leningrad residents died of starvation and severe cold). Starting with the winter of 1941, the "road of life" *(doroga zhizni)* across Lake Ladoga east of the city—by transport on ice during the winter months and by ferry during the warm season—linked the blockaded Leningrad with the mainland. The siege was fully lifted on January 27, 1944.

*A Tale about the Great Plan: Rasskaz o velikom plane* (1930); prescribed reading for Soviet children about socialist construction, by Mikhail Ilyin (1895–1953), brother of Samuil Marshak (see note to p. 5).

p. 17

*Vereshchagino . . . Molotov . . . Siva:* Vereshchagino is a district center in the Perm province of Russia, 75 miles west of Perm; from 1940 to 1957, the city of Perm, a major city of the Ural region, located 873 miles northeast of Moscow on the Kama River, bore the last name of Vyacheslav Molotov (see note p. 14); Siva is a large village (rural town) 25 miles northwest of Vereshchagino, on the Siva River.

*verst:* Old Russian-unit of distance; a verst is about two-thirds of a mile.

p. 18

*treats them to* makhorka: Also *tyutyun*; Russian and Ukrainian name for *Nicotiana rustica,* a type of cheap and commonly grown tobacco selected from wild-growing tobacco species; cf. Aztec tobacco, Indian tobacco.

p. 21

*Sverdlovsk:* From 1924 to 1991, the name of Ekaterinburg, a provincial capital and major industrial center in the Urals, located 1,036 miles to the east of Moscow.

p. 23

*"ice road":* "Road of life"; see note to p. 26.

p. 25

*Permyak:* The Permyaks or Permians are a heavily Russianized ethnic group, Christianized in the fifteenth century, historically the speakers of the Finno-Ugric Komi-Permyak language; the Permyak Komis reside mainly in the Komi-Permian Autonomous Region and the Perm and Kirov provinces of the Russian Federation.

*Esenin:* Sergey Esenin (1895–1925), Russian poet in the peasant-folkloric vein, one of Russia's most beloved lyrical voices.

*Simonov:* Konstantin Simonov (1915–1979), Russian Soviet poet, prose writer, playwright; during World War II, Simonov's poem "Wait for me and I'll return . . ." ("Zhdi menya, i ya vernus' . . .") became one of the most recited Russian lyrics; see also note to p. 69.

p. 26

*Vladimirovna . . . Antipovna:* In Russian peasant culture (and to some extent in Russian lower-class urban culture), it was customary to address a familiar person by *patronymic only,* instead of by first name and patronymic; a patronymic's contracted form was commonly used (e.g., throughout the novel, the patronymic of the Rayevs' host Andrey Mikheevich gets contracted from "Mikheevich" to "Mikheich," and people might address him simply as "Mikheich." The peasants of Siva thus address Danya Rayev's mother as "Vladimirovna"; in remembering his village childhood, Danya refers to other peasant women as "Antipovna," "Prokhorovna," "Nikiforovna," and so on.

p. 28

*Shrovetide:* Marking the beginning of Lent, Shrovetide *(Maslennitsa,* from *maslo,* "butter"; cf. Fat Tuesday) is traditionally celebrated among the Russian Orthodox with the consumption of blinis.

p. 30

*kvass:* Traditional Russian malt beverage.

p. 31

*Paskha:* Generic Russian word, from the Greek *Pascha* ("Passover"), for both Easter and Passover; to specify which is meant, the adjective Orthodox *(pravoslavnaya)* or Jewish *(evreyskaya)* is added.

p. 34

*wild plants called* "pestiki": Singular, *pestik,* literally, "pestle" or "pistil"; Russian popular name for both bistort *(Polyganum bistorta;* also called *"brylena"*) and wild asparagus (also called *"kholodok"*).

p. 41

*"Danchik, what a groys menshele you've become!":* Yiddish for "a big little man"; here used in the affectionate sense.

*Russian Folk Tales, collected by Karnaukhova:* Danya Rayev is possibly referring to the classic volume *Fairy Tales and Legends of the*

*Northern Region* (1934), collected, edited, and annotated by the folklorist Irina Karnaukhova (1901–59). Already a children's author and popular performer of fairy tales in the 1940s, Karnaukhova turned to collecting and adapting for children the fairy tales and epic poems of the Russian people and other ethnic groups of the Soviet Union. Her *Rainbow-Bow* (1946) and *Amusing Fairy Tales* (1947) were followed by other volumes for children, and Danya Rayev may be superimposing his postwar memories onto those of his wartime years.

p. 48

*Cheka:* Abbreviation for *Chrezvychaynaya komissiya* (Extraordinary Commission), the earliest post-1917 precursor of the Soviet secret police.

p. 53

*"saffron milk caps":* In Russian, *ryzhiki,* literally, "redheads"; a delectable mushroom *(Lactarius deliciosus)* and staple of the traditional Russian peasant diet.

p. 54

*November holidays:* National celebration of the October Revolution, whose date fell on November 7th after the Soviet state switched from the Julian to the Gregorian calendar.

p. 56

*Karaite:* The Karaites are a Jewish sect that rejects the Talmud, originating in eighth-century Persia. The ethnic roots of the Crimean Karaites, from which Lithuania's Karaite community originated, are debated to this day, with some theories linking the Crimean Karaites to the disappeared Khazars (see note to p. 145). In the fourteenth century, Lithuania's Grand Duke Gedyminas transferred his capital to Trakai (Troki), a town located about 18 miles west of the present-day Lithuanian capital Vilnius. The greatest Lithuanian warrior and conqueror, Grand Duke Vytautas, brought some 300 Karaite men with families from the Crimea, settling them in Trakai and making the men his personal guard. During the

Shoah, the Lithuanian Karaites survived by making a case to the Nazi authorities that they were neither ethnically Jewish nor Judaic, but rather a Turkic tribe with a sui generis faith of its own, which recognizes the Old Testament (like other Judeo-Christian religions) but also incorporates some traditions of Islam. After the war, the small Karaite communities in the Soviet Union found themselves dwindling in numbers and isolated from both the Soviet and world Jewish community and the Karaite communities worldwide (about 25,000 Karaites live in modern-day Israel). At the present time, about 400 Karaites (or Karaims, as they prefer to call themselves) live in Lithuania, mainly in Trakai and Vilnius, continuing to insist that they are not of the Jews. They speak a Turkic language and are recognized in modern-day Lithuania as an ethnic minority of Turkic origin. Two Karaite prayer houses, called "kinessa" (cf. the Hebrew *knesset*), can be seen in Vilnius and Trakai; in Trakai, one of the main tourist attractions is Karaimu gatve (Karaite Street).

p. 57

*"you can't even roll your r's properly"*: In speaking Russian, some native speakers of Yiddish (and their children) would display a characteristically uvular ("grunted") *r* instead of the lingual ("tongue-trilled") Russian consonant (in Russian, this is known as *"kartavost' "*). This speech particularity made them targets of taunting and baiting, and anecdotes about identifying a Jew by his mis-rolled *r*'s belonged to the common repertoire of anti-Jewish jokes.

p. 59

*"I doubt that this shiker"*: Yiddish for "drunkard."

p. 60

*"As the Bible says, nation rose against nation"*: Andrey Mikheich is possibly paraphrasing Mark 13:8: "For nation shall rise against nation, and kingdom against kingdom: and there shall be earthquakes in divers places, and there shall be famines and troubles: these [are] the beginnings of sorrows" (from the King James Version; cf. the Synodal Russian text: *"Ibo vosstanet narod na narod i tsarstvo na*

*tsarstvo; i budut zemletryaseniya po mestam, i budut glady i smyateniya. Eto—nachalo bolezney"*).

p. 61

*Socialist-Revolutionaries:* Known in Russian by abbreviation *esery*, from *sotsialisty-revolyutsionery*; members of a major Russian populist-agrarian political party, with a powerful "combat" organization that practiced political violence. In 1918, the Socialist-Revolutionaries won a majority in the Constitutional Assembly disbanded by the Bolsheviks; by 1922, their activities were suppressed in the Soviet Union.

*Local military enlistment office: Voennyi komissariat* (literally, "military commissariat"), abbreviated as *voenkomat*.

p. 62

*Agricultural Expo:* See note to p. 4.

p. 66

*"The Wonderful Doctor":* "Chudesnyi doktor" (1897); short story by Aleksandr Kuprin (1870–1938), fictionalizing the life of the great Russian surgeon Nikolay Pirogov (1810–81).

*The Black Book and Schwambrania: Konduit i Shvambraniya*, popular book for teenagers by Lev Kassil (1905–70), originally published as two short novels, *The Black Book* (1930) and *Schwambrania* (1933).

*The Magician of the Emerald City:* First published in 1939 and subsequently revised, the magic novel *Volshebnik izumrudnogo goroda* by Aleksandr Volkov (1891–1977) was a splendid (if unacknowledged) adaptation of L. Frank Baum's *The Wonderful Wizard of Oz* (1900); in the postwar period, Volkov created a series of magic novels, which enjoyed a cult status among generations of Soviet teenagers.

*Three Fat Men: Tri tolsyaka* (1930); fairy tale-like short novel by Yuri Olesha (1899–1960).

*Dersu Uzala:* A 1923 novel about the legendary Far Eastern guide and hunter Derchu Odzhal by the explorer of the Far East, author, and ethnographer Vladimir Arsenyev (1872–1930).

*Chapayev:* A 1923 novel by Dmitri Furmanov (1891–1926), set during the Russian Civil War and mythologizing the Red Army commander Vasily Chapayev (1887–1919).

*School: Shkola* (1929); short autobiographical novel by Arkady Gaydar (1901–41), a prolific Soviet author of fiction for adolescents. Although carrying out ideological commissions, some of Gaydar's writings, especially the short story "The Blue Cup" (1935) and the short novel *The Fate of a Drummer* (1938), are more complex and subtle than what today's students of Soviet letters are willing to admit.

. . . *Kyukhelbeker:* cion of a Baltic-German family, Vil'gel'm Kyukhel'beker (Wilhelm Küchelbecker, 1797–1846) was a Russian Romantic poet and student of German idealist philosophy; Kyukhelbeker's life was fictionalized in the novel *Kyukhlya* (1925, "Kyukhlya" was the poet's nickname) by the literary scholar and author Yury Tynyanov (1894–1943).

p. 68

*Forestry Technology Academy . . . Krestinsky. . . . Tishchenko:* See notes to p. 3. Vyacheslav Tishchenko (1861–1941) was a distinguished Russian organic chemist, Academician of the Soviet Academy of Sciences, and, at the end of his life, a research professor at Leningrad University.

p. 69

*Yury Durov:* Danya Rayev refers to Yury V. Durov (1910–71), famous Russian circus animal trainer and clown from a prominent family of circus performers, founded by Anatoly Durov (1864–1916), brother of Yuri V. Durov's grandfather Vladimir Durov (1863–1934).

*Wait for Me: Zhdi menya* (1943): Film directed by Aleksandr Stolper and written by Konstantin Simonov (after his poem "Wait for me, and I'll return . . ."; see note to p. 25); featured in the lead role was Boris Blinov (1909–43), a Soviet actor who had played the part of Furmanov in Sergey and Georgy Vasiliev's film *Chapayev* (1934); see also note to p. 66.

p. 71

*misrolled r's:* See note to p. 57.

p. 79

*Kirov . . . A Boy from Urzhum . . . Seryozha Kostrikov . . . Kirov . . . Vyatka:* Kirov (Khlynov until 1781; Vyatka until 1934; renamed "Kirov" after Sergey Kirov) is a provincial capital 609 miles north-east of Moscow, 244 miles west of Perm. *A Boy from Urzhum (Mal'chik iz Urzhuma,* c. 1938) was a popular book for teenagers, by Antonina Golubeva (1899–1989), about the childhood and youth of Sergey Kirov (born Kostrikov; 1886–1934), prominent Soviet leader murdered in 1934. Stalin and his henchmen used Kirov's murder to crush the remaining elements of dissent within the Bolshevik Party and unleash the Great Terror. Kirov grew up in the town of Urzhum, in the Vyatka (Kirov) Province. Kirov was heroized in works of Soviet literature.

*School:* See notes to p. 66.

*The Son of a Regiment: Syn polka* (1945): popular novel for adolescents by Valentin Kataev (1897–1986), set during World War II. Here Danya Rayev superimposes his postwar impressions of reading the novel on the memories of his 1944 journey back to Leningrad.

p. 84

*"Say* korova!*":* After living in the Urals for three years, Danya Rayev acquired the local accent, characterized by the so-called *okan'e* ("o-non-reduction"). In the standard Russian, which Danya would have spoken in Leningrad before the evacuation, and which his friend Borya (casual diminutive *Bor'ka*) Smorodin, a survivor of the siege, speaks, the unstressed vowel *o* is pronounced in the reduced fashion, like an short *a.* However, in areas to the north and east of Moscow, particularly in the Russian North, the Volga area, and parts of the Urals, the locals population pronounced the unstressed *o* in a non-reduced manner, close to the way a stressed (and long) round o-vowel would be pronounced in Russian. The Russ-

ian word *korova* ("cow"), with its first unstressed and second stressed *o,* is a good test for one's regional accent in Russian.

pp. 86–88

*Lanskoy Road . . . Lanskoy Pond . . . General Lanskoy:* In 1844 General Pyotr Lanskoy (1799–1877) married Natalya Pushkina (née Goncharova [1812–63]), the widow of the great Russian writer Aleksandr Pushkin (1799–1837), who was mortally wounded at a duel. General Lanskoy had a summer house, then outside St. Petersburg, and presently in Lesnoye, the section of St. Petersburg where Danya Rayev lives (see notes to p. 1). The present-day Lanskoy Road extends north from Chernaya Rechka ("Black River"), the area of Pushkin's fatal duel, ending at Engels Prospekt, the street where Danya Rayev resides, just across the street from the former "Lanskoy property." The overgrown Lanskoy Pond and a dilapidated master's house remain to this day. In the short story "The Lanskoy Road" (1985), included in his collection *Jonah and Sarah: Jewish Stories of Russia and America* (Syracuse University Press, 2003), Shrayer-Petrov depicted a young Jewish boy's mystical encounter with Pushkin on the banks of Lanskoy Pond.

*Day and night, smoke billowed out of the bread factory:* Versions of this episode also appear as an autobiographical digression in Shrayer-Petrov's novel *Herbert and Nelly* (1992; revised 2006) and in his short story "Ottorzhenie" ("To Be Ripped Away"; 1998), included in *Jonah and Sarah: Jewish Stories of Russia and America.*

p. 89

*Vyborg District:* See notes to p. 1.

p. 90

*People's Duma of the Lesnoye-Udelnoye District . . . Kalinin:* Kalinin, Mikhail Ivanovich (1875–1946): prominent Bolshevik leader, from 1919 Chairman of the Central Executive Committee (VTSiK; TsiK after 1922), from 1938 Chairman of the Presidium of the Supreme Soviet, i.e., a titulary Soviet head of state. Following the February 1917 revolution, Kalinin was elected to the Petrograd

Council (soviet) of Workers' and Soldiers' Representatives (RSD) as a representative of the Vyborg Side. The two-story mansion which Danya Rayev recollects, presently no. 13/17 Bolotnaya Street, housed the Lesnoye-Udelnoye District Duma, whose chairman Kalinin was before the October Bolshevik Revolution. On October 16, 1917, the Central Committee of the Bolshevik Party convened in the mansion to discuss the planning of the October coup d'etat.

p. 94

*Jolly Fellows: Vesyolye rebyata*; Grigory Aleksandrov's 1934 popular cine-musical.

*Chapayev:* See notes to pp. 66 and 69.

p. 99

*Mikoyan:* Anastas Mikoyan (1895–1978), Soviet leader, one of Stalin's henchmen, subsequently one of Khrushchev's close associates; in 1937–58 deputy chairman of the Soviet Council of Ministers.

*became a shock worker:* Also "Stakhanovite," after Aleksey Stakhanov (1906–77), a Don Basin coal miner who in 1935 set a production record and initiated what became a national Soviet movement to exceed the production norms set by the plan.

p. 100

*Jewish Preobrazhenskoye cemetery:* Built in the early 1900s on the southeastern outskirts of St. Petersburg.

Notes to "Autumn in Yalta"

David Shrayer-Petrov wrote the short story "Autumn in Yalta" (Russ. "Osen' v Yalte") in 1992 in Providence, Rhode Island. Originally featured in the Philadelphia-based émigré annual *Poberezh'e (The Coast,* no. 3, 1994), it was reprinted in the St. Petersburg monthly *Neva* (no. 2, 1997). The story was included in Shrayer-

Petrov's recent collection of twenty-four stories, *Carp for the Gefilte Fish (Karp dlya farshirovannoy ryby*; Moscow, 2005).

p. 102

*Every time I had met her . . . Nabokov:* The epigraph is taken from one of Vladimir Nabokov's finest Russian short stories, "Spring in Fialta" ("Vesna v Fial'te"; 1936), set in a fictitious Mediterranean resort (see the afterword).

*Kolyma:* After the Kolyma River; Kolyma was a common name of a group of labor camps located in northeastern Siberia.

*Yalta:* City on the southeastern tip of the Crimean peninsula (administratively, part of Ukraine), the largest resort in the Crimea, and the site of the Yalta Conference (February 1945). Known for their mild and dry Mediterranean-like climate, Yalta and the resort towns nearby (Simeiz, Alupka, Gurzuf) have been a traditional destination for those suffering from respiratory and lung ailments. The area houses many sanatoria. On Chekhov's Yalta and his story "Lady with a Lapdog" ("Dama s sobachkoy"; 1899), see the afterword.

p. 103

*Strogino:* Residential district on the northwestern outskirts of Moscow, developed in the 1970s–1980s.

*Tverskaya:* Old name of Gorky Street, Moscow's central artery; the name was restored in the post-Soviet era.

p. 104

*Polechka:* Affectionate diminutive form of the name "Polina."

*Alazan Valley:* Georgian red semisweet wine.

*Simeiz:* Resort town on the coast of southern Crimea, 38 miles south of Yalta; see notes to p. 102.

p. 105

*box of these* papirosy: See notes to p. 9.

p. 108

*Crimean Tatars . . . allowed to return:* A Turkic ethnic group, the Crimean Tatars established themselves in the Crimea in the fifteenth century, as a Khanate. In the eighteenth century, the Crimea became part of the Russian Empire. At the end of World War II, the entire nation of Crimean Tatars was accused of having collaborated with the Nazis and was subjected to mass deportations to remote eastern areas of the Soviet Union. Only in 1967 was the charge of collaboration—ludicrous as any such collective charge can be—withdrawn, but the Soviet government did next to nothing to enable the Crimean Tatars to return to their homeland.

p. 109

*Petrograd Side:* see note to p. 1.

p. 112

*Maundy Thursday:* Also Holy Thursday; in the Christian calendar, the Thursday preceding Easter.

p. 114

*The Petty Demon: Melkii bes* (1902); major novel by Fyodor Sologub (1863–1927).

*"The Local Hooligan Abramashvili":* "Mestnyi khuligan Abramashvili" (1963); short story by Vassily Aksyonov (born 1932).

p. 116–17

*Yauza train stop:* Yauza stop is a suburban stop of the Moscow-Yaroslavl Railroad; the Yauza, the largest tributary of the Moscow (Moskva) River, originates in the center of Moscow and flows to the northeast through the Moscow province.

*Leningrad station . . . Yaroslavl station:* Along with Kazan station, these stations form the so-called Three Stations *(Tri vokzala),* a major railroad juncture in Moscow; each station was originally named after a large city of destination.

p. 121

*Likhachev Factory:* Zavod imeni I. A. Likhacheva (ZIL; formerly, Zavod imeni Stalina; ZIS) was a giant Moscow factory whose products included automobiles and refrigerators.

p. 124

*lived through the siege:* See note to p. 15.

p. 128

*Kutuzovsky Prospekt:* Thoroughfare running to the southwest of downtown Moscow; its original houses were built in the Stalinist monumentalist style and were historically populated with members of the Soviet elite.

*Opalikha:* Railroad stop and town to the east of Moscow; the relatively pristine area around Opalikha is considered by Muscovites to be a prestigious locale for a dacha or country house.

p. 133

*"I was a merry seamstress . . .":* "*Byla ya beloshveikoy . . .*"; one of the less subtle variants of lines three and four of this popular song is: "Then I became an actress / And turned into a whore" (*"Potom poshla v aktrissy / I stala blyad'yu"*).

Notes to "The Love of Akira Watanabe"

Written in Providence, Rhode Island, in 1999, the short story "The Love of Akira Watanabe" ("Lyubov' Akira Vatanabe") originally appeared in St. Petersburg's monthly *Neva* (no. 12, 2000) and was reprinted in the Russian-language edition of the New York *Forward* (April 14–20, 2000) and in the Moscow monthly *Nasha ulitsa (Our Street)* (no. 9, 2000). In 2004, the author revised the text and added a section to the ending. The story appeared in Shrayer-Petrov's recent collection of twenty-four stories, *Carp for the Gefilte Fish (Karp dlya farshirovannoy ryby;* Moscow, 2005).

p. 137

*In the story there is a he and a she . . . Pilnyak:* the epigraph is taken from "A Story about the Writing of Stories" ("Rasskaz o tom, kak pishutsya rasskazy"; 1926) by Boris Pilnyak (1894–1937). In Pilnyak's story, set in the late 1910s and 1920s, a Japanese officer stationed in the Russian Far East marries a Russian woman, takes her to Japan, and writes a revealing book about his marriage to—and intimacy with—a Russian woman. Informed by Pilnyak's travel experiences, Oriental, and specifically Japanese motifs, are notable in Pilnyak's works.

p. 142

*Novgorod:* See notes to p. 14.

p. 145

*Karaites:* See notes to p. 56.

*Khazars:* Members of a Turkic tribe whose state, located in the lower Volga basin, with the capital Itil in the Volga delta, was a regional power broker in the eighth to tenth centuries. At its height, the Khazar Kingdom stretched west as far as Kievan Rus. In the late eighth and early ninth centuries, the Khazar ruler and several thousand Khazar nobles converted to Judaism, and the Jewish faith subsequently spread to the lower strata of the multireligious Khazar society. In the eleventh century, the dominance of the Khazar Kingdom was severed by Kievan Rus, and the remaining Khazars were dispersed in the thirteenth century, following the Tatar-Mongol invasion. Various theories, some based on historical, archaeological, and ethnographic evidence, have been advanced to identify the descendants of the Khazars among the region's Turkic and Slavic groups and among the Jewish communities of Europe and Asia.

Notes to "Carp for the Gefilte Fish"

David Shrayer-Petrov composed the short story "Carp for the Gefilte Fish" ("Karp dlya farshirovannoy ryby") in 1996 in Providence, Rhode Island. It appeared in three installments in the New York-based émigré weekly *Interesnaya gazeta (Interesting paper)* (nos. 27–29 [July-August] 1998). The story lent its title to Shrayer-Petrov's recent collection of twenty-four stories, *Carp for the Gefilte Fish (Karp dlya farshirovannoy ryby*; Moscow, 2005).

p. 150

*Borisov:* Industrial district center in the Minsk province of Belarus, 41 miles to the northeast of Minsk. In 1959–60, David

Shrayer-Petrov served as a military physician in a tank army stationed in Borisov.

*only as* shiker: See notes to p. 59.

p. 151

*Fedyushka:* Diminutive of Fyodor.

p. 152

*shock worker:* See notes to p. 99.

*plot of the "doctor-murderers":* Commonly known as the "Doctors' Plot." On January 13, 1953, *Pravda* announced the arrest of a group of leading Soviet physicians and medical researchers, the majority of them with characteristically Jewish names, who were charged with "sabotage" and with "murdering" Soviet leaders. Rumors circulated that this was a pretext to incite pogroms and massive deportation of the Jewish population. After Stalin's death on March 5, 1953, the new "collective leadership" denounced the "Doctors' Plot" as a provocation and released the falsely accused doctors.

p. 153

*Zhodino:* Town 11 miles southwest of Borisov; see notes to p. 150.

p. 154

*Shrovetide:* See notes to p. 28.

p. 156

*pirozhki:* Russian pastries; fried or baked small pies (patties) with various types of fillings.

p. 158

*"my* bobe *used to make":* Yiddish for "grandmother."

p. 161

*look at that* nekeiva: Yiddish for "whore," "cunt"; from Hebrew for "female," literally "receptacle."

*Fedenka:* Affectionate diminutive of Fyodor.

*Rayushka:* Diminutive of Raya.

p. 170

*Sun Valley Serenade:* H. Bruce Humberstone's 1941 musical comedy; "trophy" copies of this and other American films were brought to the Soviet Union at the end of World War II and continued to be shown around the country as late as the 1980s.

p. 178

*muzhik:* Russian word meaning literally "peasant" and, figuratively and colloquially, "man."

p. 180

"Genug *already*": Yiddish for "enough."

p. 182

*kasha:* Yiddish (of Slavic origin) for "gruel" or "cereal," commonly used to refer to buckwheat meal.

# Afterword

*Maxim D. Shrayer*

For many Anglo-American readers, the "Yalta" in the title of this collection readily suggests the Yalta Conference (February 1945), where the "Big Three" allied leaders, Churchill, Roosevelt, and Stalin, redrew the map of post-Nazi Europe.* Already in the Yalta of 1945, both the Eastern Bloc and the Cold War—which surrounded David Shrayer-Petrov during the first three decades of his literary career—had become a looming reality. But for many Russian readers, Yalta is, above all, Chekhov's Yalta. Writing to his sister Mariya on July 14, 1888, Anton Chekhov (1860–1904) described his first impressions of Yalta, which never fully abandoned him:

> Looking at the shore from aboard the ship, I realized why it hadn't yet inspired a single poet or given a plot to any decent artist-belletrist. Doctors and wealthy ladies advertise it, and that's its main strength. Yalta is a cross of something European, resembling pictures of Nice, with something tacky and country-fairish. . . . (M.D.S: My literal translations, here and hereafter unless otherwise noted)

Chekhov kept returning to Yalta, and spending time in other coastal resorts nearby. To the poet and translator Aleksey N. Pleshcheev,

*Parts of the afterword originally appeared in the magazine *Lifestyles,* vol. 33, no. 193 (2004).

Chekhov wrote these aphoristic lines on August 3, 1889: "In Yalta, there are many young ladies, but not a single pretty one. Many littérateurs, but not one talented person. Much wine, but not a drop of a decent one. The only good things here are the sea and the ambling horses." In Yalta, a number of women, including younger and older actresses, passed through the pages of Chekhov's life, some vanishing into the blank margins, others resurfacing in the black print of his stories and plays. Yalta's evanescent mix of "something European" and something Oriental (which also distinguishes the atmosphere of many Mediterranean resorts) did inspire Russia's greatest "artist-belletrist," as it has also inspired other Russian authors, providing them with a vibrant setting and an evocative place of composition.

Anton Chekhov in Fiume and Genoa, Ivan Bunin in Grasse and Juan-les-Pins, Vladimir Nabokov in Cannes and Menton . . . Whenever I have the good fortune to find myself on the Riviera, voices of Russian writers reach me there, dispatching long trains of biographical and literary associations. Illness and love, war and exile have chased Russian writers and their fictional representatives to the Mediterranean and Crimean shores. In Yalta, Abbazia (Opatija), Ospedaletti, Nice and other Rivieraized resorts, the very air conjures up a sense of unrecognizable, foreboding familiarity that so nurtures a literary imagination . . .

In October–November 2004, I spent five weeks at an artists' and authors' colony in Bogliasco, a Ligurian fishing village east of Genoa. Despite the charming distractions of a small Italian town still unspoiled by the development and wealth of Northern Italy, despite the view of Golfo Paradiso from my studio, I managed to work hard at Bogliasco. I was finishing a project of almost seven years: an anthology of Jewish-Russian literature from the early 1800s to the early 2000s. I faced a deadline. And I lived for the first ten days in anticipation of my wife's visit.

Because practicing primary care doctors have a difficult time leaving their patients, Karen could only come for two weeks. She arrived the fourth week in October, and the day after, we walked from our villa down to the pocket-size Bogliasco train stop. On a misty late October morning, a commuter train—graffiti, Romany women with infants, and truant Italian schoolchildren—zipped us through Genoa'a densely populated suburbs, their smatterings of clothing boutiques, *gelatterias,* and tobacconist shops visible from the train. On the right, we saw mountains, smoke (it was the season to burn branches) rising from the olive-green middle of the slopes, and the barren tops with the occasional pyramidal tree. On the left, when not in the throat of a tunnel, we saw the sea, beige and salmon villas, toothed cliffs, umbrella pines. I memorized the landscape without being conscious of its elements. During that train ride to Genoa, I thought of destiny. I remembered myself as a teenage re-fusenik reading about and imagining all the places a Soviet—especially a Jew—could only dream of visiting: the Italian Riviera, Venice, Capri. And when I saw—through the dusty windows of the train pulling into Stazione Brignole—the hilly skyline of Genoa studded with towers, domes, and palazzi, like a gilded chessboard of another life, I told my American-born wife that the odd moments of happiness come from knowing your destiny. It was mine to love her and to translate my father's stories.

The subject of a writer's destiny was still on my mind the next day, as Karen and I walked from Bogliasco to its fancier neighbor, Nervi, Genoa's easternmost suburb. We descended Via Aurelia past a now-empty Pit Bar. Bearing to the left, we passed a small baroque church. We left behind a dilapidated grand villa, sunk in a shady park. Turning left toward the water, we strolled past a former train station, now a private residence with an overgrown back garden, where overripe persimmons and bursting, forgotten eggplants hung from their burdened branches and vines. We passed a little harbor with a pebbly beach, old boats, and a boarded-up café. Enthroned on a bench, two swarthy keepers of the vessels were so engrossed in solving the affairs of the world they barely responded to our greetings. Karen and I climbed up some steps, and there it was, the locally famed boardwalk, the *passagiata al mare*.

The *passagiata* stretches along the water for about a mile, ending in the old Nervi seaport. When we first walked there, the sun was setting over the sea, to our left. Elegantly dressed Italians, many of them with lapdogs of various breeds, sizes, and shapes, sauntered back and forth or congregated around benches facing the water. Trains whooshed by, the speedy intercity trains and the slower commuter ones. The *passagiata* was built on cliff ledges and probably on remains of medieval fortresses and walls. Narrow steps with rope railings went down to pools of water that, I have heard, owes its azure blueness to the pollution level of the Mediterranean. Using bread as bait, fishermen with long poles cast their lines from the flat platforms in the cliffs. Exhausted-looking Berber peddlers offered their wares—leather goods and music CDs. Ancient pines hung over the water, the cliffs, and the villas. The cafés with pink tablecloths and woven chairs looked more Viennese than Genoese. On our right, we left behind an underground passage to the Nervi train station and, on our left, the Hotel Ristorante Marinella, a lovers' retreat, right on the boardwalk. Although late October, the evening air was still hot. Sheltered from the winds by the surrounding cliffs and the maritime pines, perched betwixt sun and cliff wall, the *passagiata* was a greenhouse by the sea, a northerner's overheated dream.

We were approaching the spot where the road curves sharply before it drops into the seaport when Karen exclaimed, "Look, Sholem Aleichem!" And she pointed to a plaque immured in a concave cliff wall. Taking in so much else and happy to be reunited with my wife, I probably would not have noticed the plaque, if it had not caught Karen's eye. Right above the plaque stood an elegant, peach-colored stucco building. I took out a notebook to write down the commemoration. "A ricordo dei lunghi anni di soggiorno a Nervi del brilliante scrittore in lingue Yiddish Shalom Rabinovitz in arte 'Sholem Alejchem' (1859–1916) [*sic*]." The plaque had been put up recently, in February 2003, it said. As I stood in the middle of the boardwalk, a small crowd of onlookers gathered around me: two disheveled mothers with strollers and screaming babies, a group of bejeweled older ladies in fur coats, two distinguished elderly gentlemen wearing fine-tailored sport coats and cravats, and a dreamy young woman with an anxious Pomeranian on a long leash. I copied the inscription slowly, trying not to introduce any errors into the Italian, and I had a chance to see that the onlookers were equally bemused by the plaque itself, which they clearly had not noticed before, and by the peculiar foreigner studiously writing down what was written on it. In "memory of the long years" that a "brilliant writer in the Yiddish language" spent . . . in Nervi?

Well, it did not take me long to discover that Nervi had been an important coordinate in the life of Sholem Aleichem, just as the Ligurian coast, where I was a lucky resident that autumn, has been for many other writers who came from Russia. In autumn of 1908, after being diagnosed with pulmonary tuberculosis, Sholem Aleichem moved to Italy with his wife, Olga, and their daughters. At the time, because of its climate and location, Nervi was considered an ideal place for pulmonary patients to winter. From 1908 until 1913, when doctors pronounced Sholem Aleichem "recovered," he would spend the cold months in Nervi, dividing the rest of the year between the "magic" mountains of Switzerland and the spas of Germany's Black Forest.

Genoa had a small, Sephardic community. During the Nervi months, Sholem Aleichem lived in isolation from his native Yiddish-speaking milieu. The Italians identified Sholem Aleichem and his family as "Russians." A Jew in Russia and a Russian abroad, despite the remoteness of home, Sholem Aleichem worked prolifically during his European exile. Those were the years of his growing fame and international reputation, especially in Russian translation and among Russia's mainstream readers and writers. The "good years" lasted until the outbreak of World War I and Sholem Aleichem's move to America, where he died in 1916.

Although Sholem Aleichem was fond of Nervi and the Ligurian vistas outside his windows, he did not take well to the contrast of hot sunny days and cold windy nights. In *My Father, Sholem Aleichem* (1968), Marie Waife-Goldberg recalled her father's first winter in Nervi:

> The nights in Nervi were agonizing, for he could not sleep for coughing. . . . On a small table near his bed lay the book which was placed there each evening and a chair for the watcher to sit down and read to him until he fell asleep. The book was usually a collection of short stories by my father's favorite author, Chekhov, in the original Russian.

A "Yiddish Chekhov," they called him at home, and Sholem Aleichem was not unaware of this comparison. He wrote perfect literary Russian and, like his junior contemporaries, such as David Aizman (1869–1922) and Semyon Yushkevich (1868–1927), Sholem Aleichem might have become an excellent Jewish author in the Russian language if he had not chosen—had not been destined—to become a great Yiddish writer instead. He imbued his works with the best contributions of Russian writers, past and present, especially Gogol and Chekhov. By the time Sholem Aleichem had gained a broad Russian-language audience in Russia, Anton Chekhov, a contemporary of his, was gone. He died at a German spa town, of the same lung ailment that would later bring Sholem Aleichem to Italy . . .

I kept thinking about our living so close to the place where Sholem Aleichem spent a total of several years. Karen went back to Boston, and I stayed on for two more weeks at Bogliasco. I focused on the editing and cotranslating of *Autumn in Yalta: A Novel and Three*

*Stories.* One of my tasks as this volume's editor was to check the translated texts against my father's Russian originals. A product of exile and a casualty of imperfect bilingualism, I could not help thinking that the Sholem Aleichem plaque, which my wife had discovered in Nervi, was a fatidic clue. One that applied to my own life as my father's son and translator, to Jewish-Russian writers' dialogue with Chekhov, and to my father's tales of exile that were gaining their final English-language contours under my laptop-tapping fingers.

*Autumn in Yalta* is the second book of my father's works that I have helped to English. In contrast to *Jonah and Sarah: Jewish Stories of Russia and America,* which appeared in the Library of Modern Jewish Literature in 2003 and retrospectively showcased his short fiction written both in the Soviet Union and in emigration, *Autumn in Yalta* features only the works my father has written in America since immigrating here in 1987. This volume is structured by the chronology, not of its composition, but of the events depicted in its works: childhood, World War II and the Shoah, 1930s and 1940s (*Strange Danya Rayev*); youth and disenchantment, 1960s and 1970s ("Autumn in Yalta"); and emigration, 1980s and 1990s ("The Love of Akira Watanabe" and "Carp for the Gefilte Fish").

Even more so than *Jonah and Sarah, Autumn in Yalta* is a labor of family love. My father wrote the stories in Russian; I edited and annotated the volume and cotranslated two of its stories. My mother translated another. My wife, herself a daughter of Jewish immigrants, both witnessed and welcomed these tales' rebirth in the English language. This book validates my family's experiences as Jewish-Russian cultural transplants from the former Soviet Union to the United States. Furthermore, the backgrounds of the other cotranslators—Arna B. Bronstein, an American-born descendant of immigrants from the Russian Empire, the Polish-born Aleksandra I. Fleszar, who has spent much of her professional career in America, and the Armenian-born Margarit Tedevosyan, who arrived in

America as a high school student, collectively underscore the extent to which today's American culture is genuinely one of multilingual émigrés and transplants.

A dual name, David Shrayer-Petrov, betokens my father's literary career. Born in 1936 in Leningrad (St. Petersburg), he descends, on his father's side, from Podolian millers and, on his mother's, from Lithuanian rabbis. As young people, both of my father's parents (he an engineer; she a chemist) made the transition, tantamount to emigration, from the former Pale of Settlement to Leningrad in the 1920s. Growing up, my father heard Yiddish in the traditional home of his paternal grandparents. Evacuated from Leningrad as the Nazi siege set in, he spent three years in a remote Russian village in the Urals, almost nine hundred miles from Moscow and Leningrad and from the front lines (the experience informs the novel *Strange Danya Rayev*). A Jewish youth coming of age in postwar Leningrad, my father formulated the questions, which his writings probe to this day: "Do Jews belong in Russia?" "Is assimilation (im)possible?"

Starting medical school in 1953, the year of the anti-Semitic "Doctors' Plot," whose evil perpetrators were interrupted by Stalin's death, my father entered the literary scene as a poet and translator in the middle to late 1950s, during Khrushchev's Thaw. In 1958, on the advice of the influential Jewish-Russian poet Boris Slutsky (1919–86), he adopted the pen name "David Petrov," the surname being derived from his father's Russianized given name "Petr" (Peysakh). This assimilatory gesture hardly facilitated the publication of my father's poetry in the Soviet Union. His first poetry collection was derailed in 1964 in Leningrad, following the trial of the poet Joseph Brodsky, with whom my father was friendly at the time. During his Soviet years, he made a name for himself mainly as a literary translator, especially from Lithuanian and the South-Slavic languages.

After graduating from Leningrad's First Medical School in 1959, my father served as a military physician in Belarus. Two years after his marriage, in 1962, to my mother, Emilia Shrayer (née Polyak; born 1940), he completed his Ph.D. dissertation at the Leningrad Institute of Tuberculosis (defending it in 1966). His dissertation studied the impact of staphylococcal infections on the occurrence of tuberculosis in white mice, and its echoes can be heard in the story "Autumn in Yalta," in the experiments of its protagonist, Dr. Samoylovich, as well as in my father's early story "Mimosas for My Grandmother's Grave" (1997; written in 1984). In 1964, my parents moved to my mother's native Moscow, where I was born in 1967, and where my father worked as a researcher at the Gamaleya Institute of Epidemiology and Microbiology, from 1967 to 1978.

From his earliest poems, my father explored the dual nature of Jewish identity in Diaspora. Although he managed to publish a collection of poetry *(Canvasses,* 1967) and two books of essays in the 1970s, most of his writings were too controversial for Soviet officials to permit them to be published. Nor did his occasional flights into prescribed Soviet subjects (e.g., space exploration, the construction of the Baikal-Amur Railroad) in poetry, essays, and song lyrics earn him the trust of the regime. Despite recommendations by prominent writers such as Viktor Shklovsky, my father was admitted to the Union of Soviet Writers only after a protracted battle, in 1976. The manuscript of what would have been his second poetry collection, *Winter Ship,* never made it through the icebound straits of the "Soviet Writer" publishing house.

By the early 1970s, relations between Jews and Gentiles had become a principal concern of my father's writing. At a spring poetry festival in Vilnius, Lithuania, in 1978, he recited a poem of protest, "My Slavic Soul" (1975). That spring, I was almost eleven. I remember a shiver passing through the Lithuanian audience as my father read from the stage about the poet's "Slavic" soul, which abandons his "Jewish" body to hide in a hayloft. Immediately after my father's return from Lithuania to Moscow, officials of the Union of Soviet Writers threatened him with expulsion. Ostracism for having transgressed the unspoken taboo on treatment of Jewish subjects weaned my father off his last illusions, pushing him to emigrate.

A family picture taken in 1978 shows my parents and me on an annual vacation in our beloved resort of Pärnu on the western coast of Estonia. Suntanned and caressed by Baltic winds, we look completely unprepared for future hardships. When, in January 1979, we applied for exit visas, my mother lost her academic teaching job, and my father his research position at the Academy of Medical Sciences. Neither my mother's dedication to her students nor my father's innovative research on staphylococcal infections, which had helped save peoples' lives, mattered to the Soviet state. My parents' careers were mutilated. We applied to emigrate when I was eleven. More than anything, I wanted to leave behind my stifling Soviet school and my classmates' habitual xenophobia. Like thousands of other Jewish families, we found ourselves in refusenik limbo. The shock of realizing that, along with my parents, I, too, had become a refusenik marked the end of my childhood.

Following my father's expulsion from the Union of Soviet Writers, the galleys of three of his forthcoming books were destroyed (he had already corrected the proofs of one of them and vetted the illustrations). The three books never appeared. My father was banned from publishing in the Soviet Union. In 1979–80, while driving an illegal cab at night and working in an emergency room lab, he conceived of a panoramic novel about the destinies of Jewish refuseniks. *Herbert and Nelly,* my father's novel exploring the exodus of Soviet Jews, will likely be his next work to be translated into English. (The complete edition of *Herbert and Nelly* was published in Moscow in 1992 and long-listed for the 1993 Booker Russian Prize; a revised edition appeared in St. Petersburg in 2006).

After we requested permission to emigrate, the KGB launched a series of measures against my parents, ranging from arrests and physical harassment to a smear campaign in the press. The persecution intensified in 1985, when plans for the publication of the first part of my father's novel about refuseniks were announced in Israel. (The first part of the Russian original appeared in Jerusalem, in 1986.) I remember the strange looks my university classmates gave me, as though I was related to a death row inmate. In central and provincial Soviet newspapers, my father was labeled a "Zionist" author and accused of "infecting" Jews with a "hostile" ideology. A real threat of being charged with anti-Soviet activity and imprisoned hung over my father's head; for parts of the fall of 1985, he went into hiding. The mounting pressures of being stalked by the Soviet secret police brought on a heart attack and subsequent hospitalization. Plainclothes KGB thugs waited for my father outside the hospital ward. On a frosty December night, my mother and I passed the open letter my father had written to his literary brethren in the West to a *New York Times* correspondent. Urgently appealing to politicians and diplomats, Jewish organizations in the United States, Canada, and Great Britain pushed for our cause. Courageous Americans, Canadians, and Britons visited us in Moscow, taking our pictures, showing their support.

A refusenik's isolation, coupled with the absurdity of being a Jewish writer who is at once silenced by and shackled to Russia, made my father's last Soviet decade prolific in spite of his persecution. From 1979 to 1987, he wrote two novels, several plays, a memoir, and many stories and verses. Permission to emigrate finally came in April 1987. After a long forced good-bye, our leave-taking was short. Our whole lives packed into five suitcases, we left the Soviet Union on June 7, 1987.

Spending the summer in Austria and Italy, we arrived in the United States on August 26, 1987. Providence, the petite capital of the smallest American state, became my parents' new home. Emigration and an outwardly peaceful life in New England accorded my father both distance from and perspective on his Russian past.

His arrival in the West brought forth new publications, including six novels and over forty shorter works of fiction. In January 2006, my father will turn seventy. He continues to divide his time between writing and doing cancer research (experimental therapy). In many of his works, notably in the title story of *Autumn in Yalta* and in the novel *French Cottage* (1999), David Shrayer-Petrov's medical interests overlap with those of a fictionist.

Before turning to the subject of my father's exilic dialogue with doctor and author Anton Chekhov, and with Russian-American master Vladimir Nabokov (1899–1977), I would like to take a step back and revisit the years of World War II, Shrayer-Petrov's formative years. It was then that the future writer experienced the unspoiled richness of the Russian language as the peasants in the Urals still spoke it. Shrayer-Petrov depicted the birth of a dual, Jewish-Russian identity in his autobiographical novel *Strange Danya Rayev*. Set in Stalinist Russia in the late 1930s–1940s, the novel focuses on the wartime childhood experiences of Danya (Daniil) Rayev, its Jewish-Russian protagonist and narrator-storyteller. Danya and his mother Stella are evacuated from the besieged Leningrad to Siva, a village in the Ural Mountains. In Siva, far away from the war front and the life he knew as a small child, Danya nearly forgets about his otherness, assimilating after a Russian peasant fashion. When he returns to the destroyed city of Leningrad in 1944, Danya confronts challenges of his dual identity while also learning that his father, a decorated naval officer, has a "second wife" and started a new family. Told in a confessional voice, the novel ends as its young protagonist regains the bitter knowledge of anti-Semitism while celebrating the Soviet victory over Nazism on the ruins of his native city and family.

Young Danya Rayev of *Strange Danya Rayev* and the older Samoylovich of "Autumn in Yalta" are in essence the same Jewish boy from the author's native city of Leningrad or, to put it differently, Samoylovich is a projection of Danya Rayev onto postwar Jewish-Soviet history. The transparent links between their names, on the one hand, and the quintessentially Jewish (especially so in Soviet Russia) names and corresponding books in the Hebrew Bible, on the other, highlight the affinity between the two characters (Daniil = Daniel; the surname "Samoylovich" derives from "Samoyla" = Samuel).

By reading *Strange Danya Rayev* and "Autumn in Yalta" in succession between the same covers, readers can best experience the transposition of the theme of Jewish-Russian identity in both texts. Danya spends the war years away from Leningrad and the Nazi siege, which extinguished possibly as many as a million lives. Although the episode with the police officer Dodonov and the mysterious Karaite Bobukh serves as an early warning, Danya does not consciously suffer from visceral, still incomprehensible anti-Semitism until after his return home in 1944. The casual anti-Semitism of an adult, the woman baker at the bread factory, shocks and literally nauseates him; the furtive, malicious baiting by his classmate Mincha transforms Danya into a Jewish fighter. Recall the episode in which the adult Samoylovich, himself a survivor of the siege of Leningrad, remembers his first day in elementary school, when he is surrounded by a group of hungry children asking for food. Nowhere in the story does Shrayer-Petrov identify his protagonist as "Jewish"—although readers are given cultural identity markers: Samoylovich's last name, the occasional Yiddish expression his grandmother drops behind the narrative scenes, the Jewish chopped herring, *farhsmak,* she prepares for him. In this brief recollection, occurring in a moment of desperate reckoning with the past, readers face the habitual anti-Semitism of a group of Russian, non-Jewish children, who stereotypically believe that their Jewish classmate has more food than they do, and that his family (Samoylovich has lost both parents in the war) is richer, better-off than theirs. The adult Samoylovich is only a partial extension of Danya

Rayev. Samoylovich never learns to fight back, to be tough, to suspect malice in others (or, as Shrayer-Petrov put it in December 2004, responding to my e-mail query), "Samoylovich becomes Danya—the fighter—too late"). A Jewish doctor in post-Stalinist Soviet Union, one who has lived as a young man through Soviet Jewry's darkest years, Samoylovich continues to cure those around him with love, with his "soul"—regardless of their origins. A writer-doctor, Shrayer-Petrov creates a privileged protagonist in Dr. Samoylovich. Having sacrificed ten years of freedom for his beloved, the actress Polechka, who is not Jewish, Samoylovich returns to Moscow from a prison camp in Siberia, seeking—or not seeking—to settle scores, to come to terms with his ruptured past. Judging by the reference to the re-renaming of Leningrad, which occurred in 1991, the story ends during the liminal years 1991–92. A former doctor and medical researcher, the Soviet Jew Samoylovich has been reduced to an underground man of sorts, a nighttime driver of an illegal cab. Yet the flourishing of Samoylovich's love for Polechka dates to the Leningrad of the late 1960s, when he was still a successful academic, and she a "promising" young actress, though also a TB patient. The story culminates in the late 1970s or early 1980s, at a tuberculosis sanatorium in the resort town of Simeiz, south of Yalta. Which brings us back to the tubercular Dr. Chekhov, his Yalta, and the biographical and historical background behind the composition of "Autumn in Yalta," the title story of this volume.

A deterioration of Chekhov's health in 1897 led the writer to move to Yalta, where he was based during the last five years of his life. In Yalta, from 1899 to 1904, Chekhov wrote *Three Sisters* and *The Cherry Orchard,* and a number of his greatest stories, among them, "Lady with a Lapdog" (1899). In October 1898, Chekhov started building a house in a suburb of Yalta. One of Dr. Chekhov's contributions was his well-publicized 1899 appeal to the public to donate funds for the construction of a charity tuberculosis sanatorium in Yalta. (Lung ailments and stories of desire between doctors and their TB patients are a notable subject of Chekhov's fiction and drama, from the early "Belated Flowers" [1882], with its Dr. Toporkov and the dying Princess Priklonskaya, to *Ivanov* [1887], with the "kikess" Anna Petrovna, née Sara Abramson, and the compassionate Dr. Lvov.)

At the turn of the century, Chekhov's presence had energized Yalta's provincial cultural life. The Moscow Art Theater gave performances in Yalta in April 1900. Some of Russia's best writers who walked in Chekhov's footsteps—Maxim Gorky, Ivan Bunin, Aleksandr Kuprin—visited him in Yalta. And so did Olga Knipper-Chekhova, an actress at the Moscow Arts Theater, both before and after she and Chekhov were married in 1901. Sometimes feeling like an exile in Yalta, Chekhov longed to see Knipper-Chekhova and pined for Moscow and central Russia. Yalta's cold, stormy winter weather was hardly good for his health. Chekhov left Yalta in May 1904, never to see it again.

In Yalta, perhaps more so than elsewhere, Chekhov socialized with Jewish (and Karaite) acquaintances, including Jewish doctors. In the fall of 1898, Chekhov stayed in Yalta at the dacha of Dr. Isaak Altshuller. Another colorful Jewish acquaintance was Isaak Sinani, owner of a local book and tobacco shop, which was a meeting place of Yalta's tubercular exiles. From the 1880s to the 1900s, Chekhov observed and described the hunger for Russian literature among acculturated Jews. In "My Life" (1896), Chekhov wrote about a southern provincial town where "only Jewish adolescents frequented the local . . . libraries." In "Ionych" (1898), Chekhov stressed again that "the people in S. read very little, and at the local library they said that if it hadn't been for unmarried ladies and young Jews, one might as well close the library." The Jewish question certainly preoccupied the creator of *Ivanov*, "Steppe" (1888), and "Rothchild's Fiddle" (1894); during his final years in Yalta, Chekhov was likely to hear from his acquaintances among the Jewish-Russian intelligentsia about the birth of Zionism . . .

Chekhov's Yalta runs like a watermark through the pages of Shrayer-Petrov's story. Reading "Autumn in Yalta," one comes across various telltale signs of its author's dialogue with Chekhov's "Lady with a Lapdog," a masterpiece of short fiction. In "Lady with a Lap Dog," the lovers Anna and Gurov first meet in autumnal Yalta. And, in a significant structural reversal of Chekhov's narrative, Polechka and Samoylovich meet for the "last" time also in the Crimean resort and in autumn, during the so-called *barkhatnyi sezon* (velvet season). This fateful meeting, which leads to Samoylovich's "crime," brings the story to the brink of a Chekhovian adultery narrative: just like Anna, Polechka (as she is quick to inform Samoylovich) is a "married lady." Indicators of this literary dialogue—occurring almost a century later and across the Atlantic—are numerous in Shrayer-Petrov's story. Consider, for instance, the scene in a Yalta café where Polechka asks if she is "contagious," and Samoylovich replies, in a seeming non sequitur, "I love you, Polechka." The scene recalls both the first meeting of Gurov and Anna in a café on the Yalta embankment and the subsequent episode with the arrival of a steamship and a festive crowd of vacationers (in a bout of hyperrealism, Chekhov has planted more generals than one would ever expect to see on any one day on the waterfront of a Riviera resort). Even Sazonova (Sazonova-Casanova?), the name of the fictitious, ageless stage diva in "Autumn in Yalta," hints at a real-life contemporary of Chekhov, the writer Sofia Smirnova-Sazonova (1852–1921), who recorded in her diary for July 1899: "I saw Chekhov on the promenade. He sits all alone on a little bench" (I quote from Donald Rayfield's *Chekhov: A Life* [1997]).

"Autumn in Yalta" might not have become an exilic, Russian-American story if, besides Chekhov's Yalta, it had not also dialogued with Nabokov's Fi(Y)alta. By taking an epigraph from Nabokov's fabled tale of love and exile "Spring in Fialta" (1936), Shrayer-Petrov signals, not only his debt to Nabokov, but also his awareness that Chekhov's "Lady with a Lapdog" had served as a major point of departure for Nabokov's story. Composed in Berlin in 1936 and published the same year in Paris, "Spring in Fialta" belonged—by Nabokov's own admission—to "the leading troika" of his stories. Comparing "Spring in Fialta" to Chekhov's "Lady with a Lap Dog" and Kafka's "The Metamorphosis," Nabokov called it an "exemplary" short story. (In 1956, the New York-based Chekhov Publishing House issued Nabokov's third collection of Russian stories under the title *Spring in Fialta*.) Mindful of Chekhov (his "predecessor," as he put it), Nabokov set his story in interwar Europe and created a fictional resort. Nabokov's Fialta, with echoes of the Dalmatian Fiume (now Rijeka) and the Crimean Yalta, hosted exiles whose lives conflated lofty memories of Russia with the quotidian realities of Europe in the early 1930s.

Nabokov's "Spring in Fialta" (the *"spring* season," the *"spring* of memories," and the "narrative *spring*") resonates through Shrayer-Petrov's "Autumn in Yalta," inviting comparatists to investigate a three-generational literary dynamic. Consider, for instance, that in "Lady with a Lapdog," omission and silence are Chekhov's chosen devices to depict sexuality. Immediately after Gurov and Anna disappear to her hotel room (to make love), Gurov is shown eating watermelon to the accompaniment of Anna's sobs and her self-flagellation as a "bad . . . woman." In Nabokov's covertly modernist text, sex is depicted partly with metaphor, partly with allusion, and partly with silence. Consider this recollection by the narrating protagonist Vasenka ("Victor" in the English version of the story, first published in *Harper's Bazaar* in 1947):

[Nina] turned and rapidly swaying on slender ankles led me along the sea-blue carpeted passage. A chair at the door of her room supported a tray with the remains of breakfast . . . and because of our sudden draft a wave of muslin embroidered with white dahlias got sucked in, with a shudder and knock, between the responsive halves of the French window, and only when the door had been locked did they let go that curtain with something like a blissful sigh; and a little later I stepped out on the diminutive cast-iron balcony beyond to inhale a combined smell of dry maple leaves and gasoline. (Translated by Vladimir Nabokov and Peter A. Pertzoff)

Even though, in Shrayer-Petrov's love story, the classical Russian chastity of Chekhov's art yields to Nabokov's more nuanced and liberal portrayal of sexuality and lovemaking, and even though Shrayer-Petrov brings a medical researcher's, rather than a lepidopterist's, eye to his tale, Dr. Samoylovich still refuses to refer to Polechka's sexual numbness in clinical terms. "That," he calls her unresponsiveness, perhaps forgetting to recognize his own lovemaking as that of an "eternal student" (pace Chekhov). It is Polechka, not Samoylovich, who resorts to medical terminology, evoking, as do both Chekhov and Nabokov in their own ways, the fundamental divide between the world of sexuality and the world of romantic fulfillment. "Maybe my own exalted imagination or how much I was actually driven to him stood in the way of my normal sensations?" Polechka confesses to Samoylovich after the New Year's party and her "rendezvous" with Kaftanov. "You know what I mean, don't you, Samoylovich? You doctors call it frigidity. I would call it waiting for a miracle. I've been waiting for it my whole life."

Thus writing on the shores of New England and modeling a life in his former homeland, Shrayer-Petrov returns from the fictionality of Nabokov's locale (Fialta) to the reality of Chekhov's Yalta. This re-fictionalized space of the resort blends the Jewish-Russian writer's own exilic recollections with layers of collective memory stored in the Russian language he has brought with him to America. When Samoylovich waits for Polechka at his Crimean seaside cottage, finally prepared to "believe" that "Polechka had deceived him," does he also recall, as I do when I read Shrayer-Petrov's story, this episode from the middle of "Lady with a Lapdog"?

> In Oreanda [Anna and Gurov] sat on a bench, not far from the church, looking silently at the sea down below. Yalta was hardly visible through the morning fog; white clouds stood motionless upon the mountain peaks. Leaves didn't stir on the trees, crickets screamed, and the monotonous, hollow sound of the sea coming up from below, spoke of quietude, of the eternal sleep awaiting us all. The same sound could be heard from down below when there was no Yalta or Oreanda, and it was still heard now and would continue with the same indifference and hollowness when we were no longer around. And in this permanence, this sheer indifference to the life and death of each one of us, there lies, perhaps, the promise of our eternal salvation, of life's uninterrupted stride on earth, of continuous movement toward perfection.

Does Samoylovich the Jewish idealist turned gypsy cab driver still believe, however faintly, in this Chekhovian "movement toward perfection" when he encounters his past after having returned from the labor camp? (Shrayer-Petrov suggested to me on New Year's morning of 2005 that the character of Dr. Samoylovich might be closely related to the self-sacrificing Dr. Dymov of Chekhov's "The Grasshopper" [1892].) "Autumn in Yalta" ends by bringing readers back to its establishing scene, where Samoylovich recognizes his beloved Polechka in one of the "classy" ladies (the other one, presumably, is Nina, the woman from the wintry dacha outside Moscow, and the men are the actor Kaftanov, who became Nina's husband, and the astrophysicist Murov, Polechka's husband). Clashing with the breakneck pace of Soviet historical time, this almost miraculous stoppage of character time can only hint at a possibility of death or revenge beyond the story's ending (Ivan Bunin's stories from *Dark Avenues* come to mind as Samoylovich strokes a gun hidden in his jacket pocket). Such an artistic choice on Shrayer-Petrov's part takes stock both of Chekhov's open ending, rife with tremulous possibilities, and of Nabokov's decision to kill Nina, the female protagonist of "Spring in Fialta," in a banal car crash. Indeed, Shrayer-Petrov's Polechka takes after Nabokov's Nina much more than she does after Chekhov's Anna (Shrayer-Petrov purposely gave the name and something of the aura of Nabokov's Nina to his own Nina of consignment store fame). And yet, no matter what outcome readers may project beyond the physical end of Shrayer-Petrov's text, in the triangulating composition of "Autumn in Yalta" it is Polechka who belongs with "those salamanders of fate, those basilisks of good fortune," as Nabokov labeled Nina's belletrist husband Ferdinand and his cohort Segur, who survive the car crash that claims Nina's life in Fialta. Shrayer-Petrov's consumptive Polechka will probably live on, whereas her driver Samoylovich . . . (Readers can speculate for themselves.)

And finally, in assessing a Jewish-Russian writer's double homage to Chekhov and Nabokov, one might consider the impact of Shrayer-Petrov's medical experiences on the making of "Autumn in Fialta." This is not only Chekhov's and Nabokov's (pre-Soviet) Yalta; it is also Soviet Yalta, where Dr. Shrayer-Petrov worked during a cholera epidemic. In the summer of 1970 a vast territory of southern Russia and the Crimean peninsula was struck by cholera. It was part of the seventh world pandemic of cholera, spread to the former Soviet Union from the Southeast Asia. Soviet newspapers, radio and TV preferred not to tell the people about the dangerous situation at home, with only a small piece of information concerning "sporadic cases" of gastroenteritis of "unknown" bacterial origin being published in the Moscow-based *Medical Gazette*. Eventually, more and more residents of the stricken areas became gravely ill. The symptoms of the disease were typical for cholera. The outbreaks occurred in Astrakhan (on the Caspian Sea), Kerch (on the

Black Sea and the Sea of Azov), Feodosiya and Yalta (both on the
Black Sea). In September 1970, soon after the outbreak had been
registered, a group of five microbiologists from Moscow's Gamaleya
Institute of Epidimeology and Microbiology was dispatched to
Yalta. As a member of this group, Dr. Shrayer-Petrov worked in
Yalta for a month in the midst of the cholera epidemic. The purpose
of their mission was to find the best ways to prevent the spread of
cholera, to provide treatment to the deathly ill patients, and to study
the biology and molecular genetics of the causative agent, *Vibrio
cholerae*. Less than a year later, in the summer of 1971, Shrayer-
Petrov's article on cholera appeared in the Soviet magazine *Nature
(Priroda)*. It was possibly the first Soviet academic publication where
the 1970 epidemic was discussed in no uncertain terms.

Many years later, first in Russia and then in the United States,
Shrayer-Petrov revisited the subject in his novel *French Cottage*,
where a chapter is set in Yalta during the 1970 cholera epidemic.
The protagonist of *French Cottage*, Daniil Geyer, shares much in
common, not only with Samoylovich of "Autumn in Yalta," but also
with Daniil Rayev of *Strange Danya Rayev*. In going back to the
wartime past and his character's childhood, Shrayer-Petrov re-
hearses aspects of the future Danya Rayev both in Samoylovich,
whose fictional existence stops in 1991 or 1992, and in the medical
journalist Geyer, who becomes a refusenik and emigrates to America in the late 1980s. Because Shrayer-Petrov's artistic method priv-
ileges Nabokov's combination of the "eye"-narrator with the
"I"-storyteller over Chekhov's dispassionate omniscience, Shrayer-
Petrov's semiautobiographical narrators both look out from within
and stare in from without. "How difficult it is," the adult Danya
Rayev remarks, "to separate those sixty-year-old impressions from
my present memories of those impressions!"

Jews and Russians are the "two peoples [who] are the closest to me
in flesh (genes) and spirit (language)," Shrayer-Petrov wrote in 1985,

two years before emigrating from Soviet Russia, in *Friends and Shadows,* a memoir-novel of the late 1950s Leningrad. Over fifteen years later, in the preface to the collection *Jonah and Sarah,* he commented:"These fourteen stories bear testimony to over fifteen years of setting roots in my new country. Whether they feature characters still living in the old country or having already arrived in the New World, these stories are a record of a Jewish writer's separation from his Russian homeland."

In a number of stories written after coming to America, love between Jews and Gentiles fuels Shrayer-Petrov's imagination. Some of the stories are gently ironic. Others, like the story "Hände Hoch!" about the legacy of the Shoah in modern America (featured in *Jonah and Sarah*), are sharply polemical, going against the grain of commonly perpetuated stereotypes. Such is also the case of the story "Carp for the Gefilte Fish" (in this volume), where love of a non-Jewish, Belarusian man for his Jewish wife endures across the boundaries of time, language, and country, whereas hers for him does not (or at least seems not to at first glance). Exile and its many forms and varieties has become a focus of Shrayer-Petrov's writing, and the author's own Jewish experience provides a point of calibration when he writes of other, non-Jewish immigrants in America (in the present volume, the Japanese protagonist of "The Love of Akira Watanabe").

Characters in the novel *Strange Danya Rayev* and the story "Autumn in Yalta" struggle with the dilemmas of their dual, Jewish-Russian selves. To complement a novel and a story written in America but set in Russia, this volume also features two tales of transplantation onto a new culture and language. Both "The Love of Akira Watanabe" and "Carp for the Gefilte Fish" depict Soviet immigrants interacting with and confronting native-born Americans—as coworkers, intellectual and romantic rivals, as lovers and non-lovers. Newcomers to the United States, arriving in the predominantly Jewish 1970s and 1980s wave of emigration ("Third

Wave") from the former Soviet Union, are habitually subsumed into two categories: Jews as "Russians" and Russians as "Jews."

The entire volume is unified by its author's obsession with identity markers and his self-conscious adherence to the canons of the European love story of Guy de Maupassant, Anton Chekhov, Thomas Mann, Ivan Bunin, Vladimir Nabokov, and Isaac Bashevis Singer. A characteristic example of how Shrayer-Petrov explores parameters of identity through variations on the traditional love story is "The Love of Akira Watanabe." In this story, told in first person, Shrayer-Petrov creates an alternative model of exile and alienation. A partially autobiographical, Jewish-Russian scientist meets and befriends a Japanese professor as they both take "English as a Second Language" at an American university, in the company of other campus-based immigrants. The Japanese professor, an estranged scion of a Samurai family, and hardly a man of his time, either at home or abroad, falls in love with their ESL teacher, only to learn that she shares her life with a female partner. In taking an epigraph from Nabokov's story for "Autumn in Yalta," Shrayer-Petrov fondly acknowledges a literary master. By contrast, in drawing an epigraph from "A Story about the Writing of Stories" (1926) by Boris Pilnyak (1894–1937), he polemically sets "The Love of Akira Watanabe" against the fictions of stereotyping. Naturally, fiction writers play with various perceptions and misperceptions of stereotypes. What distinguishes Pilnyak's portrayal of a Japanese officer married to a Russian woman in "A Story about the Writing of Stories" is the degree to which Pilnyak adheres to a simplistic and negative stereotype of a Japanese man dating back to the turn of the twentieth century and the Russo-Japanese War. (In his portrayal of Jewish characters, the talented writer Pilnyak also clung to off-putting, albeit stylistically accomplished, stereotypes.) As drawn by the Jewish-Russian narrator-storyteller, the character of Akira Watanabe serves to undermine stereotypes. To phrase this differently, Akira Watanabe is a stereotype debunking stereotypes. Ironically, the narrator-storyteller himself falls prey to stereotyping by Akira's rival in the story's love triangle, Margaret's partner, Leslie: "Like all Russians, you probably drink your vodka *straight?*"

We create our own, unique diasporas by undoing stereotypes, be they ethnic, religious, or sexual, suggests this story with a surprisingly lyrical ending. The undoing of stereotypes continues in the volume's final story, "Carp for the Gefilte Fish." Set in Rhode Island, Shrayer-Petrov's home since 1987, and nurtured by memories of his military service in western Belarus in 1959–60, this story features a tetrangle of desire linking an émigré couple, Fyodor and Raya Kuzmenko, and their American employers, widowed furniture store owner Harry Kapler and his daughter, Rachel. Hailing from a provincial Belarusian town in the heart of the former Pale of Settlement, the Kuzmenkos bring to America the contrapuntal contradictions of a mixed marriage: Raya is Jewish; Fyodor is not. The couple is without children, and Fyodor (who has no living blood relatives) periodically goes on drinking binges. The Kuzmenkos distance themselves from Raya's *meshpucha* in Providence, moving to a small town where no other Russians live, but where a small Jewish community has established itself. At the end of the story, a turn of events involving Raya's adulterous adventure with their American employer, Fyodor's fishing expedition and eschewing of temptation, and an old Ashkenazic cooking recipe, brings the émigré couple back together. (Or does it?)

A volume of Shrayer-Petrov's selected stories, published in Moscow in 2005, bears the title *Carp for the Gefilte Fish*, testifying to the privileged place the author assigns to the story. The story's debunking of stereotypes functions as an admonition to the kind of self-righteous Jewish reader who appreciates only the tales where other Jews alone emerge as positive characters. Rather than create a fictional hierarchy of ethics, Shrayer-Petrov examines his subjects from many different ethical, aesthetic, and metaphysical perspectives, often presenting conflicting and incongruous points of view. Coupled with the conviction that the author does not know much more than his characters do, this (Dostoevskian?) quality of nonnarrative analysis of the narrative events is manifest in modern Jewish writing.

"Literature can very well describe the absurd, but it should never become absurd itself," wrote Isaac Bashevis Singer (1904–91) in the "Author's Note" to his *Collected Stories* (1982). Whether or not one agrees with Singer's dictum, one can see that, at some of the most dramatic points of Shrayer-Petrov's fiction (e.g., Samoylovich's escape attempt, where a boat transmogrifies into a yard dog), Shrayer-Petrov places his characters on the brink of the absurd. This teetering on the verge of the absurd, this dybbuk dancing on the author's humanist imagination, brings to mind not only the traditions of what Ken Frieden calls "classic Yiddish fiction" (S. Y. Abramovitsh, Sholem Aleichem, and I. L. Peretz forming the triumvirate), but also the fiction of Bashevis Singer. I find Singer's post-Shoah exilic tales *Enemies: A Love Story* (1966) and *Shosha* (1974), one of America and maturity, the other of Poland and youth, especially pertinent to the career of David Shrayer-Petrov in general, and to the present volume, in particular. In Bashevis Singer's novels—as in much of Shrayer-Petrov's fiction—encounters between Jews and non-Jews (Slavs) prompt the workings of the love story.

Already gearing up for an open challenge to Soviet officialdom in 1975–76, my father composed poems where disharmonies of his Russian and Jewish selves adumbrated a conflict with the regime. Earlier I mentioned the poem "My Slavic Soul" only in passing; let me quote another poem, "Early Morning in Moscow" (1976), in its entirety. Published in English in 1993, it appeared in my father's first American collection of Russian poetry, *Song of a Blue Elephant* (1990).

EARLY MORNING IN MOSCOW

The woodpecker knocks on the pine tree
rehearsing his wooden reverie

*knock-knock-knock*
*knock-knock-knock*
On the ground
falls the deadening wooden sound.

The janitor shovels the street
rehearsing his snowy reverie
*dirty Jew dirty Jew*
*dirty Jew—*
In the camps
I'd break your head in two.

The doctor knocks on my chest
rehearsing his wishful reverie
*one day we'll*
*one day we'll*
*one day we'll*
be free to sing in the spring.

Sounds filling the dawn
keep time with my salt tears
*on the verge of life*
*on the verge of life*
*on this low verge* lies
Moscow muffled in snow.

Commenting on the translation, a product of my collaboration
with the American poet Edwin Honig, my father wrote in 1992:
"this poem of mine in English translation (I almost wrote in 'American translation') acquired a particularly revelatory and lament-like
intonation, akin to what I hear in the character of the writer Robert
Cohn in Hemingway's novel *The Sun Also Rises* [1926]." (Published
in 1935 in Vera Toper's fine translation and better known in Russian

as *Fiesta,* Hemingway's novel had been immensely popular in the Soviet Union of my father's youth.)

I confess that as I worked with Margarit Tadevosyan on the Englishing of "Carp for the Gefilte Fish," I "heard" in the emergent, translated voice of the narrator echoes of Bernard Malamud's novel *The Assistant* (1957). (Heard or wanted to hear?) And in the character of Fyodor Kuzmenko there is perhaps something of Frank Alpine, Malamud's archetypal American goy who takes upon himself the great burden of Jewishness, driven to it by a mixture of desire, love, guilt, and self-hatred. Frank Alpine, the Italian-American Catholic "holdupnik" of a measly Jewish grocery store, identifies with Saint Francis of Assisi, and Malamud engages him in an *imitation* of Morris Bober, the old Jewish grocer. Answering Alpine's question what it means to be a Jew, Morris first tells him this: "My father used to say to be a Jew all you need is a good heart." Only later does Bober share with Alpine his justification of not following *koshrut,* his notion of Jewish Law, and his idea of Jewish suffering. Referring to Alpine's circumcision, Malamud ends his American novel with one of the most enigmatic sentences composed by a Jewish writer: "The pain enraged and inspired him. After Passover he became a Jew." The "he" refers to Frank Alpine. Marking the protagonist of "Carp for the Gefilte Fish" with the name "Fyodor" (from the Greek *Theodoros,* "Gift of God"), my father remarks in the middle of the story: "He [Fyodor] had lived among Jews for many years but could never really understand them completely." Fyodor may not have "become a Jew," but he stays with "them" his whole life, loving Raya more than anything, more than his Belarusian homeland.

Four years ago, in an afterword to *Jonah and Sarah: Jewish Stories of Russia and America,* I speculated about the trajectory of my father's writing career, which has led him to writing about the Jewish-, the Russian-, and—increasingly—unhyphenated Americans. *Autumn in Yalta* is, finally, less a Jewish-Russian than a Jewish-American book, particularly in its multiplicity of cultural perspectives, its diversity of subjects, its seeking to overcome stereotypes, but also in its insistence on getting over the traumas of the past. Despite the piercing sadness that wafts through many of its pages, this American book breathes with hopefulness. Looking back at our shared past and my father's earlier fiction, I can hardly imagine his writing a book like *Autumn in Yalta* in post-Soviet Russia. Consider this passage from the ending of "Carp for the Gefilte Fish":

> [Fyodor] drove on, thinking what a happy guy he really was. Here he was, in a new country, where he came, not like some sort of a loser, but as a married man. Both he and Raya have jobs. They have their house and a garden. And they haven't hit old age. It's too bad, of course, that they don't have a boy or a girl. But who knows, maybe they'll get lucky? Here in America, even worse kinds of ailments get cured. If it's all from his drinking, then he's practically on the wagon. And what if?

*What if?*

A literary translator is someone who couches the original in the words of another language while also interpreting its meaning. As someone who has translated works by many writers from a number of languages, my father knows this well. When an author's son is also his translator and editor, he wants to represent more than his father's voice. Before me on the page were not only my father's words. In my mind's eye was my father's life story.

I first tried my hand at translating my father's work into English when we were still refuseniks, in 1986. One of his poems that I had rendered into English, quite awkwardly, was smuggled to the West, printed on a leaflet, and recited as a supplemental 1986 Passover reading in synagogues in the United States and Canada. My first serious attempts at translation go back to my undergraduate years at Brown, 1987–89, when, under the sympathetic gaze of John

Hawkes and Albert Cook, I was making a transition from my native Russian to my adopted English. In the late 1980s and early 1990s, translations of my father's prose and poetry began to appear in American periodicals. In 1999, having collaborated with other translators on several of my father's stories, I began to put together and translate a collection that eventually appeared under the title *Jonah and Sarah*. The idea for the present volume emerged during a series of readings and book signings my father and I did together in the fall, no, in *autumn* of 2003, after the publication of *Jonah and Sarah*. In preparing *Autumn in Yalta*, I was lucky to have the contribution and collaboration of four devoted translators, Arna B. Bronstein, Aleksandra I. Fleszar, Emilia Shrayer, and Margarit Tadevosyan.

Now that *Autumn in Fialta* is heading for publication—and plans for translating other works are under way—my father and I joke about loving disagreements that arose when I edited the final text. This was no ordinary translation project for me. Over the years, I have had the privilege of translating works by a number of Jewish-Russian writers, among them, David Aizman, Vladimir Jabotinsky, Lev Ginzburg, and Boris Slutsky. But this was not simply a writer whose work I admired, but my own father. I wanted the translations to capture his intonation, his breath, and his silence, in the most fitting Anglo-American idiom. And I wished them to stand as a memorial to our ancestors, carrying on Jewish thought and spirit. While working on the translations, I was often transported to the past. In one of my father's favorite stories, "Dismemberers," from the collection *Jonah and Sarah,* my father's Olympia typewriter continues to type subversive stories even after her owner has left Russia for good. The tale was composed in May 1987 in our Moscow apartment while Dan Rather and a CBS crew were filming a segment about my parents for the special *Seven Days in May.* The typewriter story took me back to the lessons my father gave me when I was four. He sat me at his writer's desk and let me bang out my first compositions—Cyrillic characters, arranged on a page like a Dadaist manifesto. He simply let me be myself in language, and he still does today.

Something that has always sustained me as a son and my father's translator is his belief in a form of universal harmony, in a "saving proportionality," as he termed it in the preface to *Jonah and Sarah*: "Not a harmony in the grand poetic sense of the word, but a proportionality, intended for the purpose of distributing happiness and unhappiness among people." As I worked on Englishing my father's prose, I would call him frequently, asking to make small alterations. "This is my story, and this is how I came to know it—no, how my characters did," my father would reply. I know he has helped preserve this harmony by saving me from the temptation of knowing better than the author himself.

A book's future is alluring, enchanting . . . My wife and I are visiting my parents in Providence, about a mile from where Karen grew up. We are sitting in the backyard of my parents' house. It's the end of September, a summery afternoon. Maple leaves fall at our feet, keeping time with our conversation.

"They are going to love *Autumn in Yalta*," I say with what is supposed to be the smile of a tireless promoter.

"You think so?" asks my gentle father.

"What do *you* think?" I reply.

"What do I think? I wrote the book, but it also wrote me," says my father. And he pauses, before adding, "And the same for you: you edited and cotranslated it, but it also edited and cotranslated you. A book is a destiny."

October 2004–January 2006

# About the Translators

Arna B. Bronstein and Aleksandra I. Fleszar (translators of *Strange Danya Rayev*) are professors of Russian and Slavic studies at the University of New Hampshire. Longtime collaborators, they have coauthored acclaimed textbooks of Russian widely used across the Anglophone world, including *Making Progress in Russian*. Their translations from Russian include *Five Russian Stories*.

Emilia Shrayer (translator of "The Love of Akira Watanabe") works at the Rockefeller Library, Brown University. Her translations into Russian, with David Shrayer-Petrov, include works by Erskine Caldwell, Maxim D. Shrayer, and Australian poets. She has translated into English Shrayer-Petrov's monograph *Staphylococcal Disease in the Soviet Union* and a number of her husband's creative works.

Maxim D. Shrayer (translator of "Autumn and Yalta" and "Carp for the Gefilte Fish")—see the editor's biography following the copyright page.

Margarit Tadevosyan (translator of "Carp for the Gefilte Fish") is completing a Ph.D. dissertation about writers in exile and literary bilingualism. She has published articles on Aleksandr Grin, Vladimir Nabokov, and Evelyn Waugh and has translated fiction from Armenian and Russian, including stories by David Shrayer-Petrov.